A SINGULAR FURY

A SINGULAR FURY

A SAM BENEDICT MYSTERY

by
Howard L. Oleck

THE WORLD PUBLISHING COMPANY
CLEVELAND AND NEW YORK

Published by The World Publishing Company
2231 West 110th Street, Cleveland, Ohio 44102
Published simultaneously in Canada by
Nelson, Foster & Scott Ltd.

FIRST PRINTING—NOVEMBER, 1968
SECOND PRINTING—JANUARY, 1969

30784149
Mys C1 DB296

A SINGULAR FURY

CHAPTER

1

"Mr. Benedict, my name is Janet Duffield Porter. I am being held by the police. They say that I killed my husband. Can you come here to talk with me . . . ?"

Sam Benedict cradled the telephone between his chin and shoulder, and lit a cigarette. Midnight phone calls were put through to his apartment only when his night answering service was sure that they were important.

"When were you arrested?" he asked.

Her voice was surprisingly calm and controlled when she answered. It sounded cultured and precise. Well educated, he thought, as she spoke, and remarkably cool for a person being held on a homicide charge. "About ten o'clock this evening. I was at home and it's all rather confused," she said.

"Don't tell me about it now," Sam interrupted. "Telephones can have more than one receiver. Just answer my questions 'Yes' or 'No.'"

That name—Porter—had a familiar ring. Wasn't there a prominent Porter family in town? A professor who had married some socialite from a well known Eastern family? Something in the *Examiner* not long ago about a grant to a Professor Kevin Porter by some research foundation?

"Are the police treating you decently?" he asked.

"Yes."

"Have they questioned you?"

"Yes."

"Have you told them anything?"

"There is nothing to tell. I don't understand all this."

"Good. Say nothing. Discuss nothing. And above all, sign nothing."

But how had she happened to call him? He asked her.

"Your name somehow came to mind. Perhaps my husband had mentioned it. He was a law professor. The police said that I should call my attorney. So I called you."

Sam grinned. Shades of the Supreme Court! The Escobedo Case and the Miranda Case had shaken every police officer and prosecutor in the country. They were taking no chances on having convictions thrown out. The court had said "no pressured confessions and no defendants without lawyers to protect them." The police were following the rules; at least in San Francisco they were.

"All right, then," he said. "I'll see you in the morning, about ten o'clock. Get some sleep and try to take it easy."

She protested, "Can't you come now?"

"Hell, no." His temper stirred. "This call could have waited until morning anyhow. A lawyer's wife should know better. What do you expect me to do at two in the morning? I'll see you at ten. Goodby now." He hung up, dialed Hank Tabor's number, and smiled faintly as he heard Hank's querulous "hello."

"Sorry, Hank. You guessed it. Something for you to do, first thing in the morning. Make it early. Get me a rundown on the Kevin Porter family here in town. I particularly want to know about Janet Porter—P-O-R-T-E-R. Get it to me by eight or nine at the latest. See what you can find in *Who's Who*, the newspaper morgues, the *Social Register*, and that sort of thing. I want to know when they came to San Francisco, where from, what they do—everything. This is urgent."

"What's it all about?" Hank asked, his voice suddenly interested.

"Can't be sure yet," Sam answered. "Sounds like Murder One. They're holding Janet Porter."

Hank whistled. "I'll see what I can do. Eight o'clock, then." He said "good night," and hung up.

Sam crushed out his cigarette, lit another, and walked to a window. He looked out at the fog spotted with bright patches of red and yellow neon light. He opened a window and sniffed the air, cool and salty with the aroma of sea foam. Foghorns moaned from down in the bay below. It would be a short sleep tonight, until his habitual wake-up time—five o'clock in the morning.

On his way to the bedroom Sam stopped for a moment in front of a mirror and looked at his reflection quizzically. He wondered, staring at his image in the glass, why he—a successful, middle-aged lawyer—would get involved in another murder case at all. He certainly didn't need the money or the probable publicity. He had too many clients and too many cases as it was. He inspected his snowy shirt front and dark silk necktie, and looked down at the razor-sharp creases in the trouser legs of his conservatively gray, summer-weight suit. Then he extended his arms, popping his cuffs as was his habit, to expose his silver cufflinks, each shining and inset with a small white pearl.

He wondered if others saw him as he saw himself—trim and lean despite his middle-age years, a kind of greyhound-looking man. His face was deeply lined with the strains of many a hard fight: in the ring as a young man, in war, and in many a hard-fought trial in many a courtroom. His slim and well-proportioned body—not very tall in fact—gave him a look of alert, youthful vigor. He suspected that his gray hair and now receding hairline, widow's-peaked in the center, made him look older than his lithe body and posture suggested.

He was no matinee idol or pretty boy—that was for sure, he thought. But he had an appearance that inspired respect and attention. Those hard, wise eyes, alone, caught and held the attention of everyone who saw him; he knew that.

He moved on. It was late. Time to get to sleep.

At eight o'clock in the morning Hank Tabor came into Sam's office. He had a piece of paper in his hand and began to tick off his information about the Porter family. Hank was Sam's good right arm in his law practice, as big and strong as a grizzly bear, but wise and gentle and keen-minded. He had been with Sam for years, and wasted no time in starting his report.

"Item one, from *Who's Who*. Kevin Wilson Porter. Born in San Francisco. Age, forty-six. Bachelor of Arts, Stanford. Law degree, Harvard. Master of Laws, Yale. Member of the Bar in

New York and California. With a big Wall Street law firm for years. Taught at Cleveland-Marshall Law School for two years, and professor at University of California Law School in Berkeley since then. Holder of the Bostwick Chair of Constitutional Law for the past four years. Wrote many articles for legal journals. Married to Janet Duffield Porter. No children. Lives on Telegraph Hill." Hank looked up. "All kinds of memberships and professional societies."

Sam nodded. "The usual route for a smart boy from a family with dough. What else?"

"Item two, from the newspapers. Porter got a grant of ten grand from the Wallenstein Foundation a year or so ago to do a book on the Supreme Court, Oliver Wendell Holmes, Jr., and modern corporation law. It's not finished yet; at least it hasn't been published yet."

Sam leaned back in his big swivel chair and adjusted the carefully folded handkerchief in his breast pocket. "He needed the money like I need six fingers. Dozens of bright, hard-working researchers and writers, and they give the grant to the one who doesn't need it."

Hank bridled. "Does his family's money rule him out?"

"No. I didn't say that. It just would have been nicer for him not to apply for a grant if he didn't need the money."

"Well, he certainly wasn't headed for the poor farm. According to the social columns, his father was a director or trustee of a dozen banks and business firms—big ones. Kevin Porter was an only child and sole heir. He inherited it all when his parents died."

"Hold it a minute." Sam pressed the intercom buzzer, as he heard footsteps in the outer office. "The girls must be getting in."

"Yes, Mr. Benedict. Good morning." It was his secretary, Trudy Wagner.

"Trudy, start a file on a new case. Title is *People of the State of California versus Janet Duffield Porter*. I'll be going over to the Hall of Justice at nine-thirty, so cancel all engagements for the morning. I'll be back in the office between two and three in the afternoon."

"Yes, Mr. Benedict. What about rescheduling your appointments?"

"Hold them off," Sam said. "Tell them we'll be in touch in a day or two. I'll know more about what we can do later in the day. Hank will give you some notes for the Porter file."

He turned back to Hank and nodded.

"So much for Kevin Porter," Hank continued. "Janet Porter is another matter. All I can find about her is in the *Blue Book* and the society pages of the papers. For a society hotshot she doesn't seem very social. She's listed as a committee member for this and that charity, but never seems to be very active. No 'among-those-present' listings for debutante soirees, charity balls, and so on."

"So what's so social about her?"

"Her family. The John Duffields of Park Avenue and the North Shore of Long Island were very big in the old Cholly Knickerbocker columns. But the *Social Register* doesn't tell much about Janet Duffield Porter, except her list of society memberships."

"What kind of clubs?"

"The usual. D.A.R., Colonial Dames, and stuff like that. No golf club, no hobbies that you can spot. No nothing."

"How about schools?"

"That's a funny thing. I was sure it would be Vassar or Smith or one of the Seven Sisters. Maybe a Swiss finishing school. But no. Nothing. It's hard to believe, but it looks as if she never went to college or finishing school. One thing, though: her father was Daley Professor of Law at Harvard Law School for some time. Did you know that?"

Sam frowned. "No, I didn't connect it. So the Duffield of Harvard was her daddy. One of the great scholars of the century and a social lion, too. There's something there, Hank. Get me all you can on the old boy. I have a feeling about the old prof. . . ."

Hank nodded. "Okay. Now, according to the papers, Janet Duffield and Kevin Porter met in New York. It was a quiet courtship, if you go by the space it received in the social columns. They were married. No hoopla; no big wedding blowout reported in the papers. They got married and they went to Cleveland and then after a while to San Francisco. That was nine or ten years ago."

"Then what?"

"Then they seem to have settled down quietly in the Porter mansion and that's all—until now."

"Anything else?"

Hank leaned back and stretched wearily. "That's all, so far. After all, I only had a few hours to scrounge for this poop. Talking about poop, *I'm* pooped. Not much sleep last night."

Sam grinned. "All right, Hank. Take a nap if you're tired. I won't need you at the Hall of Justice. See what else you can dig up, later. I'll see you about three or four."

Hank rose heavily and trudged out. Sam swung his swivel chair around and gazed out the window. The case was beginning to show promise. Law professors, blue-blood society, wealthy people—and homicide. Quite a combination. He pulled a wafer-thin gold watch from his vest pocket and looked at the time. Then he leaned across the desk and buzzed Trudy to get him a taxi.

The new Hall of Justice was a big, pale-gray, slab-sided block of a building. Nothing like the old one, he thought regretfully. The old one had had character; not much for efficiency, maybe, but style and feeling. With all its crowding and heaviness, it had had a dignity that stark modern architecture could not match.

He pushed through the big doors and went in. The halls were busy with people coming and going. As Sam walked across the lobby toward the elevators, he was greeted by a man from the Prosecutor's Office.

"Hi, Master." It was Barney Rosvalley, tough old war horse from the D.A.'s Office. "What brings you to our fair jail house today?"

"Don't know for sure yet, Barney. How's with you?"

"Can't complain. Going up? I'll go along with you."

The elevator moved upward silently and, when the doors slid open, Sam stepped out. "See you around, Barney," he said, and walked down the hallway to the Women's Division interviewing room. He went in and talked to the policewoman attendant. She was all politeness.

"Would you like a cup of coffee, Counselor? They'll bring Mrs. Porter in in a few minutes."

Sam shook his head. "No, thank you." He sat down at the table and got out a cigarette. The policewoman went out. The room was stark and almost bare, its walls painted pale green; a table and two chairs were its only furniture. The door opened, and Sam stood up.

Janet Porter had style and grace, even after a night in the county jail. She was pale, but her straight, brown hair was brushed and the whites of her eyes were clear. Not a great beauty, Sam thought, but handsome and dignified. She still was wearing a dress, not a prison uniform.

Most women would have been upset and emotional in such a situation. But Janet Porter seemed to be the picture of calm, self-possessed dignity. She hesitated for a moment just inside the door and waited for the woman deputy sheriff who accompanied her to give some directions. The square, stern deputy motioned her toward Sam and then stood discreetly at the door.

Sam put out his hand. Janet's hand was cold and her palm was damp. "I'm Sam Benedict, Mrs. Porter. Please sit down." He turned to the guard. "You can wait outside the door, Deputy. There's no other way out of here, and I want to talk with my client privately." The policewoman went out and closed the door behind her.

"Now then. Would you like a cigarette, Mrs. Porter?" Sam sat down at the table, facing her.

"Thank you. I have no more." He gave her a cigarette, lit it for her, and tossed his pack to her side of the table. "Keep these. The guard will get cigarettes for you if you want them. Do you have matches?"

"Yes. Thank you. I have some in my purse."

"All right now. Take your time, and tell me all about it."

"There really is not much to tell. My husband is dead. I know. I saw his body. But that's all I know. The police were there and they brought me here. I don't remember much else. It's all blurry. They say that I killed him. But that can't be so, can it?"

Sam's eyebrows lifted slightly. Was she pulling his leg? Her face was calm and expressionless, almost stiffly impassive. The hand holding the cigarette was steady. The pupils of her eyes did not shift or dart as she spoke, but were fixed steadily on him.

"You said that the police arrested you at about ten o'clock, Mrs. Porter. Let's back up a bit. Did you spend the evening at home?"

"Yes."

"Alone?"

"No. With Kevin."

"Did you have dinner with him?"

"Yes."

"What time?"

"About six, as usual."

"Then, after dinner . . . ?"

"We went into the library and read the evening paper. We always do that after dinner."

"How long did that take?"

"Perhaps half an hour."

"Then . . . ?"

"Then Kevin went out to some meeting—at Hastings Law School, he said. I started to work in the library."

"What work?"

"Well, Kevin is working—I mean, was—on a paper about constitutional aspects of corporation law. I, myself, have been busy for some time on my father's notes and papers on the history of the Supreme Court, in the manuscript for his autobiography."

"Did you and Kevin work together?"

"In a sense. We each have a desk and a worktable in the library. I work at mine and sometimes he worked at his. But he did most of his work at Berkeley."

"All right. So you were working. Then what?"

"That's all. So help me God, Mr. Benedict, that's all. Next thing I knew it was ten o'clock. The hall clock was chiming ten, I remember. I was in the hall. The police were there. Rogers was there, too, I think."

"Who is Rogers?"

"He's our houseman. What you used to call a butler. But he

runs the house. Kevin has no use for a butler's uniform. Rogers drives for us sometimes, but mostly he manages the house."

"How long has he been with you?"

"Oh, a long time. He worked for Kevin before we were married. A long time."

"What's his full name?"

"Paul. Paul Rogers."

Sam leaned back in his chair, and looked at her reflectively. "Do you mean that you can't remember anything between seven-thirty and ten o'clock?"

"No. Believe me, Mr. Benedict. No, I can't remember anything."

"Had you been drinking?"

She was startled. "Good heavens, no. Kevin and I had a glass of wine with dinner, and that's all. I remember, we had one glass of Chablis. That's all. Neither of us is a drinker, Mr. Benedict."

"Forgive me, if I offend you, Mrs. Porter, but tell me—did either of you use drugs or sedatives?"

"No. Never. What do you take me for . . . ?"

"All right, let it go." He flushed. "I'm sorry, but I have to ask."

She had shown a flash of emotion for a moment. Now it was gone. Once again she was composed and her brown eyes were expressionless. Sam got up and walked slowly toward the door. He turned suddenly and shot another question at her: "Had you quarreled about anything that evening?"

"No."

"During the day?"

"No. It was an ordinary day. Kevin was over at Berkeley and came home at five as usual. I was at a tea early in the afternoon. A dull day and I was glad to get home. Then I worked alone at home for a while. I didn't see Kevin until about six. We had nothing to quarrel about."

"You just don't remember anything after he left, then?"

"No. Nothing. It's all a blank."

"All right then. That's enough for now. There'll be an arraignment hearing right away. I'll plead you 'not guilty' of course. Maybe I'll ask for a postponement."

She nodded.

"Now, Mrs. Porter, let's talk about fees. Maybe you know and maybe you don't, but I only take three or four real cases a year, nowadays. My fees are high." He waited for her to speak.

She nodded and murmured, "Yes."

"I will want a retainer of ten thousand dollars, and we'll talk about the full fee later." She nodded again.

Sam continued, "Expenses of investigation and preparation are not part of the fee. Is that understood?"

"Yes."

"And there is nothing contingent about my fee. It's not on a win-or-don't-get-paid basis. Later on, when the case gets clearer, I'll tell you what the total fee will be. Is that agreeable?"

"Yes." She hardly seemed to hear him.

"Mrs. Porter, do you understand what I am saying?" Sam's voice was a notch higher than his usual slow, low tone.

"I don't care, Mr. Benedict." Her tone was almost hostile, and she looked straight into his eyes. "Really, I don't care. Maybe I ought to plead 'guilty.' They say I did it, anyhow."

Sam winced. "Never plead 'guilty,' Mrs. Porter. Never plead 'guilty.' Certainly not in this kind of situation."

He paused. "Let's see what tomorrow brings." He walked away from the table and knocked at the door. "All done, Deputy," he said, loudly.

Janet stood up, silent. She walked to the door, where the guard was waiting. Then she turned and gazed at Sam.

"Thank you, Mr. Benedict." Her voice was flat and toneless.

As Sam came out into the hall, a familiar figure came toward him. It was Barney Rosvalley. Barney stopped in front of him, hands on his hips, and his head cocked to one side. "Say it isn't so, Sam."

"Meaning what, Barney?"

"I hear that you are taking the Porter case."

"Looks like it."

"You'll spoil your record with this one."

"How so?"

"You've never lost one to the gas chamber yet, but this may be the first."

Sam shrugged noncommitally. "What makes you so sure?"

"Oh, Sam. This one is brass-bound. A lead-pipe cinch for any half-decent prosecutor. You'll hear it at the preliminary hearing tomorrow morning at ten, so I might as well tell you now. Eyewitness murder, Sam, eyewitness murder."

"You don't say." Sam's tone was sarcastic.

"I do say. As the Greeks put it: *In flagrante delicto*. Caught in the act. Dead to rights."

"Doing what?" Sam challenged.

"Busting his skull, no less. Clobbering him."

Sam adjusted the snowy peaks of the handkerchief in his breast pocket, and stared down at the floor.

Barney went on, in a rush: "I tell you, Sam, be smart. Plead her 'guilty' and get it over with."

Sam's head snapped up. "You know better than that, Barney. You'll get no gift convictions from me."

"But what's the point of making a big production out of it? There's no point to it."

"There *is* a point." Sam's voice was slow and very low, but very clear. "You have to convict, Mister Prosecutor. You have to prove, Mister D.A. Nobody is guilty, *nobody*, until the jury comes in and says so. And that isn't the end of the line either. There are lots of points, lots of points."

Barney shrugged. "Okay. Don't get peeved. I was only trying to be decent and to save the State and your client some time and money. But have it your way, if you insist—the hard way."

"That's the way it will be." Sam started toward the staircase. "Going to lunch?"

Barney nodded, and walked along with him.

"How about the Nob Hill Room at the Mark Hopkins? I hear that they're real good on roast beef."

"Fine, we'll catch a cab. What's new with the Giants? Friend of mine said he almost froze in the draft at Candlestick Park yesterday. If they don't do something about that wind at that ballpark. . . ."

They disappeared down the stairway.

After lunch Sam took a taxi to McAllister Street, and got out before a big, yellowish-gray stone building set back from the sidewalk. Across its façade were carved letters: "Hastings College of The Law, University of California." He went into the law-school building, his footsteps echoing in the high, marble-faced lobby, stopped for a moment to greet two professors whom he knew, and went on to the dean's office. He spoke to the receptionist.

"My name is Benedict. I'm a lawyer. Can you tell me if there was some sort of meeting here last night, and who was in charge of it?"

The girl thought for a moment. "Oh, yes. There was a meeting of the Constitutional Law Society. Professor Dombroski was supposed to make the arrangements. He would know about it. He's in; just got back from lunch. His office is on the third floor. You can take an elevator."

Sam thanked her, and went up to the third floor. Professor Dombroski was glad to tell him about the meeting. There had been about fourteen people, mostly law teachers and judges, and some practitioners, and they had discussed the possibility of starting a new journal on constitutional law.

"Was Professor Porter from Berkeley at the meeting?" Sam asked.

"Oh, yes. The tall, white-haired law professor from Berkeley. He was here. A very active member of the Society. Yes. He was here."

"Did he take part in the discussion?"

"Of course. He was quite helpful, as he always is."

"Did you happen to notice . . . was he ill or upset?"

"Why, no. He was quite normal. Seemed to be perfectly all right." Dombroski seemed to be surprised by the question.

"What time did the meeting break up?" Sam asked.

"About nine-thirty."

"Did Professor Porter leave with anyone? Did you happen to notice?"

"No. I didn't notice. Why? Is he all right? Is he ill?"

"No, no. Nothing special. Just a personal matter." Sam

thanked him and left. Dombroski stared wonderingly after him as he walked out.

Sam stopped again at the dean's office to leave a word of greeting for Dean Gabler. Gabler had invited him to deliver a lecture at the law school some time before, and he had done so.

It was almost three o'clock. Sam went upstairs again, to the library. He asked the desk attendant for a copy of the current *Law Teachers Directory* and looked up the biographical sketch of "Porter." It was much the same as the story in *Who's Who*. A blank. Sam sighed and went out. He would have to send Hank to make some discreet inquiries about Kevin Porter from faculty colleagues at Boalt Hall in Berkeley.

Out in the street, he hailed a taxicab and told the driver, "Drive to Montgomery Street." The visit to Hastings Law School had confirmed that Kevin Porter had not lied to his wife about where he had gone the night before. It had not been to a tryst with another woman, nor to a poker game with the boys.

The outer waiting room on the sixteenth floor of his office building was full of people as Sam came out of the elevator. His offices occupied the entire floor. He walked quickly through the panelled reception room, and Trudy buzzed the door open for him. Inside, he leafed through the pile of messages, and instructed Trudy on how to handle them. Then he went into his office, opened his vest, sat back in his high-backed swivel chair, and put his feet up on the corner of the desk. He inspected his short, gleaming, black leather boots, flicked a spot of dust off one, and buzzed Hank to come in.

Hank tossed a newspaper on Sam's desk when he came in. "The afternoon papers have a story," he said. "Page one, no less. Nothing much in them, really, except social background, which we already know. They do say, though, that Kevin Porter was bludgeoned to death. I didn't know that this morning."

"Neither did I. What else?"

"They say that the family butler discovered the body. Man named Rogers. Been with the Porter family for sixteen years."

"I know."

Sam filled him in on the conversation with Janet Porter. "She claims absolute amnesia. Doesn't remember a thing. She obviously was unhurt, so that rules out a 'masked-intruder' angle."

"What do we do now?"

"Check out this Rogers fellow, first. Where was he when the killing occurred? Does he have an alibi? Was there any reason for him to have attacked Porter?"

"Okay." Hank scribbled notes in his pocket notebook.

"Also, get over to Boalt Hall at Berkeley. Visit with the boys on the law faculty. Find out how Porter got along with them. Any jealousies? Any personal animosities or rivalries? Anyone who might have had it in for him?"

Hank looked dubious. "Law professors are hardly the type to beat someone to death."

"Anyone is the type to beat someone to death, given enough reason, or enough imagined reason. It's not likely, but we had better make sure." Sam paused, and drummed his fingers on the desk for a moment. "Then I need to know a lot more about Janet Porter; a lot more. Who are her friends? What did she do with her time? She didn't have to clean house or scrub floors. What did she do with herself? Did she have a boy friend, maybe? Was she in any trouble? Did she ever act odd or irrational? Check it all, as much as you can. You've got your work cut out for you."

Hank stood up and began to walk toward the door. "Okay. I've already started on some more background on her, but there's a lot to do."

The phone buzzed and Sam picked it up. It was Trudy. "A Mr. Kennedy, a reporter, insists on talking with you. I think it's about the Porter case."

Sam motioned Hank to stay, and told Trudy to put the call through. He knew Bud Kennedy, a reporter with the *Chronicle*.

"Hello, Bud. What can I do for you?"

Bud's voice was crisp and self-confident. "Good afternoon, Master. I'll get right to the point. The story is out that you are going to represent Janet Porter. Is that true?"

"Yes. It is true."

"How are you going to plead her?"

"Don't know yet."

"Did you see her this morning?"

"Yes."

"How is she? Is she hurt?"

"Now, now, Bud. . . ."

"Does she have any statement for the press?"

"Nope."

"Do you?"

"Nope."

Kennedy's voice became less self-confident, and almost pleading in tone. "Oh, come on, Sam, give us something. We have to make a living, you know."

"Sorry, Bud. No comment."

"Do you know that the arraignment is on for ten tomorrow morning?"

Sam cupped his hand over the mouthpiece and spoke to Hank. "Did we get word of a preliminary hearing tomorrow on the Porter case?"

Hank nodded. "Yes. Ten in the morning, tomorrow."

"Who's sitting?"

"Judge Harper."

Sam spoke into the receiver again. "I have to go now, Bud. That's all for now. Probably see you at the hearing or in a couple of days. Goodby, now." He hung up. The newspapers were going to play up this case; that was certain. It had all the elements of a good yarn, the kind that would sell lots of papers.

Sam turned in his chair and stared out the window. It was much too soon to tell for sure, but the case was beginning to take shape and direction. He spoke, half to Hank and half to himself. "She claims a blackout—amnesia. That means that she claims either illness or mental trouble—assuming her story to be honest, of course. Now, does she have a history of diabetes or something? Who's her doctor? Has she been under treatment for anything?"

Hank made a note. "I'll check on it."

Sam continued. "But if it's really mental, we'll need a lot more than a blood-pressure or blood-sugar record. That will mean a detailed search of her whole history, back to her childhood. A hell of a job of investigation. It also will mean psychiatrists, and maybe lots of them."

Hank nodded. "Do you want me to call one?"

Sam shook his head. "No, let that wait a bit. There's something else we'd better do, first."

"Yes?"

"Let's go look at the scene of the case—the Porter house. Call Barney Rosvalley and ask him to tell the police officer on duty there that it's all right for us to go in and look around."

Hank nodded, and picked up the phone.

The Porter house was a big, square, red-brick bulk, set back from the street behind a tall, wrought-iron fence. It had a narrow but well-manicured lawn, flower beds, and evergreens set in heavy profusion around the foundation. It was an expensive and exclusive-looking house, aristocratic, and in a turn-of-the-century style. "Bastard Greek Revival," Hank guessed, as they walked towards the gate. A police officer was standing at the door, looking very bored and glad of any visitors. "Mr. Benedict?" he asked.

"Yes. This is my assistant, Mr. Tabor."

"Go right in." The policeman opened the door for them, and followed them inside. "There's nobody in the house. Please don't touch anything. But Mr. Rosvalley said you could look anywhere you want. I'm to stay with you, though."

"Trusting bastard, that Barney, isn't he!" Sam stepped past the vestibule and looked around the center hall. A staircase ran up the right wall, just beyond a double, glass-panelled sliding door which closed off a large dining room. On the left was another glass-panelled sliding door and a sitting room full of furniture and paintings. At the end of the hall two more oak doors were visible.

They walked through the living room, a beige-and-gold rug muffling their footsteps. Chinese, Sam guessed, or a Chindia. Latticed, curved Italian chairs, massive coffee tables done in antique off-white, and impressionistic paintings in heavily carved gray frames, all spoke of expensive good taste. He picked up one figurine from a lamp table. It was about six inches high, made of gold-washed silver, and represented a knight in full armor, with movable visor and face of carved ivory. German, he thought, old, and probably cost plenty; maybe a museum piece. It had semiprecious stones set into its teakwood base. There were half-a-dozen other such figurines on that table.

From the sitting room a pair of open double doors led into the library. Bookshelves lined all but one wall. Big, heavy oak tables and two desks, and leather chairs in brown and dark green filled the room. Oriental rugs were scattered about on a polished oak floor. A picture window, with drapes drawn back, overlooked a garden, behind which a tall hedge closed out the world. Sam looked appreciatively at the other furniture: an antique globe map, hassocks, lamps, a television set standing on a radiator enclosure—in all, very nearly the picture of a scholar's retreat. Papers were scattered over the desks and tables along with open books, buckram-bound and with gold-lettered, red-and-black title markers on their spines.

"That's where the body was, Counselor." The policeman pointed to a spot on the floor near the doorway.

Sam picked up a sheaf of papers in a blue manila folder from one table, and riffled the pages. They were annotated copies of the opinions of Justice Holmes. "I suppose the D.A. has the murder weapon," he said, as he put the folder back on the table.

"Oh, sure. It was a bronze statue of a woman—Lady Justice or somebody holding up a pair of scales in one hand." The officer was glad to have somebody to talk to.

Sam and Hank looked at each other quizzically. A statue of Justice, no less!

"Who called the police?" Hank was pleased to oblige the talkative policeman.

"Oh, that was the butler, they say. He heard a noise, the story is, and came in to see what it was. He found old-man Porter flat on the floor, near the door, with his head bashed in. Old-lady Porter was sitting in one of these chairs, holding the statue. Anyhow, that's the story I got. So this guy calls in for a wagon. That was just last night. I've been on duty since one o'clock today. Won't be relieved until six. A hell of a way to spend a shift, just standing around."

"Where's the butler now?" Hank pressed his luck.

The policeman went on happily. "They say he's being held as a material witness, at some hotel down on Market around Fifth or Sixth. Pretty nice for him, loafing in some hotel."

"Was there anyone else in the house?"

"Yeah, the cook or somebody. They're holding her, too."

Sam looked up sharply. Another witness! This was news—

probably bad news. Janet Porter had said nothing about a cook. Why?

He pulled Hank's arm. "That's new—the cook. When you talk to Janet Porter, or anybody else, find out about her. Why in hell didn't Janet tell me about the cook? Never mentioned her."

The policeman was rambling on, about day shifts and night shifts. They walked through the big, spacious rooms, upstairs and down to the basement. Nothing. Just rooms and furniture and knicknacks. There was nothing more to be learned here.

They thanked the policeman and left. No taxis were in sight, so they walked back toward the financial district and the office. Anyhow, Sam felt the need to stretch his legs. He would take a nap when they got back to the office.

Trudy was gone when they returned. She had left another pile of message slips. One message particularly interested Sam. It was from Justice Radcliffe, "about Janet Porter—will call again." Now what did the eminent Justice Radcliffe have to do with this?

Sam said "good night" as Hank left to go home. Then he took off his coat and vest, and leaned back in his swivel chair. An hour's nap before dinner would be fine, but it was nearly seven o'clock—time for calling home. The evening call was a regular ritual, every day and wherever he was. His wife called it "Sam's daily check-in." He leaned forward, picked up a phone, and dialed his private home number. A woman's voice answered, and Sam's face softened. "Hi, darling, I'm at the office. How are you? How was your day?"

His wife's voice was calm and sweet, as always. Like she is, he thought, peace and sanity and kindness incarnate. "Hello, dear. Just another day. The usual busy, busy, busy. A nice day, all in all. Are you coming home soon?"

"In a while, honey," he said. "Maybe about nine. How are the children?"

"Fine. Busy with their own friends and affairs, of course."

"I'll see you soon. 'By, now." He waited for her goodby, and hung up. Then he leaned back in his chair, crossed his feet on the corner of the big desk, and closed his eyes. The sounds of the city, sixteen stories below, were a faint hum. He dozed, head tilted down and chin on his chest. He dreamed.

Ground mist clung to the shattered walls of broken houses in a battered farm village. It was a gray November morning in the foothills of the Vosges Mountains. Squat, gray-brown tanks were spread in a half-circle in the fields, their long cannon pointing east, like antennae of monstrous beetles. Sam saw himself—Captain Sam Benedict—climbing heavily up a rough wooden ladder. The staircase to the church tower was hanging crazily from the roof. Gaping holes in the walls told of artillery fire the day before. The climbing figure pulled himself up to what remained of the belfry floor, tugged his binoculars loose from a leather case, crouched behind the low belfry wall, and stared out over the dun hills.

There was a patch of woods, nearly bare now under the cold November wind. Something moved there. Sam saw himself turning the knob of the glasses and straining his eyes. He saw heavy forms under the trees—trucks; then there were two figures moving together, and there was no mistaking the coal-scuttle helmets—they were German soldiers. Then there were more of them, and the trucks were beginning to move.

Captain Benedict picked up the walkie-talkie and spoke into the mouthpiece, calling his company executive officer. "Blue Fox, Blue Fox. This is Benedict. Do you read me?"

Electric crackling, and the radio answered into his ear. "Benedict, Benedict, this is Blue Fox. Pearson speaking. I read you loud and clear. Over."

Sam spoke quickly to his tank company's second in command. "There is a patch of woods about three thousand yards east of the village, direct front. Looks like a Kraut bivouac area. Range in on it. When you bracket it, lay all guns on it—the whole company. Azimuth about two—niner—zero. I say again, two—niner—zero. Range three thousand. Got that? Over."

"Roger. Got it." There was a pause while Pearson talked to the tank commanders. Then his voice again: "Loaded and ready. Over."

"Fire one." Sam snapped the order, and a gun cracked behind him. Beyond the woods a geyser of earth erupted suddenly.

"Over," Sam shouted. "Pearson, you were over. Azimuth is okay, but you were over. Down two hundred. Down two hundred. Fire one."

"Roger." Another thud behind him, and another geyser just in front of the woods.

"Bracket." Sam's voice.

Take it slow, he was saying to himself, slow and easy does it. "You have a bracket, Pearson. Now, up one hundred. Up one hundred and fire one. Over." Another crash behind him, and smoke and dust in the trees—on target. Now Sam shouted into the radio, "You've got it. On the nose. Lay all guns, Pearson." He looked back. All of the tank guns were moving slowly, like feelers. He heard his own voice, like that of a stranger. "Fire for effect. I say again, fire for effect." The air behind him moved and bellowed as fifteen cannon blasted out into a roaring crescendo of sound.

The woods were suddenly full of eruptions, gouts of flame, and shaking clouds of dust and smoke. Men were running from the edges, and pieces of things appeared in the air above the trees and fell slowly back into the inferno below. He fixed his glasses on the hellish scene. A human form appeared suddenly on the top of one geyser, spinning in the air like a rag doll. Roaring noise enveloped him, like the buzzing in the ears after a strong drink on an empty stomach.

And Sam was laughing.

He was laughing.

Waves of laughter washed through him. His head was thrown back, and he was roaring with laughter.

Was this Sam Benedict, he thought dimly? Or was this some fiend from Hell, bubbling with joy at the sight of killing and destruction? An icy calmness came over him. Shame bathed him, and his face was wet and cold. He mumbled into the radio. "Pearson. Cease fire, Pearson. For God's sake, cease fire, Pearson!"

Then there was dead silence, and his face was cold. A telephone was ringing. Sam sat upright in his chair. He hadn't dreamed about that for a long time now. Had he gone mad that day in France? Was he really sane, he wondered, if he once had done *that?* Everyone knew, and he knew, that logic, reason, and sanity were the very essence of his life—but if *he, too,* could do something like that . . . ! He picked up the phone.

Hank was on the line. After dinner he had decided to check out the story about the cook in the Porter house. He had gone to the hotel on Market Street. Shot with luck again. The desk clerk had told him what rooms the police had reserved for their two witnesses. Barney Rosvalley might raise hell about talking to State's witnesses, but Hank had gone up to her room and found her there happily watching television.

"She's a pleasant Mexican gal," Hank reported. "Middle-aged and a simple soul. Been cooking for Kevin Porter for over ten years. She was in the kitchen and pantry until about eight, and then in the recreation room in the basement, watching TV until the police came. Her name is Hernandez. And that's all there is to her. She and Rogers spend a lot of time in the recreation room, watching idiot-vision. That room is considered pretty much for their use only."

Sam was interested but not surprised. "It figured that a woman cook would not clobber her boss with a bronze figure. If she was sore at him, she'd probably use poison. Maybe a knife, or even a meat cleaver—not a bronze statue. But what about Rogers?"

"No luck on that. He was not in his room. But—get this—the Hernandez woman gives him a perfect alibi. He was with her in the kitchen in the early evening. And then he was in the TV room from nine to ten. She's sure about that: some program he always watches at that time."

"Well, we'll double check that. But it sounds conclusive."

"Yep. If Porter was killed just before ten that lets Rogers out."

"All right, Hank. Enough for today. See you tomorrow."

After talking with Hank, Sam closed the office and left the building. It was after eight. Paoli's restaurant was handy, so he stopped in there for a light dinner. Then, about nine, coming out onto Montgomery Street, he decided to walk home instead of taking a cab. It was a nice evening and he started walking up the slope of Nob Hill. He felt fine.

"My town," he thought, as he strolled leisurely along Sacramento Street. "What a lovely city is San Francisco!" It was dusk, and colored lights were beginning to shine here and there in the half light. He walked slowly up the slope, alone. There was nobody else on the street. He passed Chinatown and kept on walking. Then he neared the corner of Powell Street; a chill wind seemed to touch him. Suddenly his senses were alert. He had an odd feeling, like moving with infantry again, creeping around a bend in a road where an ambush might be waiting.

Three pairs of boots were there, in front of him on the sidewalk. Dirty, shabby boots with high heels, and tight bluejeans on the ankles above them. The light was dim. He looked up, and shifted the rolled-up copy of *Newsweek* magazine that he often carried in his hand when walking at night. It was held tightly in his right hand, grasped in the middle like a short stick, the ends protruding from his fist.

Three slim young men stood before him. Two of them moved, one slightly to his right and one to his left, hemming him in. Black leather jackets. One had a scruffy, short beard—the one in the middle. That was the one that grasped Sam's coat lapel and said:

"Where ya goin', daddyo? Got any bread with ya?"

Sam said nothing. Instead he stepped forward suddenly and lashed out at the beard, with his clenched left hand. It was a total surprise. He caught the beard full and hard, with all of his weight behind the blow. The bearded one catapulted back. His head hit the pavement with a thud, and he lay still. Sam's left hand hurt horribly.

He spun to the left. That one stood frozen, utter astonishment etched on his face. Sam swung the magazine in a short, tight arc, end forward, hard, into the solar plexus of the frozen figure. Down he went, gasping, his hands folded across his stomach. He rolled on the ground, writhing.

The third one, on the right, was moving, fast, right past Sam and down the hill. He was running as though the hounds of Hell were after him. Sam stood still. His heart was pounding and his left hand burned and throbbed. Then a policeman was there. He had not seen the little tableau, but the picture was clear. He knew who Sam was.

"Goddam punks," he said. "I'm glad they got what was coming to them. Are you okay, Counselor?"

Sam nodded. "I'm all right. They can give you the name of the other one. There were three of them."

The policeman was frisking the two on the ground. "This one that was asleep is coming to. The one with the sick stomach is real unhappy." He held up two switchblade knives. "Shiv carriers. Nice boys! Did you know that this one had a bicycle chain in his pocket?"

Sam shook his head. "No. I didn't see it. The new generation that the world owes a living to." He felt dull and tired.

"Do you want me to help you home?" The officer was solicitous. "A squad car will be along soon. I'll get rid of these two."

"No, thanks." Sam wanted to be alone. He felt depressed. "I live just a bit up there. I'm fine. I'd rather walk." He thanked the policeman. "You know where to find me, if you want a complaining witness. I want these people prosecuted."

"You bet, Counselor. Leave it to me. I'll take care of them. The sergeant'll probably call you about them. You go along home if you like."

Sam said "good night" and started walking again. His hand ached.

CHAPTER

Trudy rarely pressed Sam on anything about clients or cases. She was a gem of a secretary, efficient and reliable—never a nuisance. But she was pressing him now.

"You ought to talk to her, Mr. Benedict. She's been waiting since eight o'clock."

Sam swallowed a surge of irritation. "Trudy, you know better than that. I've got enough to do. This Porter case is going to be enough in itself. Tell Belle Larkbey to take it somewhere else. There's no shortage of lawyers in this city."

"But she's an old client, Mr. Benedict, and she's very upset." Trudy was almost insistent.

He pursed his lips. Belle Larkbey really was a good client, though not a rich one. She was always in and out of some business deal, and she had referred quite a few people to his office. "All right," he conceded grudgingly. "Tell her to come in. But I shouldn't do it."

Belle was a character. Bleached blond and loud, she did not look her forty-plus years. She had been running a small gin mill in North Beach, years ago, when she had brought her first case to him. That had been an involved dispute about a contract for furniture and fixtures, and she had fought an attempted gouge by the seller. Belle was a fighter, and she had been right that time. Since then she had bought and sold half a dozen small night clubs and bars, and Sam guessed that she was involved in another contract dispute. Belle was likeable, but he really was not interested in a squabble about some North Beach bar.

Belle came in with a flourish, tossed her worn mink jacket

over the back of a chair, and slapped a newspaper down on his desk. "Hi, Sam. Get a load of that." She pointed at a caption on an article at the bottom of the front page: BELLE LARKBEY'S CLUB RAIDED.

"Hey. That's pretty good." Sam was impressed. "Great publicity, Belle. You've never made the front page before."

"Oh, yeah." Belle's indignation boomed through the room. "Great. Just great. I'm closed up, Sam. Padlocked. Shut tight. Out of business. Great. Just great." Her voice was heavy with sarcasm and outrage.

Sam skimmed through the story. "Sale of liquor to minors. . . . Violation of statute. . . . Complaints from angry citizens . . ." and so on. He looked up. "I'm surprised Belle. Selling liquor to kids! That's not like you. Is it true?"

Belle exploded again. "Minors, schminors. Three goddamn spoiled brats with expensive clothes and fake I.D. cards. What am I supposed to be, a den mother? They had I.D. cards. I asked to see their I.D. cards. They showed me their I.D. cards. So I sold them some drinks. They make damn nuisances of themselves. I go to throw them out of the joint. And next thing I'm raided and padlocked. How in hell was I supposed to know that they were minors and their I.D. cards were phonies? Tell me that."

"When was all this?"

"Yesterday. I was padlocked yesterday. The three stooges were in my place last night and got me closed up last night."

"Even so," Sam wondered aloud, "how come all the fanfare? Why didn't they just slap a fine on you and let it go at that? Have you been nailed for selling liquor to minors before?"

"Never, Sam. Never, as God is my judge. Not many bar operators can say that."

Sam was puzzled. "It's a pretty commonplace, routine thing. Must happen all the time—kids looking older than they are, and being sold a drink."

"Yes. Every bar slips up on that once in a while," Belle said. "I've been very careful. Usually, when it happens it means a fine. A *fine*—not a padlock."

"Then, why all the hoopla?"

"That's what I want to know."

"And why a page-one story about a routine little sale-to-minors incident?"

"That's what I want to know, too. What the hell is going on? Why are they leaning on me?"

She became quiet and serious. "It ain't funny, Sam. It's bad. A little publicity is one thing, but a reputation as a dive is something else again. And every day I'm closed cuts down business in the future. I need some help. This thing can ruin me."

"I'm pretty tied up, Belle." Sam was hesitant. "Maybe you can get someone else to handle it."

"No. I want you. This is life-and-death to me. I've put a lot into this tavern, and I can't afford to lose it."

"Be practical, Belle. I'm an expensive lawyer. You know that. It doesn't pay, from your point of view."

"This is important to me, Sam." Belle was very earnest. "I know you don't work for peanuts. But I need this pub, and I need a clean name. You can get them back for me, if anyone can."

He gave up his resistance. "All right, then. I'll see what I can do. Do you have a copy of the order closing your place?"

She dug through her handbag, extracted a wrinkled sheet of paper, and handed it to him. "Here."

He smoothed it flat on his desk and scanned it quickly: "Three counts . . . three sales . . . minors . . . namely and to wit: Ralph Waldo Hibbes, James Madison Canfield, III, and Walter S. Finchley. . . ." He looked up at Belle. "Who are these kids? Do you know them?"

"Never saw them before, and I hope never again. I don't know them from Adam. Pure transient trade."

"This one in particular—Canfield—is there anything you can tell me about him? That's a big name in this town."

"I don't know which is which." Her voice rose again. "They looked like college boys to me. Expensive-looking clothes, and they ordered martinis. That's all."

"All right, Belle. I'll take care of it." He walked her to the door. "I'll be in touch." She stalked through the outer waiting room like a brigantine under full sail, bleached hair and open fur jacket fluttering in her wake.

Hank Tabor had seen the morning papers and had noticed the piece about Belle Larkbey. But he was much more interested in the headline story about Janet Porter. That was natural headline material. Big, black letters shouted SOCIALITE . . . TELEGRAPH HILL MANSION . . . BLUDGEON MURDER . . . He added his copy to the one already on Sam's desk.

"Looks like the papers are going all out on this story," Hank remarked. "Some of them already have Janet Porter in the death house."

"So I see." Sam was noncommittal. "Trudy tells me that reporters have been hanging around the office. Be extra careful, Hank. The courts and Bar Associations have been real hard-nosed ever since the Supreme Court reversal of the Sheppard conviction in Cleveland. The day of trying cases in the news-papers seems to be over, and I for one am glad of it."

Hank smiled. "Aren't you the man who said that the court-room is only *one* of the places in which a case is decided?"

"Yes, I've said that," Sam replied, "and still say it. But I was not talking about making a public circus of a case. Anyhow, right now anything the press says about Janet Porter can't be good for us. All the facts we have so far look bad for her. Don't let's make it look any worse." Then Sam told Hank about Belle Larkbey's problem and showed him the padlock order. "I want you to work on this one, too, while you're digging on the Porter case. Find out who's behind this and, if possible, why. Check particularly on those three youngsters and their backgrounds. How did they happen to wander into Belle's place, and just what happened there?"

Hank took the paper and glanced at it. "Okay."

"Find out who's handling the case in the Prosecutor's Office, and when the hearing is scheduled. Also, who's sitting then."

Sam's hands rested on the desk top as he spoke. A strip of tape was wound around the knuckles of his left hand. Hank turned and looked at the tape.

"What happened to your hand?"

Sam grinned and told him about the incident on his way home the evening before. "It doesn't hurt much now, just the skin bruised. It'll be all gone in a day or two."

Hank was concerned and angry. "You can take good care

of yourself, boss, I know. But you're not getting any younger. You used to carry that little, two-barrel Derringer in your vest pocket. I haven't seen it there for quite a while. Don't you think you ought to carry it, on general principles?"

"No." Sam stood up and showed Hank a rolled-up magazine like the one he had carried the evening before. "Watch this." He walked around the desk to a clothes-closet door near one of its corners. With a sudden turn he smashed the end of the magazine into the heavy wood panel in the center of the door. A dented circle, paint knocked off, showed on the panel where he had struck it. "I don't need a gun. This is weapon enough for anyone. It can be deadly. But I don't want to kill anyone —even young thugs who waylay people in the streets," Sam said.

Hank whistled softly. "Oh my! Look at that dent!"

"Don't misunderstand me," Sam went on. "Those miserable pups are going to get the full punishment that the law allows. Violence in the streets is just not to be tolerated. It is the end of any decent society if that sort of thing goes unpunished. I mean to press charges to the limit. I happened to be able to handle them. What if I had not been able!"

Hank rolled up a sheaf of paper in his hands and struck one end experimentally against his left palm. It hurt, though he had not hit it very hard. "I'm convinced. From now on I'll carry a magazine when I go out at night."

Sam smiled and tossed the magazine onto a chair. "You'd better be on your way. You have a lot of checking to do."

Hank grunted, heaved his big frame out of the chair, and started for the door. "You can say that again."

"You have a lot of checking to do."

"Okay, boss; I know, I know."

They grinned at each other affectionately as Hank pulled open the door.

Trudy buzzed on the intercom. "Mr. Benedict. Justice Radcliffe is here. You have an appointment to see him."

"Tell him I'll be right out." Sam got up and went to the door. Radcliffe was a good judge, one of the best. This one is what a good judge is supposed to be, he thought; not one of the political hacks that got paid off with a seat on the bench. A real judge, and a good one. He opened the door. "Mr. Justice Radcliffe. Welcome. Do come in." His voice was warm, and he held the door open for the austerely dignified man who came in with his hand extended in greeting. "It's always good to see you." They shook hands.

The old judge walked in and looked around. "I've always liked your office, Sam. It's like you—simple but solid, uncluttered and direct in spite of all the things in it." He looked closely at the mementos resting unobtrusively on a table and on the bar—a doorknob from the old Hall of Justice, set in a plaque engraved "To the Master—Sam Benedict . . ."; a framed letter from a former President of the United States starting with "Dear Sam,"; a picture of a famous movie star, inscribed "With heartfelt thanks to Sam Benedict, who saved my life. . . ."; and more.

Sam offered the judge a chair. "Would you like some coffee, Mr. Justice, or a highball?"

"No, thank you. I'm not here on a social visit, Sam, though it's always a delight to chat with you. I'm here on serious business, and to ask a favor of you." For a moment he remained standing near a window; then he walked to the opposite side of the room and paused at the doorway. It led into a conference room, every wall of which was lined with shelves solidly filled with law books. There was a large conference table and leather-covered captain's chairs surrounding it on all sides.

Radcliffe looked around, almost sadly. "It's good to see a real law office again. A place where a man can breathe. Not the marble-lined tomb where I work. A man can be alive here. He can try, and experiment, and improvise. He can even make a mistake and then correct it."

"You don't make many mistakes, Mr. Justice." Sam meant it.

"Don't dare to, Sam. Don't dare to. Have to live like a machine now, like a computer. Dry and mechanical, and everlastingly accurate. No blood or tears or human sweat or emotion any more. Bloodless logic and law—nothing else. Oh, how I miss all this." He swept his hand around. He drew a deep breath, and turned back toward Sam. "You know that I called you yesterday."

"Yes."

"It was good of you to see me on such short notice. I'll get to the point." He paused.

Sam waited.

"I want you to defend Janet Porter," the judge resumed. "You've seen her already. I know that. I want you to take this case, hopeless as it seems. Name your own fee."

The buzzer rang suddenly. Sam snapped the switch. "No calls, Trudy. No interruptions. Please." There was silence for a minute between the two men. "It's not like you, Mr. Justice, to get involved in a trial-level case. May I ask why? What is Janet Porter to you?"

The judge's ice-blue eyes looked hard at him. "Her father was the best friend I ever had. Maybe the only man in all my life who was my close and good friend. I owe his memory whatever I can do for his daughter."

"Is Janet Porter a special friend of yours?"

"I have known her since she was an infant. Knew her mother too. Have known her well and watched her—from a distance, of course—since she was about twelve years old."

"Twelve years old?" Sam's voice showed surprise.

"I was a law professor at Columbia then, Sam. The law school was in Kent Hall in those days, not in that modernistic pile on Amsterdam. I was giving the Buchanan Lectures that year." He seemed to be lost in thought.

"And she was twelve years old!" Sam repeated.

"Yes. Twelve years old, and John brought her to the Buchanan Lectures. She was very bright. She had just finished grammar school, and he brought her with him. Her mother had died. She had no one else. I remember that her hair was in two braids, one on each side of her face. She was very quiet and sober, for a child. Looked like Alice in Wonderland."

"Did she attend all of the lectures?"

"Radcliffe nodded. "Yes. Every one. She sat in the front row with her father each day, very quiet and serious. I think that I talked mostly to her in giving those lectures, just as you pick one main face in a jury box to talk to. I delivered the Buchanan Lectures to this child, and she understood me perfectly. I know she did."

"But that was years ago."

"I've seen her often, since then. More often since her father died. I was named executor of his will, you know. Handled all of her estate and business affairs then, while she was still in New York and working at New York University, and when she married and moved here. Since I've been in the 'mausoleum' at Sacramento, of course, I can't do that any more."

"I understand."

"But I can see that she gets the ablest help there is, Sam, and that's you. Will you look out for her now?"

"Mr. Justice, I would defend Jezebel if you asked me to."

"I'm glad."

"Tell me, though. Did she kill Kevin Porter?"

"Not a doubt of it. The evidence so far is all circumstantial, but it is as conclusive as any I've ever seen."

"Why did she do it?"

"I don't know." The old judge was suddenly tired and bewildered.

"Then what defense does she have?"

"I don't know. It's up to you to find one, if there is one. Or find out if there isn't any. It's all up to you."

"All right then," Sam said. "I'll do what I can."

After the judge had left, Trudy brought in a pile of phone messages and memos. There were affidavits to check, motion papers to draw up, memoranda of law to dictate, letters to send, and all the busy minutiae of an active law office. On top of it all, Sam had to finish a paper that he had promised to deliver before the National Academy of Trial Lawyers. He swore at himself for his reluctance to say no to such requests. Well, there was no help for it. He told Trudy to bring the files he needed. "Bring your book, too. I have some things for you to do."

Before they began he made some mental calculations aloud. "The American Bar Association Annual Meeting begins in New York next Monday. The N.A.T.L. meeting is the day before. Get me a flight to New York on Saturday afternoon. Make a reservation at the Regency. The Waldorf and the Americana must be booked solid by now." He paused. "By Tuesday afternoon I should be able to leave New York. Get me a flight to Cleveland for then, and make a reservation at the Sheraton.

Then, early Thursday morning I should be able to move on to Chicago, so get a flight to there. Book me at the Ambassador East or West there, but I'll probably start for home the same day. For that afternoon, a flight back to San Francisco."

Trudy read back his instructions.

Sam nodded. "All right. Let's start with the Vanderjagt file. The same caption, dated today; 'Motion to Appoint a Special Referee as to the assets of the insolvent Maddox Corporation. Pursuant to the order of this honorable court, dated. . . .'"

Hank phoned in while Bud Kennedy was coming into the office, late in the morning. Sam told Bud to sit down and make himself comfortable while he took the call. "Yes, Hank. I'm talking with Bud Kennedy."

"I have two items of information that you wanted," Hank reported. "First, the D.A.'s Office has assigned Jerry Spangler to the Belle Larkbey matter."

"Gerald! He's a pretty heavy gun to be assigned to that kind of petty business." Sam was surprised.

"That's what struck me, too."

"Have you talked with him yet?"

"No. Do you want me to?"

"Yes, but carefully. Find out his attitude toward it. That's all you'll get anyhow."

"Okay. Now the second item. Janet Porter had only one close friend here in town, as far as I can find out. Her name is Elizabeth Holdridge. She's a divorcee, it seems—twice over. She has an apartment at the Mark Hopkins."

Sam jotted down the name. "Sounds interesting. Call her and ask her if she'll be at home later today. I'd like to talk to her. Anything else?"

"That's all for now."

"All right, Hank. Keep in touch." He hung up, and turned to Bud. The newspaperman was listening eagerly, trying to get the drift of the conversation.

"I know that you want a story, Bud. I understand." Sam was sympathetic. "But there simply is no story to give. It's just too soon."

"Oh, come on now, Sam," Kennedy pleaded. "You've been

digging into it. I know that. That was Hank Tabor on the phone, wasn't it? He's legging it around, and it must be on the Porter case. I can add two and two, you know."

Sam smiled. "Bud, when there is any story to give out, I'll give it out. You know that, too. I've never been unfriendly to the papers. You are entitled to print the facts. But there just aren't any facts worth printing."

Kennedy leaned forward, and his voice was earnest. "There are facts and facts. My editor expects me to bring in a story. At least what's going on so far. This is a front-page item, after all. I don't expect secrets. But you can tell me at least if she denies the murder charge."

Sam's lips tightened. "There'll be a hearing tomorrow. That's public record, and official. If Mrs. Porter enters a denial that will be when and where she does. I have no right to speak for her now."

"I'm not asking you to speak for her," Kennedy pressed him. "Just tell me whether or not she denies the charge. She must have done that, to the police. You know that Barney Rosvalley won't tell me anything."

"He can't. The Supreme Court lays down the rules, not Barney or I. They just won't have any big hoorah in the papers in such cases. It's prejudicial. The Sheppard case made that pretty clear. Are you asking me to risk a contempt citation?"

Kennedy snorted. "That will be the day, when Sam Benedict is afraid of a contempt citation. I've seen you tell off prosecutors and even judges, right in the courtroom."

"That's different. Protecting a client's right is my job, even if it means fighting a D.A. or even a judge, when he's wrong. Get that—when he's wrong. Being wrong myself, and defying the law or proper procedure, is not the same thing. You ought to know that."

The reporter's face reddened. "You don't have to lecture me, Sam. I wasn't born yesterday."

Sam stood up slowly, his eyes hard. "And don't you get lippy with me, young fella. I didn't invite you in here. It was your idea. Now you can get the hell out."

The newsman winced. "I'm sorry, Sam. That was childish of me. Don't get sore."

Sam sat down again. His face softened. "All right, Bud, but don't needle me."

Bud was contrite. "When you're right, you're right. I was out of line. You know how it is, trying to get a story."

Sam replied. "The thing that annoys me is the idea that a reporter has an absolute right to know everything that goes on. That is a crock of you-know-what. It gravels me when a reporter gets arrogant and demanding."

"That may be so, but there's another side to the picture. 'The people's right to know' may be a corny phrase, but there's a lot of truth in it."

"'The people's right to know' is not a synonym for a publisher's right to build circulation with sensationalism. Kid me not." Sam's voice was icy. "You are interested in a story for the sake of a story. I have to think of a human being who is in peril of her life. She isn't grist for a newspaper mill. She's a living, breathing human being, no matter what she did or didn't do."

Bud shrugged his shoulders. "Okay, okay. For my salary I'm not going to crucify anyone."

"Damn right you're not. At least not with any help from me." Sam grinned. "What do they pay you now?"

"Not enough. Not nearly enough."

Sam changed the subject. "By the way, did you have anything to do with the story on Belle Larkbey in this morning's issue?"

Bud's head lifted suddenly, like a hunting dog sniffing a scent. "No, that's not mine. Why? Are you interested in that one?"

Sam picked up a notebook and leafed through its pages as though looking for something. "Just curious. Seems like an unusual bit for the front page. Not much of a story, one sale of intoxicating liquor to some minors, in a bar that never was in trouble before. Hardly seems worth a page-one story."

The reporter looked at him doubtfully, and then said, "Well, Belle Larkbey is an interesting character. Colorful. Good material for a story, more than once."

"True, true. But page one, for such a petty incident?"

"A story's a story, Sam. The public loves stories about misguided youth, and it likes stories about colorful characters."

Sam shook his head. "For the columns, maybe. But the bloomin' front page. Come on, Bud. There's more to this than meets the eye, isn't there?"

"If there is, I don't know about it."

"Whose story was it?"

Bud looked at the paper. "I don't know. There's no byline on it."

"No, there isn't," Sam said, "and isn't that odd. A page-one, human-interest story, and no byline . . . ?"

Bud's memory was beginning to register. "Say. Didn't you once represent Belle in a case? You're her attorney, aren't you?" He spoke carefully, aware that he might be getting into deep water.

Sam shrugged. "I handled a matter or two for her a while ago. You're right in that. But I haven't handled anything for her for some time. I'm just curious about an old client, that's all."

Bud was unconvinced. "I'll ask about it when I get back to the office. You don't have anything to do with it, eh?"

Sam was all innocence. "How could I? It just popped in the papers today."

Bud looked back doubtfully as he went out. "Just who was interviewing whom, Master?"

Elizabeth Holdridge lived at the Mark Hopkins. That, in itself, told something about her—not many people could afford a permanent suite in this lordly hotel. A maid in silver-gray uniform met Sam at the door of the suite. He waited for a minute or two in a sitting room furnished and decorated in gilded Empire style. It was early afternoon and the room was bright with sunlight.

She came into the room very much the *grande dame*, wearing a lace peignoir and holding a long ivory cigarette holder in her hand. Her face was thin and fine-featured, and she had closely cut blond hair. "Only her hairdresser knows for sure," Sam thought, surmising that the color was the result of skillful bleaching. He bowed slightly as she approached, and said, "Mrs. Holdridge, my name is Sam Benedict. It was good of you to see me."

She motioned him toward a chair. "Not at all, Mr. Benedict. Please call me Betty. You're here about Janet, aren't you? Please don't be formal. Do sit down. Would you care for some tea?"

"Thank you, no." He sat down on an ornate, tapestry-covered chair that had a round, upholstered seat and was not very comfortable. A Baccarat crystal cigarette urn stood next to him on an inlaid table. Sam took out one of his own cigarettes and lit it.

"It's dreadful, simply dreadful." She adjusted the folds of her dressing gown as she settled into the corner of a couch. "It is simply inconceivable. There must be some mistake. Kevin and Janet simply are not that sort of people."

"These things can happen to anyone, Mrs. Holdridge."

"Betty, please; not Mrs. Holdridge," she reproved.

"All right, Betty. I was saying, these things can happen to anyone. People are people, pretty much the same kind of animal under the skin, everywhere."

"Not really, Mr. Benedict. There are people and there are people. Some people just don't do the kind of thing the papers are saying about Janet."

"Sam, please; not Mr. Benedict."

She smiled. *"Touché,* Sam. I'll try to remember."

"What kind of people would you say Kevin and Janet Porter were?"

"The better kind, I would say. Distinctly not of the common herd."

"Oh?" He waited for her to continue.

"Yes. He was a distinguished scholar, you know. A professor in the best sense of that term. And a gentleman. A gentleman in the finest sense of *that* term."

"And Janet?"

"Fine breeding. A woman of breeding. She comes from one of the best families in the East. Nothing *nouveau* about her. A bit quiet and plain, perhaps, but definitely of good family. Definitely."

"Yes."

"We were very close friends, you know. Very close. Many's the afternoon I spent with Janet. Many."

"When did you last see her?"

"No more than three or four days ago. We had lunch together at the St. Francis. Then we went shopping at Gump's. Janet had to buy a gift for somebody. A wedding anniversary, I think."

"How did she seem to be, then?"

"Quite as usual. Nothing at all unusual. She was very quiet, you know. A women of few words, you might say. A good listener rather than an interesting conversationalist. That is a nice way to be, really. Better than to be like me. I love to chatter, as you can see. It would be rather tiresome if everyone were like me—fond of gaiety and laughter and bright conversation."

"Did you spend the whole afternoon together?"

"No. Janet did her shopping and then she went home. Said she had to work on her book. It's not really her book, you know, it's her father's. He never finished it, and she has been working on it for a long time. She was always rushing home to work on that awful book. Dreary business, it seemed to me, but she was forever at it."

"Did you speak to her after that?"

"No. I was going to call her today, or she me, about doing something over the weekend. That's off now, of course."

"Of course." Sam's voice was faintly sarcastic. There was something about this woman's manner that irritated him.

She went on. "But she seemed perfectly fine then. Nothing at all to suggest that this terrible thing was going to happen. But then she always was quiet, almost secretive sometimes."

"Yes. How long have you known her?"

"Since she came to San Francisco. We became friends right after she arrived here."

"How did you meet?"

"At a Hunt Club breakfast, I remember," she said positively. "Not that Janet could ride. Kevin brought her, to get her to meet some people and make some friends. She was very shy, you know."

"Was she?"

"My, yes. For someone who came from a family quite well known in social circles she was extraordinarily shy and withdrawn. Kevin had quite a time getting her to go out and meet people."

"You had known Kevin before that?"

"For years. He was almost one of my beaux, years before. He was in the stag line at my coming-out party. He was not really a beau, of course, but I've known him for years. No. It couldn't have been my debut. It must have been some other party. He's quite a bit older than I, you know."

"Was he?"

"Yes. Rather a bit. He was quite gray-haired, you know. That was premature, really, his gray hair. He's quite a bit older than Janet, or than I, for that matter."

"Much older than Janet?"

"My, yes. White-haired now, you know. He must have been ten or twelve years older than Janet, at least. Almost a May-and-December marriage, everyone said."

"You had not known her in the East?"

"No. She lived at Great Neck. I know some people on the North Shore, but never had met her."

"Did she meet Kevin there?"

"No. From what they told me, they met in Manhattan. She was a research fellow at New York University and Kevin was visiting there on some project or other. That's where they met."

"And got married, and then came to San Francisco?"

She shook her head. "Not directly. He was teaching at some university in Ohio. In Cleveland, I think. They lived there for a short time, and then they came here."

"Did they love each other?" he asked.

Betty Holdridge smiled broadly. "Now that's a real question, Mr. Benedict—a real question. That is the kind of question I like. Who loves whom, or when. Who really loves whom? You're speaking to an expert on love, you know. Did you know that I have been married three times? Three times, Mr. Benedict, and three divorces. Yes, indeed, I know all about love."

Sam repeated his question. "Did they love each other?"

"Who really loves whom, Mr. Benedict?" Her voice was suddenly acid and shrill. "Does anybody really love anybody? Do talk and fine phrases mean love?"

"What about Kevin and Janet?"

"How do I know! Who knows? As much as people usually love each other, I suppose. You don't ask people that sort of thing; really, you don't. Besides, they'd lie to you anyhow."

"Did they seem to love each other?"

"They were polite to each other." Bitterness edged her voice. "After all, they were both people of good breeding. They didn't paw each other in public, if that's what you mean. Neither did they quarrel in public. Yes, I suppose they loved each other, insofar as married people love each other." She stood up suddenly. "Will you excuse me, please. I'll be back in a moment." She walked quickly to another room, shutting the door behind her.

Kind of upset, Sam thought. Jealous of Kevin and Janet? So this was Janet's best friend. Some friend!

A few minutes later she came back into the room. As she walked by him, Sam thought he caught a whiff of alcohol. That was probably it. She must have gone to the other room to steady her nerves with a few shots of booze. Quite a lady!

She plumped herself down on the couch, in the same corner, facing him, and said, "Now, where were we? You were pumping me for information, Sam, weren't you? Let's get on with it."

Sam took another tack. "May I say that you are a very handsome woman."

Her lip curled. "Handsome, the man says. You've come to a pretty pass, Betty. Now you're handsome. It used to be lovely, Sam, or ravishing, or at least beautiful. Now, it's handsome. *Sic transit gloria*—or Betty."

Sam said nothing. She must have taken two or three drinks.

"You'd be surprised, Sam, though," she rambled on, "there's life in the old gal yet. Did you ever read *Archie and Mehitabel?*"

He nodded.

"*Toujours gai*, kid, *toujours gai*. That's my motto. I'll have you know that there are still some pretty eligible men who think I'm quite something."

Sam agreed. "I'm sure there are."

"And I'll have you know that I'm still listed in the *Blue Book* in spite of my sad matrimonial adventures."

He was silent.

"Yes, indeed. California society may not be quite as la-de-da as the North Shore or Back Bay, but it has its rules, Sam. It has its rules. Do you know them?"

"I'm afraid not," he said.

"One of them is that a New York Stuyvesant outranks a Barbary Coast copra trader. Did you know that?"

"I don't follow you."

"Did you know that Janet Porter is related to Peter Stuyvesant? And to God-only-knows who else! She's a princess from away back. You didn't know that, did you?"

"No, I didn't."

"But take me, on the other hand. My grandfather made it big in the South Seas trade; and he owned a big place in San Francisco when the Barbary Coast was swinging. Can you picture it? They say that grandmother wore tights. But the fire of nineteen six wiped out the records. Lucky for me."

"How so?"

"That's why I was Queen of the May, in San Francisco—until Janet arrived. But when she got here I was demoted. There wasn't any vote on it, and there was no coronation ceremony for her, but she was Queen, believe me, from the day Kevin brought her here."

"She didn't seem to be much of a social butterfly."

Her face was bright with alcohol and anger. "She isn't. That's the final irony of it all. She couldn't care less. But she's the Queen Bee here. Have no doubt of that. And I'm her faithful attendant."

Sam looked at her with barely concealed dislike. "It must be very hard for you." His sarcasm was wasted.

"Oh, don't you worry about me, Sam." Her voice was suddenly hard. "Worry about her. I didn't murder my husbands, though God knows I should have."

Anger rose in him. "She murdered her husband, eh? You know that."

"What else! Everybody knows that now. The papers are full of it."

"And you believe everything you read in the papers?"

"Oh, come now, Sam. I'm not a child, you know. Facts are facts, and the facts are quite plain. That holier-than-thou manner of hers can't change the facts."

Sam stood up. "It has been very interesting, Mrs. Holdridge. Thank you for your assistance." He started to walk toward the door.

"Not at all, Sam. Not at all. Always glad to help a friend in need." Her voice was becoming slurred.

In vino veritas, he thought. He felt soiled.

She stood up and followed him. "Your honorable opponent, the District Attorney, is pretty sure of the facts about Janet. You know that, don't you?"

He stopped and turned to face her. "How do you know?"

"He has been sniffing about, too. I thought that you certainly knew that."

"Did he discover anything?"

"Not from me. After all, what is there to discover? Janet and Kevin were *sans peur et sans reproche.* Not a breath of scandal ever touched them. Not a cotton-pickin' breath."

He looked her up and down as he opened the door. "They say, to coin a phrase, that a good friend is more precious than rubies. Goodby, Mrs. Holdridge."

She glared at him, her face taut and white. "You can go straight to hell, Mister Lawyer." Then she slammed the door shut.

North Beach isn't a beach at all, although at one time, nearly a century before, it had been a popular resort area. But those were the days before the city had decided to fill in the land along that part of the Bay. In reality, North Beach forms a narrow valley between the slopes of Telegraph and Russian Hills, and contains most of the Italian, a large part of the Mexican, and a good measure of the Bohemian population of San Francisco. As the cab moved from downtown San Francisco into North Beach's colorful neighborhood, Sam reflected that here the past was a living part of the present. No historical markers or guano-encrusted statues heralded the glories of the past. But the shop windows that were crammed with odd and fascinating merchandise, and the foreign tongues and Old World traditions gave living proof that the past, at least in this section of the city, was a living, breathing thing, something real that one could touch and hold onto.

As the taxi neared Belle Larkbey's tavern, Sam ordered the driver to stop, deciding that it would be more advantageous to be seen approaching the building on foot. To get out from the cab in front of Belle's place might make it seem as if he was on a special mission, which in fact he was. As he walked toward the tavern he noted that it was a two-story, stucco structure, with a narrow frontage on the street. He guessed that the upstairs must be living quarters. The paper tacked to the front door announced that the City and County of San Francisco had ordered the establishment sealed closed. Nobody answered when he knocked on the door.

He walked down the street to the next block and stopped in front of a bar with a gilt-on-black sign over a door that announced "The In-Crowd Place." He went in. There was a bar, a few tables, and a man behind the bar mopping it with a wet cloth. Sam ordered a scotch-and-water and sat on a high stool at the bar. When the drink arrived, he stirred it and then turned to the barman. "Too bad about Belle Larkbey's place being shut down."

The bartender looked at him. "Yeah."

"She's a good egg. Pity that it happened to her."

The bartender nodded. "She's a pretty good one. I'll buy that."

"Never had a bit of trouble before. Many's the time I've rested my elbows there, and a nicer place you couldn't want."

The bartender agreed. "It's a good, clean spot."

Now that Sam had the man talking, he invented quickly. "Except for the time the two sailors tried to break up the joint."

The barman was puzzled. "What sailors? When did that happen?"

"Oh, no more than two, three weeks ago."

Disbelief showed on the barman's face, and he seemed annoyed. "You makin' a mistake, Mister. Nobody broke up Belle's place. Not ever. Not that kind of a place. You must be thinkin' of some other place."

"Oh, Belle's place always has lots of action."

"Mister, that's a nice, quiet place. You got it mixed up with somethin' else."

"You're kidding me!"

"No, I'm not. Real nice place. I'd like it if Belle would put me in that bar. Real good spot. Quiet and nice—except maybe for that Gladys."

"What Gladys?"

"The waitress. You know, the red-headed one. She's a tramp. Don't know how Belle ever hired her."

"What do you mean, 'tramp'?"

The bartender grinned sourly. "Come on, Mister. She must have hustled you if you ever spent an evening there. How she gets away with it with Belle, I can't figure out. They tell me that Belle doesn't even know. Well, that's Belle for you. If she likes someone, she trusts him all the way."

Sam agreed. "That's the truth." He swallowed his drink, and got up. "See you."

The barman resumed his mopping. "Drop in again."

They brought Janet Porter into the attorney's interview room again. The same woman deputy sheriff was with her. This time Janet was wearing a prison-uniform dress. Her hair was neatly brushed. If it were a little longer and tied back in a bun behind her head, she would look just like a post-Civil-War chromo of a proper housewife, he thought. "How are they treating you, Janet?"

"Well enough." She was composed and quiet. She sat back from the table, her hands folded tightly in her lap. There was a plain gold wedding band on her left hand. No other rings, and no diamonds.

Sam pointed at the ring. "Did the police take your rings and handbag?"

"My handbag. Not my ring. This is the only one I wear."

"Has the District Attorney spoken with you?"

"Yes."

"What did he say?"

"He asked me many questions. Much the same as you did."

"What did you tell him?" he asked.

"What I told you. That's all I know. Was that wrong?"

"No, as long as that's all. But from now on you should not discuss anything with him. If he wants to know anything, tell him to ask me. He's not likely to talk with you again, but if he does, tell him that I told you that he is to ask me."

"I understand," she said.

"Are you more rested now?"

"Yes."

"Do you remember anything more, that you haven't told me?"

"I've told you everything I can remember, Mr. Benedict. Everything."

"Did you see Rogers or the cook at any time after Kevin left, after dinner?"

"No. I'm sure of that. I was alone, working in the library."

"And you don't remember Kevin coming back in?"

"No."

"Have you ever had blackouts or amnesia, Janet?"

"No, never."

"Have you ever had any serious illness—diabetes, or high blood pressure maybe?"

"No, never."

"Do you have a family physician?"

"Well, yes. But I rarely called him; only for a cold or something trivial like that. Kevin had no real illnesses either."

"What is your doctor's name?"

"Dr. Kramer. Josiah Kramer, on Powell Street."

"I'll talk with him." He asked her to sign a note he had scribbled on a page in his pocket notebook, authorizing any doctor who had treated her to answer any questions he might ask.

After she had signed the note, he resumed his questioning. "You were born in Great Neck, New York?"

"Yes."

"Did you ever live in New York City?"

"Yes."

"Went to college?"

"No. My father had tutors for me, at home. And he himself tutored me."

"You assisted him in his work?"

"Yes."

"At New York University?"

"No, at Harvard. Then I worked at N.Y.U."

"You stayed on there after your father died?"

She nodded. "Yes. I worked as a research assistant. No salary worth mentioning, and I never was part of the faculty. But they let me work there after my father died."

"For whom did you work?"

"Various faculty members."

"And you met Kevin there?"

"Yes."

"And were married?"

"Yes."

"And lived in Cleveland for a while?"

"Yes."

"You never had any children?"

"No."

"Why?"

"We didn't want any."

"Oh."

This was no good, Sam thought. She was becoming more and more withdrawn; answering in monosyllables when he had hoped that she might open up.

"Did you love Kevin?" That ought to get a reaction, he thought.

"Yes." Her face was an impassive mask.

"He was quite a bit older than you, though, wasn't he?"

"Yes."

It was no use. He rose to go. "All right. I'll see you tomorrow, at the hearing. This is only a preliminary, you understand. Don't worry about it."

"Yes."

He shook his head. "Did the guard get you some cigarettes? Do you have what you need?"

"Yes. Thank you."

He called the deputy sheriff. Janet walked away without a backward glance.

"Getting nowhere, rapidly," he thought glumly. "Well, tomorrow is another day."

It was late afternoon when Sam arrived at Dr. Kramer's office on Powell Street. It was a typical general-practitioner's office, after hours, and empty. Dr. Kramer was a friendly fellow, anxious to be helpful once he saw Janet's note.

"I read about it in the papers. Shocking business. Janet Porter would have been the last one in the world one would expect to do such a thing."

"For what have you treated her, Doctor, or Kevin Porter?" Sam asked.

Kramer pulled two cards out of a desk file. "Very routine kind of thing. Persistent cold and postnasal drip, last winter. That was Mrs. Porter. Minor eye infection, Kevin Porter, a year ago; a tear duct was blocked and I used a probe. Nothing of any consequence. No major matters at all. Saw them seldom, and for nothing important, really."

"Any kind of personal problems that they might have talked over with you; either one?"

"No. Mrs. Porter is rather reserved, you know. Hardly the type to air her personal problems with me—or with anyone else, I would guess. Her husband was always in a hurry. He was the kind of man who thought a visit to a physician was a waste of time that interfered with his work." He paused, then added as an afterthought, "She had some minor recurrent premenstrual trouble, but many women do. It's commonplace."

"Anything significant about it?"

"No. Lots of women have it. About all they can do is bear it and curse 'the curse.' You know, that's what many women call the menstrual cycle—the 'curse'."

"Did either of them ever get a complete physical checkup?"

"Not from me."

"Any record of anything that you might classify as in the psychiatric area of practice?"

"Not a thing."

"Any record of prior hospitalization or medical record?"

"Well, perhaps. I have a notation from Mrs. Porter's first visit. She said that she had had a physical examination at the Cleveland Clinic. So had he. That was when they lived in Cleveland, before moving here. But it is unconfirmed. I never had any reason to send for a copy of that record, if there is one."

Sam sighed. No help here. Maybe something would turn up in New York or Cleveland, when he got there. He thanked the doctor, and headed back to his office.

Sam was changing his shirt when Hank came into his office.

"Been moving around," he remarked, as he buttoned up the shirt front. "How do you like these cufflinks?" He showed Hank the ornately worked, silver links before inserting them into the cuffs.

"Very handsome, boss."

Sam adjusted the dark-blue silk necktie, put on his vest and jacket, opened the vest buttons, and settled back in his swivel chair. "What have you got?"

"About the Larkbey case. I've been scouting around in the North Beach bars."

Sam nodded. "So was I."

"There's a story going around that Belle's place was held up the night the kids bought liquor there."

"Held up? Belle didn't say anything about that."

"No, she didn't. I even called her and asked if there was any truth in it. She said it was pure baloney. No such thing."

"How would such a story get started?"

"Beats me."

"Maybe with the police cars being around, and all that, someone added it up wrong. Then someone else embroidered the story. It could have started that way."

"Could be."

"Belle never lied to me." Sam said, "She never held out on me before. If she did this time, I'll have her hide."

"I can't see why she would lie." Hank shook his head.

"Neither can I. But you know how it is with clients. They sometimes think that if they can fool you, they can fool everybody. Or they think that what you don't know won't bother you. It's a wise lawyer who doesn't trust his own client too far. I'll have words with Belle, and make sure."

"Okay. I'll do some more checking on that."

"Do that. What else?"

"You know, those punks who jumped you yesterday. . . ?"

"Yes."

"They're going to cop a plea—plead 'guilty' to 'attempt.' . . . They identified the third one. When they heard who they had picked on, they spilled . . . said they'd plead 'guilty.' "

"Good. My hand still aches a little."

"I went out to Berkeley and visited around in Boalt Hall," Hank continued. "It's pretty quiet. The law school is on summer vacation and most of the faculty are away. A few of the men are in and out every day, but there's no schedule. Matter of luck if you run into one or two of them at any particular time."

"Did you talk to anyone who knew Porter?"

"Just one. A new man, name of Sorenson, just joining the faculty. He knew Porter by sight, but that's all. We'll have to talk to the old timers."

"Keep after that. Let me know who you talk to. I'll pay a visit there myself, first chance I get."

"By the way, I heard a good one in one of the bars today. Do you like Polish jokes?"

"Not much."

"Well, why are there only two pallbearers at a Polish funeral?"

"Why?"

"Because a garbage can has only two handles."

"Oh, brother!"

"And do you know how you can tell which one is the bride at a Polish wedding?"

"No, I don't."

"She's the only one with the hair under her armpits braided. Isn't that a sweet one!"

Sam scowled at him. "That's nauseating. Enough of the bad jokes. Got anything else?"

"Rosvalley has been grilling Janet Porter. Got that from one of the people at the jail."

"Of course. Anything more concrete out of that?"

Hank shook his head. "That's all. No details." He paused for a moment, and then said. "I'd like to knock off a bit early tonight, boss, if it's all right with you."

"Probably. Anything special?"

"My eldest boy is getting ready to try out for the U.S.F. football team this fall, and I want to show him a few things."

"You played for the University of San Francisco when you were a student, didn't you, Hank?"

Hank grinned. "You know I did."

"Take off, then. I'll see you in the morning. You have the file ready for the hearing tomorrow, no doubt."

"All set."

"Good night, then." Sam put his feet up on the desk, as Hank left, reached for a phone, and called home for his "check-in." All was well there. He hung up the phone, settled back in his chair, and closed his eyes.

CHAPTER

At the Hall of Justice, in the morning, there were half a dozen newspapermen waiting at the entrance when Sam arrived. Two photographers snapped pictures of him as he stood at the doorway for a moment, parrying questions that came at him from all directions.

"How are you going to plead her, Master?"

"Will you give us a statement?"

"Any new developments?"

Sam was patient but close-mouthed. "No statement, fellows. Nothing new to tell you. Maybe later; not now." He went inside. There was time to have a brief talk with Janet Porter before the hearing began.

The Court Calendar had the Porter hearing scheduled for "Municipal Court Room One, Judge Augustus Manning presiding." That was good, he thought. Manning was a methodical, careful judge. This would be a by-the-book hearing.

Room One was busy as usual. Sam lifted his head like an old war horse as he entered. People were bustling about, trying to be quiet, and whispering to each other—lawyers, defendants, bailiffs, and sundry clerks. Judge Manning already was behind the Bench looking down at Docket notes spread before him, and glancing up through his heavy glasses every once in a while. A defendant and his attorney were standing at the Rostrum, just inside the rail, in front of the Bench.

Behind the big Prosecutor's Table, at the left inside the rail, Barney Rosvalley and several other prosecutors were at work, a copy of the Docket spread before them. Rosvalley was calling out a case: "Line twenty-four. Number sixteen four-four-six-nine. Milton S. Williamson. Assault and Battery."

A lawyer stood up behind the Public Defender's Table, on the right, and walked to the Rostrum which had just been vacated. The judge motioned to the bailiff, "Williamson. Bring him up."

The bailiff spoke into the microphone attached to his desk. "Milton S. Williamson." A police officer brought a sad-looking man to the Rostrum.

Rosvalley pointed to the officer and to the raised witness stand near the Bench. "Take the stand, please." Then he began to read out the charge. Nearby, a court reporter was fingering his stenotype machine's keys.

Hank was sitting in the spectator's section, a briefcase on his knees. He lifted his hand as Sam spotted him, pointed at the angular Attorney's Table near the Rostrum, and then moved his open hand up and back toward Sam, five times. Twenty-five minutes before they would be called.

Sam would have to walk through the section inside the Bar, to get to the Holding Room on the left behind the Bench, where Janet Porter probably was waiting. The other back door, to the right, led to the Judge's Chambers. He walked quietly down the aisle to the rail gate, whispered an explanation to the attendant there, and waited for Rosvalley to finish reading the charge. When Barney finished, Sam caught his eye and pointed at the Holding Room door. Barney nodded understandingly, and Sam walked quietly and quickly toward the door. The judge looked up as he went by, nodded silently to him, and resumed his reading. Sam respectfully returned the nod as he went by. He closed the door quietly behind himself.

Janet Porter was sitting motionless in a chair in the Holding Room, her hands clasped in her lap. A guard from the Women's Division of the County Jail, standing behind her, recognized Sam, said "good morning," and then moved to a far corner of the room. Janet looked up at him, her face expressionless. Her lips had a bit more color than he remembered from the day before. She had put on a little lipstick, perhaps. He sat down next to her and went right to the point.

"We have a few minutes, Janet. There are a number of things that I'd like to ask you."

She nodded, and he went on. "Do you remember anything, now, that you didn't remember yesterday?"

"No."

"Can you think of anyone who had any reason why he might have killed your husband?"

"No."

"You told me that you loved your husband."

She hesitated for a fraction of a second. "Yes."

"Did he love you?"

Had she hesitated? Sam was not sure. Then she was answering, "Yes. He did. I am quite sure of that."

"What makes you so sure?"

"Nobody can really explain that. But I was sure. There were many things. . . ."

"Of course." Sam felt uncomfortable. "You are an attractive woman, Janet."

Her eyes stared into his. "Not really, Mr. Benedict. Perhaps wholesome looking, perhaps poised, or well groomed, but not attractive. I have never deceived myself about that."

"I think that you are a handsome woman, Janet." He was sincere.

There was a faint glow of warmth in her face and voice. "Thank you. It's kind of you to say. But not many men have thought so. Kevin was the only one."

He was silent. She went on. "In my world, before Kevin came along, there were none who courted or flattered me—not for my looks or fatal charm."

"Come now, Janet." He was unbelieving.

"They thought that I was quite intelligent; good to work with on some research project. That they did—young men and older ones too, but that was all. After all, the daughter of the distinguished Professor Duffield was worth knowing. But that was a special world of its own, where charm and attractiveness didn't matter, or even exist."

"Did that trouble you?"

"Not really, Mr. Benedict. I had interesting work to do, and the men I knew were good companions, usually. Not every girl wants to be the belle of the ball, you know. I didn't."

"What did you want to be?"

"I wanted to be a great scholar of the law. You know, like Maria Personov, of the University of Georgia Law School. She married Paul Welsh there, you remember, and they were a famous pair of scholars. I wanted to be like her. Not a Portia, not a trial lawyer like you. Not even a great law teacher, like her. But a great researcher and writer. That's what I wanted to be."

"You are very nearly that now, aren't you?"

"No. Not yet."

"Justice Radcliffe told me that your father took you to the Buchanan Lectures at Columbia when you were only twelve years old."

"Yes. I remember that." Her voice was low and slow, remembering years long past. "But even before that, I remember—perhaps I was eight or nine years old—hours and hours waiting in my father's office at Harvard. I remember the big, gray, law-school building, and the big table and brown bookshelves in his office, and all the dim portrait paintings on the walls of the corridors, and even of the stairways."

"You remember that?"

"Yes. And the books with the buckram bindings, and the red-and-black labels, and the gilt letters printed on them."

"Did you wait for him often?"

"Often. Always." Her hands trembled for a moment. "We had no one else but each other. I waited and read his books. Did you know that I learned the Code of Hammurabi when other girls were reading *Alice in Wonderland?* My father taught it to me. I remember the big, black column in the corridor of Northwestern Law School in Chicago. They have a reproduction of the original column there, you know."

"Your father took you many places with him?"

"Everywhere. I've been to half the universities and Bar Association buildings in the country, it seems to me—and in Canada."

"Your father taught you?"

"Yes. But don't deceive yourself, Mr. Benedict. I don't. He was not trying to make me into a Portia. He was a practical man. He often used to say, 'The life of the law is experience, not logic.'"

"That's from Holmes, isn't it?" Sam knew that it was.

She ignored his remark. "He was very practical. After mother died—I don't remember her at all—he needed an assistant, sounding-board, secretary, what have you. That's what I was to him, all those years, until Kevin came along." A change seemed to come over her. Her voice became softer, almost tender. "Kevin changed all that. You think perhaps Kevin was a dry, pedantic scholar? You are wrong. He was a romantic man, in his own way. And we had romance, in our own way, Mr. Benedict. We did."

There was silence for a few moments. Then she spoke again. "He asked me to marry him the second time he saw me. Did you know that? Of course you didn't. And he took me into a different world. We laughed, and we danced. You think that I'm not like that, but we did. He did, too."

Sam was silent.

A soft smile touched her lips. "We used to meet at the Oak Room in the Plaza Hotel, in New York. Then we'd go to the old Sherry Netherlands Bar and drink whiskey sours—sometimes more than we should. Then we'd go to the Essex House or the St. Moritz Roof and dance and look down at the lights of the city. And the coffee and sandwiches at Rumpelmayer's, and cheesecake at Lindy's, and poetry readings at the Vanguard in the Village, and tango music at Spanish-speaking little places, and so many, many things. . . ."

Her voice trailed off into silence for a minute. The guard in the corner was looking at her wrist watch. Janet seemed to be talking to herself. "Then we went to Cleveland, and we were happy there. We made friends. And then to San Francisco. Kevin would not take an airplane. He said that we should drive, and we did, the cities and plains and mountains unrolling before us like a panorama as we drove. And we came over the mountains, and around a curve and we saw this beautiful city. Fog came rolling in like a white wall as we drove past Berkeley towards the Bay Bridge, and I loved it, and I knew that I was home at last. . . ."

Silence echoed in the room, as she stared at her hands.

"And they say that I killed him. Killed Kevin? Oh, my God, my God."

Sam stood up. Her face was taut, but her eyes were dry, he saw. No tears, but her voice had sobbed. "We'd better go.

They must have about reached us on the docket." He opened the door for her. Barney Rosvalley was looking at him and beckoning to them impatiently.

Sam motioned Janet to a chair at the Defense Table, and then he stood erect and attentive, facing the Bench, while Barney Rosvalley read off the line and title of the case: "Line twenty-nine. Number sixteen four-four-seven-three. Janet Duffield Porter. Charge is murder."

Sam straightened his already straight necktie and pulled the snowy points of his breastpocket handkerchief a little higher. Trudy once had remarked that he did that when about to go into action, like a soldier checking his weapons before battle. The icy-calm surface that he presented hid the tense, sharp concentration and alertness beneath the well-tailored surface. His silver-gray hair gleamed under the lights.

Rosvalley was reading rapidly, Judge Manning silently following him on his copy of the Information: "In the Superior Court of the State of California, in and for the City and County of San Francisco. The People of the State of California versus Janet Duffield Porter. The District Attorney of this County hereby makes and files this Information and charges Janet Duffield Porter, of this City and County, with the commission of a felony, to wit, Murder in the First Degree, in that on or about the evening of the Second Day of August of this year, in this City and County, she did unlawfully and with malice aforethought murder her husband Kevin Wilson Porter, contrary to the form of the statute in such cases made and provided, and against the peace and dignity of the State."

He handed a copy of the Information to the bailiff, who walked over and handed it to Sam. Sam put it on the table in front of Janet. She did not look at it. Her eyes were fixed on a corner of the ceiling.

Rosvalley continued. "Janet Duffield Porter, do you appear with counsel?"

Sam answered. "If the court please, I represent Mrs. Porter. The name is Sam Benedict."

Judge Manning peered at Janet and then at Sam. "Are you ready to proceed? Do you wish the case put over in order to have more time to investigate the facts, Mr. Benedict?"

"For the purposes of a preliminary hearing we are ready, Your Honor." Janet was silent.

"Mr. Prosecutor," the judge said, "I take it that you are ready."

Barney Rosvalley answered. "The State is ready, Your Honor."

"Proceed, then."

Rosvalley beckoned to a man sitting in the spectator's section, behind the rail. "Lieutenant James Francis O'Keefe."

The police officer, a stock, broad-faced man with thick, black hair, came to the witness stand, was sworn in, and faced the prosecutor. While he was being asked the opening questions about his name, position, and authority, Sam whispered to Janet, "Don't be worried. This is not a trial. It is only a preliminary hearing."

She looked at him coolly. "I understand that, but I would like to talk with you about the plea to the charge. Don't you think that I ought to cast myself on the mercy of the court?"

Sam's eyebrows rose. "You think so? Let's talk about it after the hearing." He turned to watch Barney Rosvalley's questioning of the police lieutenant.

"And you proceeded to the Porter house immediately after receiving the telephone call from this man Rogers?" Rosvalley asked.

"Yes. It was a little before ten in the evening. We were there in a few minutes—Officer Davis and I. Rogers let us in. The Mexican woman, the cook, was sitting on a bench in the hall, counting her beads and saying her rosary. She was crying. Rogers was pretty excited."

"Then what did you do?"

"Rogers led us back to the library, a room in the back of the house. I sent Pete Davis to search the house—to see if there was anyone hiding, broken windows, jimmied doors, or anything like that."

"What did you see in the library?"

"There was a body on the floor, near the door. It was later identified as the body of Kevin Wilson Porter. He was dead. His forehead had been smashed by some heavy object."

"How long had he been dead, did you estimate?"

Janet touched Sam's arm. "Isn't that an improper question?"

He looked at her quizzically. "Maybe so. Let me worry about things like that. I'll object when I think that I ought to object." Even ignorant and illiterate defendants seemed to think that they knew better than he how their trials should be handled. She was a strange one, though, and certainly far from ignorant of the law. He looked at her again. She was cool as a cucumber.

O'Keefe was answering the question. "It was easy to see that he hadn't been dead more than minutes. There was a cut on his brow and the blood was fresh, hardly had begun to congeal. I'm no coroner, but I've seen enough of them to know a fresh stiff when I see one."

Janet seemed to wince. The judge leaned forward and reproved the lieutenant, "Please choose your language more carefully, officer. There is no need for slang."

O'Keefe gulped. "I'm sorry, Your Honor. I mean 'a body.'"

Rosvalley came to his rescue. "What else did you see in the library?"

Relieved, the lieutenant answered firmly, "Mrs. Porter—that woman—was sitting on the floor, her legs curled up under her, leaning against the desk." He pointed at Janet.

"What was she doing there?"

"Just sitting there, staring at the bookshelves." He paused.

"Yes?" Rosvalley prompted him.

"She was holding a statue in one hand. It was resting on the floor—a bronze statue of a woman in a robe. It was a statue of Justice, we saw later."

"Yes. Go on."

"The statue had a streak of blood on one side of the base. Later the coroner told us that the blood matched Mr. Porter's blood type."

Rosvalley looked back at Sam, sure that an objection would be hurled. Nothing. Sam rolled a silver pencil back and forth in his fingers and said nothing. No point in objecting, he thought, when the coroner was certain to back up the blood identification.

Rosvalley turned back to the officer. "Did you speak to the defendant?"

"Yes. Might as well have talked to the wall. I asked her what had happened. She didn't answer, didn't say a word. I thought that she might be drunk or injured, but she wasn't. No liquor smell, and no liquor around. She was not hurt in any way; not that anyone could see. She was steady on her feet when I helped her stand up. Just stood there, not saying a word."

"Then what did you do?"

"I led her to a chair and she sat down. I tried to question her. No dice. She wouldn't say a word. Just sat there, staring."

"Yes. And then?"

"Pete came back. Said there was no intruder, no sign of breaking or entering. Everything was shipshape—except in the library."

"Then?"

"That's about all. We called for a wagon, reported in, left a man to wait for the coroner, and took Mrs. Porter in. We booked her."

"Did she say anything all this time?"

"Not until we were at the Hall. Then she seemed to come to when we asked her if she wanted to call her lawyer. She called Mr. Benedict."

Barney Rosvalley turned to Sam. "Your witness, Mr. Benedict."

Sam sighed, and stood up. "No questions at this time, Your Honor."

Judge Manning was folding the Information he held in his hand. "Anything more, Mr. Rosvalley?"

Rosvalley was cocksure. "Not now, if the Court pleases. This is as open-and-shut a case as I have seen in all my years in practice. About the only things lacking is an eye-witness to the actual killing. Why, the evidence of premeditated murder is so overwhelming that . . ."

Sam was on his feet. "If the Court pleases, my learned opponent seems to think that he is summing up to a jury. This is quite improper. Would Mr. Rosvalley like to take the stand?" His voice was heavy with sarcasm.

The judge banged his gavel, as Sam and Barney glared at each other. "Gentlemen, gentlemen . . ."

Rosvalley's face was scarlet. "Mr. Benedict is not going to patronize me," he snapped. "I have been very restrained in this hearing. I could put on witnesses to sounds of quarreling between the victim and Mrs. Porter, just before the murder, if I wanted. . . ."

Sam slammed the table with his open palm. "I demand that Mr. Rosvalley be properly sworn before he continues with his testimony. This is not a preliminary hearing. This is an attack by Mr. Rosvalley. How gross can a Prosecutor get . . . ?"

Rosvalley swung around toward Sam, almost purple-faced. Sam was pale with anger. The judge's gavel banged again and again as they faced each other furiously.

Irritation sounded in Judge Manning's quiet voice as he surveyed the tense adversaries. "Gentlemen. We will have no more of this. Mr. Rosvalley, you were wrong to become argumentative. Mr. Benedict, this Court is perfectly capable of properly appraising evidence and argument, and needs no help in so doing. You will both please be seated and we shall announce our finding. Gentlemen?" He waited, and leafed through some papers while they sat down and began to cool off.

The judge put aside the papers before him. Then he spoke, slowly, in order to be sure that all was decorous and proper.

"It appearing to me that the offense in the within complaint mentioned, to wit, murder, has been committed and that there is sufficient cause to believe the within named 'Janet Porter' is guilty thereof, I order that she be held to answer for the same." He paused, then continued. "The case presumably will be set down for a day certain for arraignment, in Superior Court, within a few days. Counsel will be duly informed, no doubt." He paused. "Is there any other business relating to this hearing, to be brought forward now? Are there any motions or other matters?"

Rosvalley looked triumphant. Sam's face lost some of the tense combativeness of the moments before. The judge continued, "I shall hear motions or proposals regarding bail."

Barney Rosvalley stood up and walked around to the front of the Prosecutor's Table. "This is a capital offense, Your Honor. The People cannot agree to bail of any kind. This is not a bailable offense."

Sam arose, and his voice was again calm and controlled. "Ordinarily, Your Honor, I would agree with my learned opponent, who is also my good friend despite our difference of opinion of a few minutes ago." He grinned at Barney. Barney winked one eye at him and waved his hand deprecatingly. "But under the facts shown here, all that is clear is that there was a homicide, not that Mrs. Porter committed it. Certainly there is no presumption of guilt, and the proof of any guilt on her part is purely conjectural. I ask that reasonable bail be set."

Barney returned the courtesy. "With all respect for my distinguished colleague before the Bar, I must disagree with him about the weakness of the State's evidence of guilt. We oppose the granting of bail in a death-penalty case, and will cite law to that effect if it be desired by the Court."

The judge tapped his gavel once, lightly. "That's not necessary. The request for bail must be denied." He motioned to the deputy sheriff to take Janet Porter out.

Sam whispered to the deputy to wait a moment in the Holding Room. Then he turned toward Rosvalley. Barney grinned broadly. "You don't let me get away with a thing, do you, you old war horse."

Sam touched Rosvalley on the shoulder, half affectionately. "And you don't miss a trick if you think that you can use it, do you, you rascal."

They looked at each other appreciatively, two gladiators who respected each other's mettle.

Janet was waiting in the Holding Room. She burst out, even before Sam had closed the door. "You pleaded 'not guilty.' How can that be? It doesn't seem that I can deny that I killed Kevin, even though I don't remember. Everything says that I did, everything."

"Did you want to plead 'guilty'?" Sam asked, evenly. "Were you?"

"No, not really. I don't know. But should I not cast myself on the mercy of the court, in these circumstances?"

"What would that gain?"

"Mercy. I don't understand what happened, but I don't want to die, Mr. Benedict. I don't understand what happened, but I'm alive, and I don't want to die."

"Precisely. And if you plead 'guilty' to premeditated murder that is exactly what you will do. Mercy! For premeditated murder without cause? That is what the charge reads, you know."

"And if I plead 'not guilty'?"

"Then several alternatives are open to us."

"Such as?"

"Such as proving that you didn't do it, in the first place."

"But they seem sure to prove that I did."

"Or we can argue that you were not aware of what you were doing. . . . We can use that by showing that your mental state was such that you could not have formed the intent to kill your husband."

"Are you saying that I am insane?" Her eyes were wide. "It isn't true. I am not insane. I am *not*."

"I didn't say that you are."

"Then what are you saying?"

Sam raised his hands in impatience. "You don't seem to have heard him."

"Heard what?" She was bewildered.

"Rosvalley. Didn't you hear what he said when he lost his temper? He told us what was what, all right."

"I don't know what you mean."

"He said that he had witnesses to a quarrel between you and your husband, just before it happened. Don't you understand what that means?"

Comprehension began to dawn on her. "I think so."

"Then understand it clearly." He pointed his finger at her. "It means that he has a complete case. Absolutely complete. Motive —a quarrel. Opportunity—perfect. Weapon—found in your hand. Explanation—none but silence. He has a perfect case. He'll get a conviction as sure as God made little apples— unless . . ." He paused.

"Unless I am insane?"

"Unless you were insane."

She walked to a chair, sat down carefully, and folded her hands in her lap. Then she looked coolly into his eyes, and said, "But I am not insane, Mr. Benedict. I am as sane as you are."

He tried again. "That is not the issue, Mrs. Porter. Have you ever heard of the M'Naghten Rule? You did study some law, you have said."

She nodded. "I have heard of it. But criminal law was not my field."

"Then let me tell you something about it. It may concern you, believe me." He pulled up a chair, took out a cigarette, gave one to her, lit them both, and began to explain. "Let me sum up the present law this way. First, if a person commits a felony while insane, he cannot be deemed guilty of that crime. If he is legally insane, he cannot have the *mens rea,* or criminal intent, that is required in order to spell out the crime."

She nodded impatiently. "I know that."

"But then that leads to the real question in such cases, namely, 'What is legal insanity?' In most courts, legal insanity is described as a mental disorder, or a disease of the brain, as distinguished from mere disorder of the feelings or emotions. To have conclusive effect as a legal defense against a charge of crime, it must render the person incapable of distinguishing between right and wrong. Or it must render him unconscious of the nature of the act he is committing. In other words, he must be unaware that what he is doing is wrong."

"Yes."

"This, in rough outline, is what is usually called the M'Naghten Rule, from the leading English case of that name of over a century ago. Most American courts follow that rule. I hardly need point out that that rule was established before the development of modern psychiatry. In the light of modern knowledge of the human mind it is a crude, primitive rule."

She shook her head angrily. "It certainly doesn't apply to me, anyhow. I am not mentally ill. My mind is not diseased. It is rather a good one, I should think. My IQ is about one hundred and thirty-five. That may not be genius rating, but it is certainly not the mind of an imbecile."

"IQ has nothing to do with it," he said emphatically. "But let me add some points. In a few courts a new rule has been adopted in recent years. This is the Durham Case Rule. It views as legal insanity any mental derangement that makes the person incompetent of having criminal intent, or incompetent of so controlling his will as to avoid doing the act in question. That is better than the M'Naghten Rule, but not much better. In a few cases—for example, in Michigan—courts have followed the 'irresistible-impulse' concept as a defense. But the M'Naghten Rule continues to be the main rule of law, though it has been bitterly criticized by many, many lawyers and by practically all psychiatrists."

"That is all very interesting, Mr. Benedict, but I fail to see what it has to do with me."

Sam leaned forward. "It may or it may not apply to you. I don't want to offend you by suggesting that you are mentally ill. But I do want to be able to defend you on that ground or any other legal ground that may apply. You hardly retained me to stand by and watch you convicted and sentenced to death, did you?"

"No."

"Then leave your defense to me. That is my job. It may require having you examined by a psychiatrist.

Hesitantly, she nodded.

He touched her lightly on the shoulder. "Don't fret, Janet. I am a supreme egoist. I want to win for you, as a matter of pride if for no other reason."

Sam was on the phone, making an appointment with Irwin Rubenfeld, a psychiatrist who had worked with him on several cases, when Hank returned to the office. Sam waved him to a chair and concluded the conversation with "I'll see you at the Mark in about an hour." Then he turned to his assistant. "How did you make out at North Beach?"

Hank slumped wearily into a chair. "Not so hot, boss. It seems that everyone is clamming up for some reason. I talked with the bartender from Belle Larkbey's place, and he told me exactly nothing. 'Yes, he sold some drinks to the three boys. Yes, they had I.D. cards. No, he didn't know that the cards were fakes.' And that's all. About anything else, he doesn't know from nothing, he says."

"Did you talk with people in the neighborhood?"

"Several. All they know is that the police were at Belle's place that night. Nothing else concrete. . . ."

Hank shrugged. "A couple of people said they had heard something about a holdup at Belle's that night. But nobody knows anything about it. Just 'Somebody said,' and nothing more."

"Did you check the police blotters about that?"

"Yes, I did. No record of any call or complaint or anything about a holdup there. The desk sergeants haven't heard of anything like that, either."

"Have you talked with Belle? Has she called?"

"No, to both. And she's not at home, and nobody knows where she is. You'd think that she was holed up somewhere, to stay out of sight. But why should she do that?"

"Beats me. Have you talked with any of the boys who bought the drinks?"

"No. Can't locate them either. I tried to talk to the father of one of them and got an ice-cold brush-off. It gets foggier and foggier, and nobody's talking about anything."

"But I see that the papers are still raising a hue and cry about Belle's place." Sam slapped his hand down on an afternoon paper on his desk. "I've never seen the newspapers so hysterical about a minor, everyday violation. Now why is that? Hank, go visit with the reporter who wrote this bilge. Find out why the papers are so hot about this case, if you can."

Hank looked at the paper and the article about Belle. "No byline, you notice," he said. "That makes it tough."

"The City Desk will tell you who wrote it. Also, keep trying to get hold of Belle. I want to talk to her again. I have an idea that there's a lot about this affair that she hasn't told me. Another thing—get me the record on any prior arrests or trouble for the three young pups who started this business."

"Okay."

"I have an impression that I've seen pieces in the paper about some hell-raising by these kids before. While you're at it, check their records at school. They are college age and probably are registered at some universities. Look for suspensions or reprimands in their records. And keep trying to talk to their parents."

"Okay, boss." Hank heaved himself up out of the chair and started forth again. Sam smiled affectionately at his broad back.

At the Top-of-the-Mark lounge, in a quiet corner, Sam and the psychiatrist sipped their drinks and exchanged thoughts about Janet Porter and insanity. Sam always enjoyed the Top-of-the-Mark, nineteen floors high above its hilltop, and its fifty-mile panoramic view of San Francisco and the Bay area. His old friend, Dr. Rubenfeld, was in his mid-forties, and was soft and pudgy in appearance, his pink face almost boyishly friendly looking; but under the soft exterior was a mind as hard and practical as a steel trap. The psychiatrist was full of doubts.

"From all that you have told me, Sam, I gather an impression of a well-balanced, rather sound personality. Nothing that you have told me suggests mental instability. This woman seems to be a healthy girl who had a quarrel with her husband about something. In the emotional stress of a domestic quarrel people easily can lose their tempers and strike out at each other. It happens thousands of times, every day. To read insanity into such an incident is to strain credibility, on the facts you have given me."

Sam sighed, and took a sip of his scotch. "But what about the hint of repression by her father, and suggestions of hostility to him?"

"There is little to go on there. It's a possibility, but a slim one. We need to know a lot more. Until I have spent some time with her, it's impossible to tell. For example, what do you know of her physical condition?"

"Not much," Sam admitted. "Her family physician says that his records show her to be normally healthy. She looks healthy enough, Irwin. He did say something about premenstrual tension."

"I'll check that. A physical check will be part of my examination, of course. Premenstrual tension should be fully investigated."

Sam tapped the table for emphasis. "Remember, in a court of law evidence of insanity has three aspects: First, was she sane at the time of the commission of the crime? Second, is she sane enough now to stand trial? And third, if convicted, will she be sane enough for sentencing at that time? Any one of these points may be critical."

"I understand that." Rubenfeld was no amateur in testifying as a medical expert. "You want me to concentrate on the first two aspects, I suppose?"

"Yes. There are certain things that may be particularly worth investigating, as possibilities, if I may make bold suggestions, Irwin. For example, from a lawyer's point of view, paranoia is a primary question."

Rubenfeld shook his head. "Not likely, Sam. Paranoia is basically diagnosed from delusions held by the patient. I see no suggestion of delusions in Mrs. Porter's history, so far."

"Couldn't it be based on a single obsession, such as one concerning her husband, or her father?"

"Could be, but more usually it involves a whole pattern or group or system of disorders. But I'll grant you that paranoia does not destroy mental capacity, though it may dominate it."

"Good enough."

The doctor smiled wryly. "Not so good. Usually the monomania refers to wrongs or persecutions supposedly inflicted on the patient. Where is the persecution here?"

"Maybe her husband. Maybe her father."

"Maybe. I'll grant you that it is possible. I'll look into it."

"Then there is the possibility of melancholia," Sam added. "She's not a cheerful person. Rather dour, in fact."

"That, too, requires a history of delusions or hallucinations. Otherwise everyone who gets depressed would be classified as insane."

"How about schizophrenia, with this state of facts?"

Rubenfeld frowned. "She does seem to show the symptoms of indifference and withdrawal, from what you tell me. But there, too, the factor of fancied or real persecution is involved. She's not old enough for a probability of dementia praecox. Her intelligence is apparently unimpaired; which fits."

Sam sighed. "Anyhow, you see what I'm after."

"I understand, Sam. I'll look into all the possibilities. But from what you've told me it looks like you are on the wrong track, at least for forensic-medicine purposes."

"Look and see."

"I will."

Sam signaled the waiter and made ready to leave. "I'll be digging out more information from her family and friends, here and back East. As I get more data that seems significant, I'll pass it on to you."

"Do that, Sam. The more the better."

"Just remember this, Irwin," Sam concluded, "Something tells me that this case will turn on the psychiatric angle. I'm depending on you—and so is Janet Porter."

It was late afternoon when the taxi deposited Sam in the street outside Boalt Hall on the University of California campus at Berkeley. As he walked up to the big, slab-sided law-school building, he thought, sourly, how drab modern architecture had become. Huge cracker boxes—that's what the architects are designing nowadays, he thought. Egg crates laid on their sides, like this building, or egg crates stood on end in central-city construction. Pretty dismal. He could see the big University of California campanile tower jutting up above the nearby houses and university buildings. The tower dominated that part of the East Bay area, across from San Francisco. At least the tower had some grace and style, but even that was a copy of the classic old Italian campanile. He shook his head and entered the echoing hallway of the law-school building.

Professor Smith was waiting for him in his office, as he had promised. He was a happy-go-lucky fellow, chomping on his big pipe, sitting behind his desk in his shirt sleeves, his shirt collar open. "Welcome, Mr. Benedict." He pushed half a candy bar toward Sam. "Have a bite."

Sam declined with thanks and sat down across from Smith. "I'd like to ask you what you can tell me about Kevin Porter, one of your colleagues. You must have read about him in the papers—and about his wife, if you were acquainted with her."

"Sure, sure. Glad to," boomed Smith. "Nice guy. Too bad about that. Really shocking. But that's how it goes. *Morituri salutamus*. What do you want to know, that I can tell you?"

"Did you know him well?"

Smith shook his head. "Not intimately. We were not bosom companions, if that's what you mean, but I knew him. I saw quite a bit of him in the everyday routine of the faculty since he came to Berkeley a few years ago. And I know Janet, though not very well."

"What kind of man would you say he was?"

"Good man. Able. Competent instructor and pretty good legal scholar. Quiet kind of fellow. Good appearance. Distinguished looking, you might say, what with that white shock of hair and tall, upright bearing. But then, of course, *de mortuis nil nisi bonum*, I always say. You know what I mean."

"Yes. And Janet?"

"Quiet woman, too. A little mousey, maybe, but always well-turned-out, alert, and well-mannered. I didn't see much of her, you know, just at an occasional cocktail party at somebody's house, or at some starchy faculty reception. Not my type at all. I like the sexy-looking type myself. I'm a bachelor, you know. Never gave a hostage to fortune, myself."

"How did Kevin Porter happen to join your faculty?"

Smith settled back in his chair and said, "Well, therein lies a tale, as the saying goes. We're always looking for outstanding scholars to add to the faculty, you know. Somebody suggested his name. Don't recall who. He had a fairly good academic background and was teaching on the faculty of some small school back East, in Ohio, I believe. His background looked fairly good on paper, though he had not done anything earth-shaking. He must have had influential friends, because his name was pushed. His family had quite some social standing here-abouts, I think."

"What did he teach, here?"

"Constitutional Law, a seminar on constitutional questions—the Warren Court, or some such subject, and Federal systems. I believe that he used to teach Sales and Agency, but I'm not sure. I can look it up for you in the Stud Book, if you want to know."

Sam was puzzled. "Stud Book? What's the Stud Book?"

Smith grinned. "That's what we call the *Law Teachers' Directory*. It is put out every year by one of the law publishing companies. It gives a thumbnail history of every full-time law teacher in approved law schools."

"Oh, that. I'm familiar with that," Sam said. "But I never heard it called the 'Stud Book' before."

"Yes, indeed. Very important in this game, Mr. Benedict. The law schools are a private world in themselves, you know."

"So I am beginning to see, Professor Smith, A curious little world it is, too."

"You can say that again." Smith chewed on the stem of his pipe reflectively. "We're a close-knit family in some ways, and absolute strangers in others. A man may have close friends in law schools in ten different states, and maybe not one close friend in the school where he is. Or, he may be buddy-buddy with some men on his own faculty, and ships that pass in the night to other professors in other schools. But one thing is true about every man in this business—about every man. . . ."

"Yes . . . ?"

"We're all howling egotists, Mr. B., absolute prima donnas, every one. Every law teacher, almost by definition, thinks of himself as the best in the world, and really believes it. It's the nature of such men, you might say."

"Was Kevin Porter like that?"

"Oh, sure. Of course he was. So am I." He grew serious for a moment. "Makes us pretty hard to live with. I can tell you that."

"How so?"

"Every one of us loves the center of the stage," Smith said gravely. "Each of us doesn't like to listen to what someone else has to say. Some of us are pretty hard to take—arrogant, and all that. The hell of it is that a lot of law professors really are pretty sharp. But that doesn't endear us to other people. No. Pretty hard to take."

Sam tried to get him back on the track. "And Kevin . . . ?"

Smith frowned. "Oh, yes. He was as self-centered and egotistic as any. Not a bad sort, though. Not really more self-assured than most others. Well-mannered, though. A gentleman, not like some of the pompous asses in this racket. Always courteous and friendly, though in a stand-offish kind of way. He had money of his own, you know. That makes a difference."

"How so?"

"Well, law teachers are always complaining that they don't

get paid enough. They get higher salaries than any other kind of teachers, but that makes no difference to them. They're always saying that they could make a hell of a lot more money in practice, or as corporation counsel, or with government. They're always demanding more money. Drives university administrators crazy, because it happens to be true. It makes professors in other departments green with jealousy, too. But Kevin never cared what his salary was. He had an independent income, apparently, so he could afford not to give a damn about salary-rank scales. He never helped out much with the annual push for higher salaries."

"Did that make him unpopular with the faculty?"

"Not really," Smith admitted. "Everybody understood that he was a sort of a special case. We didn't really care. But I can tell you that when he got that research grant, that did really gripe some of us. He didn't need the money, and there were quite a few other men here who could have used it."

"Did anyone actively resent it?"

"Enough to murder him?" Smith's eyebrows rose. "Lord, no. We might gripe and cuss a little, but nobody really got steamed about it. Besides, he was really earning the grant. He worked like a Trojan on it, burning the midnight oil, and all that sort of thing. No, he was not a phony. Don't ever think that. He worked, and he'd probably have produced something to show for the grant if he ever had finished it."

"What about his personal habits? Did he ever gad about as far as you know?"

Smith shrugged. "He was a conservative sort of fellow. No liquoring up, and no vices, as far as I or anyone here ever knew. He didn't even like an occasional off-color joke. Rather stuffy, you might say, rather than a gay blade. Not much fun to be out with, really. Kind of a work-and-go-home type of fellow."

Sam wondered if he was not wasting his time with the professor. "What about Janet Porter?" Sam didn't see that the garrulous Smith was getting him anywhere.

Smith relit his pipe, and a thick cloud of smoke hid his saturnine face for a moment. "I didn't know her very well. Saw her in the library now and then, doing some sort of research work. Pleasant gal, but uncommunicative. There was some talk, a couple of years ago, about some sort of faculty-adjunct position for her, in research. Nothing ever came of it, though. She has no law degree, you know, and not even a B.A." He was enjoying his role as a raconteur and was clearly making the most of it.

Sam pressed him. "They tell me that she is quite a scholar. She did research work for faculty men at New York University and in Cleveland."

"You must have the degrees, Mr. Benedict, for university work. Absolute must, you know." Smith looked loftily over Sam's head.

Sam smiled. "No matter how learned the person, nor how valuable!"

Smith pursed his lips. "No matter. Degrees are the passports in the Halls of Academe, today. No tickee, no shirtee. No degrees, no university positions."

Sam smiled sarcastically. "It would be pretty rough for Tom Jefferson, or Lincoln, or Blackstone today, wouldn't it?"

Now it was Smith's turn to smile. "Yup. Old Solon or Augustus wouldn't be admitted to this law school as a student, today, let alone as a faculty member."

"We progress, don't we?" Sam remarked sarcastically to the wall.

"Oh, yes," Smith said, seriously. "Standards, Mr. Benedict. You have to have academic standards."

Sam returned to the subject of Janet Porter. "Did you know anything of how she and Kevin got along?"

"Seemed to be a normal married couple." Smith sucked on his pipe. "They didn't have any children, though, and they had been married for quite a while. I think that they didn't want any. They didn't seem to care much for kids."

"What makes you say that?"

"I recall a couple of times when some faculty man would have his kids drop in to visit. He'd take the children around to say 'hello' to the others, usually, and to kind of glow over them —the proud-parent bit, you know. Everyone always made a fuss about the kids. Not Kevin, though. He'd pay no attention to them, let alone make a fuss about them. One time Professor

Gardner's little boy was visiting him and wandered into Kevin's office, and Kevin put him out in the hall. Gardner got a little huffy about it, but Kevin said he was busy working."

"Did Kevin or Janet ever say anything about why they had no children?"

"Yes. Once or twice Kevin did say something or other about children—something like 'who needs it!' I have an impression that he just didn't want any. I don't know about Janet."

There was nothing more to be learned here, it seemed. Sam got up to go. To be polite, he asked Smith how it happened that the professor was working at his office so late on a summer afternoon. That was a mistake. Smith glowed with appreciation of his interest.

"Let me show you," he boomed. "I'm working on a paper for a law review. Leading article. It's on the effect of the Statute of Uses on modern trust law. Look here. I found a piece on that in *Kent's Commentaries* that nobody has ever followed up. Just think. . . ."

Sam interrupted him. "The Statute of Uses is centuries old, and *Kent's Commentaries* are pretty old too, aren't they?"

"Why, sure." Smith was off and running. "The Statute of Uses was enacted by Parliament in 1534. Now that statute was construed as not governing uses in personalty, for women, or for conveyances where active duties were imposed on the transferee. But Kent said . . ."

Sam begged off politely, with a story about another engagement, and got out after thanking the eager Smith. An hour of listening to the history of an old statute was not exactly what he had in mind. It would be hard enough finding a cab back to San Francisco. Dusk was settling over the sprawling university campus as he came out. At least there were no noisy demonstrations of bearded beatnik students to contend with this summer evening.

There was a note from Trudy, on top of the pile of messages on his desk in the office. The trial in the Belle Larkbey case was scheduled for tomorrow morning. Also, Belle had phoned while he was out, and had left a number for him to call back. Hank had left the Larkbey file on his desk, ready for the morning. He dialed the number Belle had left, after ringing Paoli's downstairs to send up some dinner. Belle's loud voice rang in the phone. He seemed to be destined to talk only with loud-voiced people this day.

"Where have you been, Belle," he demanded, querulously. "How do you expect me to prepare your case if I can't find you? Hank Tabor has been looking for you everywhere."

"I'm right here, Master," she chortled. "In my little old hide-out at the Flamingo Motel on Mission at Seventh. This is where I like to stay when I want peace and quiet. What's up?"

"I'm the one who should ask that," he snapped. "What the hell is all this I hear about a holdup at your place? Why didn't you tell me about that?"

Injured innocence trickled from the phone. "What holdup? Would I try to kid you, Sam? You hurt me. What holdup?"

"There have been several reports of a holdup at your place, Belle." Maybe it was just gossip, he thought. "Kid me not."

"Would I kid you, Master?" She seemed to be in earnest, but he wished that he could see her as she spoke. He let it go.

"Your case is on for trial tomorrow at ten in the morning," he told her. "Meet me at the entrance to the Hall of Justice at nine-thirty. I want to talk to you before the hearing."

"Why sure, Sam. I'll be there. You know I'll do everything you say." She was contrite. Then suddenly outrage sounded in her voice. "What in the goddam hell are the newspapers trying to do to me, Sam? Did you see the piece in the paper about my place this morning? Why don't they let up? Who have I killed?"

He tried to reassure her. "We're trying to find out. We're working at it." Someone was out in the waiting room—probably the messenger with the sandwich he had ordered. "I have to go now. Somebody waiting for me. See you in the morning."

He hung up, went out to get his dinner snack, and poured himself a pre-dinner scotch-and-water at the bar in his office. Then he called in at home, ate his sandwich without interest, and settled back in his chair for a much-needed nap. It had been a wearing day, again. He dreamed.

There was a long, narrow, dirty-white road between two rows of tall, bare poplars, under a gray autumn sky. It ran straight northwest toward the hills in the distance. Sam remembered dimly, Lorraine—the road from Rheims, back toward the lines.

The jeep ran swift and smooth in spite of the cracked and unkempt road. It was getting cold, and he huddled down in his seat to get out of the wind. With luck they would get back to division headquarters in about half an hour, in time for hot chow. He was hungry.

In the distance ahead he heard and felt the rumble of the big guns. The jeep driver was a stranger, loaned with the jeep, but he was hard-faced and poised, his gear well kept though worn. Looked like a good non-com. They were silent as they rode. The noise of the exhaust and the roar of the wind made talking difficult even if they had wanted to talk.

Up ahead the road seemed to disappear off to the left. As they moved closer he saw that it made a sweeping "S" turn about half a mile ahead. Then he saw a sprinkle of flashes dancing over the tree tops, just over the S bend. A half-second later a series of sharp, crackling explosions reached them. Sam knew what it was, now—timed fire bursts of artillery shells over the S. The driver knew, too. The jeep skidded to a stop at the edge of the road. They waited. Two minutes later, again, the bright flashes danced over the tree tops. Then the cracking "whap-whap-whap" of shellbursts echoed in the cold air.

"Time the next one," he said to the driver, and pulled his field glasses out of the case for a better view. "Looks like off-and-on-interdicting fire to block the road." The driver nodded and shook his left hand to get his wrist watch down from his sleeve.

Sam peered through the binoculars, searching the bleak, flat landscape up ahead. Nothing. They were firing by map co-ordinates—long-range, he thought. They couldn't see that the road was deserted and that they were wasting their shells. Three minutes later another series of bursts came out of no-where. Seconds after it, another salvo snapped and crashed over the "S" turn. Sam looked around at the fields. Too soft and soggy to go around. They'd mire the jeep, for sure.

The driver looked at him questioningly. "Nothing regular

about their timing," he said. "Maybe they'll quit in a while." His voice was flat and tired, and that was a good sign. He was no green replacement or rear echelon soldier. Artillery fire was an old story to him, and Sam felt better.

"We go through or we miss chow," Sam said, and thought to himself that it was rather like saying we must catch the next bus or we'll be late for dinner. "Move up a little closer." Sam put the glasses back in the leather case. "After the next burst we'll run through. Keep her in the middle of the road and open her up."

The driver nodded and jockeyed the jeep up to about a hundred yards from the first turn.

"Close enough," Sam cautioned. They stopped and minutes ticked by. Nothing happened. It was very cold, sitting still.

"Race the engine," Sam ordered, making up his mind. "We can't sit here all day. If nothing comes in the next minute we'll go through."

He watched the sweep-second hand on his watch, and glanced at the tree tops. "Let's go."

The engine roared as the driver shifted gears and pressed down on the accelerator. Tires spun and caught. Wind smacked their faces as they turned into the first bend.

"Whap-whap-whang," smashed startlingly overhead. "Whee-wisp-spptt." Steel fragments whistled and hissed past them. "Wham-wham-crack," the air leaped and pounded them. Dirty puffs of smoke dissolved in the air overhead. They squeezed down, hunched their necks down, cringing, their bellies taut. The jeep swung sickeningly for a moment, bit down again, and careened rockingly out of the last turn, into the straight road beyond. Wind roared in their ears as they raced down the road, away from the bend.

They straightened up a little and grinned furtively at each other. Sam's stomach quivered a little, then was all right. No damage. They were untouched. They pulled up, and looked around the jeep. Not even a scratch. He looked back at the bend. All quiet. Nothing. They grinned at each other again, but *they knew that death hovered invisibly over the trees back at the bend.*

"Nice driving," Sam said, and meant it. They got into the jeep again and started up the road. "Guess we'll make it for chow, after all," he added.

The driver nodded.

Sam felt good all over.

Sam woke with a start. It was eight o'clock. Time to go home. He walked through the office, closing up. He wondered why dreams of war kept coming back to him. The human mind was complex indeed. The experiences of battle seemed to leave indelible marks on the brain. War was the supreme test of a man's courage, people said, and maybe it was so. Maybe it was true of all human conflict.

"Call it a day," he said to himself. He locked the door and started for home.

CHAPTER

Belle Larkbey was waiting for him when Sam came through the entrance door at the Hall of Justice. He was relieved to see that she was wearing a plain black dress. Sometimes her clothes were loud enough to be heard. But the inevitable broad and slightly threadbare mink stole was draped around her neck, as usual. Her hair was electric yellow, as always, courtesy of peroxide; but there was nothing he could do about that.

She boomed a greeting to him, over the heads of the people in the lobby. "Hi, Counselor. Here I am."

He walked over to her, took her aside to a corner, and looked her up and down. "I'm glad to see that you dressed conservatively for the hearing, as I told you," he said. "Can't you park the mink stole somewhere? You're supposed to be the solid citizen falsely accused, you know, not Texas Guinan come back to life."

She looked aggrieved. "What's the matter with my stole? It's the height of fashion."

"A nice stole, Belle," he reassured her. "But we want you to be sedate, prim, and proper today. Have you seen Hank Tabor around?"

"You bet. He's somewhere around in the hall." She looked around, raised a hand overhead, and suddenly let out a stentorian shout, "Hey, Hank. Over here!"

Sam winced, as half a dozen people turned and glared at Belle. Hank Tabor waved at them from down the hallway, and then threaded his way to their side.

"All set, boss," he said as he joined them. "We're in Room Two. Judge Newland is sitting today. I think that it will be a good hour before we're reached on the Calendar."

"Better go up there, Hank," Sam directed, "and wait for us to be called, just in case they move along faster than you expect. I'll be in the hall, just outside the courtroom, when you want us. I want to talk with Belle a bit, and maybe with some of the reporters if there are any upstairs."

Hank nodded. "There are. I saw Bud Kennedy and another reporter upstairs, and there may be some others, too. See you in a while." Hank left them and headed for the elevators.

Sam guided Belle slowly toward the elevators too. "Let's go upstairs where it's quieter."

On the Municipal Court floor, which was just as crowded as the lower-floor hallway, he found a relatively quiet corner and resumed his conversation with Belle. "I have a strong feeling that you've been holding out on me, Belle." He looked her sternly in the eye. "If you think that kidding me along is going to help you somehow, get it out of your mind. What I don't know *can* hurt you. If we get surprised by something because you got cute and didn't tell me about it, I'll have your hide. Do you understand me?"

"Why should I hold out on you, Master?" She was all wide-eyed innocence.

Sam shrugged. There was no use in pressing the point. If she was holding back information for some reason, it was plain that she meant to go on holding it back. Then again, maybe she was not holding out anything. He had done what he could about it.

Bud Kennedy and another young man wearing horn-rimmed glasses appeared out of the crowd in the hallway, walking toward Sam and Belle. Bud nodded to Belle, and spoke to Sam. "Isn't it unusual for you to be working on a case like this one, Mr. Benedict? I thought that the Porter case was more your cup of tea."

"Yes and no, Bud." Sam was cool. "An attorney is supposed to help anyone who is being persecuted, whether the case be big or little."

"Who's persecuting whom?" Bud acted surprised. "Is someone persecuting this little flower?" He waved his hand toward Belle.

Belle's chin jutted out aggressively and she started to move toward the reporter. "Get snotty with me, you crummy . . ."

Sam restrained her with one hand and snapped at Bud, "Mind your manners, young fella. Don't let that press card go to your head as well as your hat. If you want to get anything to print in your rag, you'd better behave."

Bud was apologetic. "No offense, Belle. Just kidding."

"Don't kid with me, Mister." She snorted and straightened her stole belligerently.

"Anyhow, Master," Bud said, "you asked me to check on something for you. Remember? Well, I did."

Sam nodded. "Yes. Who's been writing the pieces about the padlocking of the Larkbey place?"

"Right here." Bud grinned broadly and pointed to his companion. "Paul Roper. Have you two ever met?"

Sam shook hands with Roper. "Glad to know you. I've been wanting to ask you about that. Why all the headline treatment of a run-of-the-mill misdemeanor case? How come the feature story follow-up on the Larkbey-place padlocking?"

Roper raised one shoulder half apologetically. "It's just another story to me, Mr. Benedict. I only work for my paper, you know. I don't own it. The city editor says 'follow up this story and stay with it.' So I follow it up and stay with it."

"Even though it ruins this woman?"

"I don't want to ruin anyone, Mr. Benedict. I'm just doing my job. Anyhow, what have I written that's so bad? Is there anything not true in my stories?"

"There's such a thing as decent proportion, Mr. Roper. A series of stories that 'view with alarm' hardly seems the proper proportions for a minor case of a kind that happens every day in the week."

The reporter drew himself up defensively. "It *is* a violation of law, you know. And there have been too many such cases of selling liquor to minors lately, with nobody doing anything about it."

"The law provides the punishment for such violations," Sam pointed out. "The punishment is a small fine, not public pillorying day after day, and not financial ruination."

"Some punishment!" The reporter was scornful. "A two-bit slap on the wrist."

"That's what the law provides, Mister Reporter. The *law*, not a newspaper editor."

"Some law!"

Anger flared on Sam's face. "Whether you like it or not, that is the law. Until the legislators elected by the people decide to change it, that is the law. It is not for you or for your newspaper to decide what the law is, or should be. It is not for you, nor for your city editor or publisher, to add to the punishment provided by the law."

"Are you saying that we can't print the story?" Roper persisted.

"I'm saying nothing of the kind," Sam replied evenly. "I'm saying that you can print a story that is in reasonable proportion to the facts, not a campaign of harassment. I'm saying that you and your paper are badgering my client, Mister Reporter, and I'm saying that I, for one, won't stand for it. I mean to find out why your paper is picking on my client."

They faced each other angrily. Bud stepped into the awkward silence. "We'd better go, Paul."

Sam relaxed and slapped Bud on the back. "I appreciate your help, Bud. Do the same for you some time." He turned back to Roper. "I understand that you have to earn a living, Mr. Roper. But tell your editor, for me, that he doesn't have a sitting duck to shoot this time. And tell him that two can play at the game of harassment. Glad to have met you. Drop in at my office anytime, and have a drink." They shook hands with barely polite formality, hardly touching, for an instant. The reporters moved away, and Sam and Belle walked toward the doorway of Municipal Court Room Two.

Hank was waiting for him at the Defense Counsel's Table in the courtroom. Sam adjusted the points of his breastpocket handkerchief fastidiously as he sat down. Hank leaned over to him and whispered, "Look behind you. See that young fellow in the black blazer with pearl buttons? That's James Madison Canfield the Third, one of the boys who bought the drinks from Belle. How do you like that?"

Sam turned and studied the young man for a few moments, then swung back to Hank. "He looks nervous. And what's he doing here? The prosecution isn't likely to call him today. Go back to him, quietly, and ask him to wait for me after the hearing. I want to talk to him for a minute." Hank nodded and moved discreetly toward the young man.

Judge Newland was studying the charges before him. The judge was a heavy-set man with close-cropped gray hair. The Chief Assistant Prosecutor started reading off the title of the case from the morning Calendar, and Sam beckoned to Belle Larkbey. She was waiting in the first row of seats in the spectators' section. They took their positions at the rostrum.

The clerk called out the first line of ritual to Belle. "What is your true name?"

"Belle Larkbey."

"Where do you live?"

"The Flamingo Motel, at Mission and Seventh."

The judge looked at her and said somberly, "Belle Larkbey, you are charged with a violation of the Alcoholic Beverage Control Act, in that you did serve alcoholic beverages to minors —three minors. I note that you were released on your own recognizance." He turned toward the Prosecutor's Table. "Isn't that somewhat unusual? Who is appearing for the Prosecutor's Office in this case?"

A man in his forties with a surprising shock of red hair stood up at the Prosecutor's Table. Sam smiled ruefully. His information had been correct. It was Jerry Spangler. But why was the D.A. using such heavy artillery for a routine misdemeanor case?

Judge Newland seemed surprised, too, at seeing one of the big guns of the D.A.'s Office on such a minor case.

Spangler stepped forward. "If Your Honor please, the defendant is a long-time resident of this city, and not likely to try to evade the jurisdiction. Moreover, the State has taken possession of her establishment with a Padlock Order, duly issued by Judge Robert L. Stafford. We have what amounts to jurisdiction *in rem*, through possession of her assets, should a fine be levied or should she seek to avoid the jurisdiction."

The judge shook his head. "Somewhat irregular, Mr. Spangler. Might be questionable procedure. But the defendant is here, and so the point is moot. I take it that you will make no objection to the procedure, Mr. Benedict."

"No objection to the release, Your Honor. Indeed, we thank the Prosecutor for his courtesy to the person of the defendant. As to his seizure of the defendant's place of business, that is another matter. We most certainly do take exception to that, and shall ask that the Padlock Order be quashed as excessive and unusual action in view of the statute's purpose and provisions."

Newland heard him out patiently, but again shook his head negatively. "We cannot go into the facts of the case at this point. Do you waive reading of the complaint?"

"Yes," Sam agreed, "I have seen the complaint. It is the precipitous and harsh action of the Prosecutor's Office that disturbs me, Your Honor. Granting that the statute does authorize such action in special cases, it is quite unusual, not justified by the facts here, and amounts to severe punishment of my client without due process of law. Her livelihood has been cut off. Moreover, we have not had adequate time to prepare, and ask that this trial be put over for a few days."

"I understand." The judge seemed sympathetic. "But we do have a proper order for the seizure, duly issued. And we must rely on the discretion of public officers unless and until an abuse of that discretion is proven. There is no choice, Mr. Benedict. That is why the point cannot be settled here and now. I will put the case over for trial, and will try to set it for as prompt trial as possible. Meanwhile, I must know how you mean to plead the defendant."

"We plead 'not guilty,' Your Honor, and respectfully protest."

"Very well, Mr. Benedict. Do you waive a jury?"

"No, Your Honor. And I request either that the defendant be continued at liberty on her own recognizance, or that some small bail be set."

Spangler was all politeness. "May it please the Court. In view of this questioning of the action of the Prosecution, and the plea entered by the defendant, the People ask that bail be set, and that it be set at three thousand dollars. I am sure that my learned adversary will agree that his charge of questionable conduct of the Prosecutor's Office requires that the interests of the People be fully protected, and that therefore the usual procedural proprieties be followed precisely."

Before Sam could answer, the judge tapped his gavel. "Your request is denied, Mr. Spangler. In view of your release of the defendant on recognizance, I see no need for bail at this time."

Sam broke in. "This is a simple misdemeanor charge. . . ."

"Yes, I understand," the judge went on. "The defendant is continued on her own recognizance. Trial is set for August tenth, ten o'clock, Department Fifteen." Judge Newland had lots of other matters to worry about. "Next case," he said briskly.

Sam walked up to Spangler, before leaving the courtroom, and whispered, "I'll call you later at your office, Jerry. This thing is developing into a big question mark."

Spangler shrugged his shoulders, and bent over the Docket sheet. Outside, in the corridor, Paul Roper and a photographer were waiting for them. The photographer began snapping pictures.

Sam saw the young man in the black blazer, standing alone on the other side of the corridor. He tossed a "goodby" over his shoulder to Belle, and said, "Smile pretty for the camera. I'll be in touch." Then Sam walked over to young Canfield.

The young man looked at him doubtfully as Sam touched his shoulder and said, "Mr. Canfield? My name is Benedict. I'm the attorney for Belle Larkbey. I'd like a few words with you, if you will. You don't have to talk to me if you don't want to, but I'd appreciate it if you would."

Canfield was short and stocky, with curly, black hair topping a round face. He looked at Sam appraisingly. "I know who you are." He put out his hand, and they shook hands. "Of course I'll talk with you if you want."

"I understand that you are one of the young fellows involved in this matter."

"Yes."

"Are you sore at Belle Larkbey for any reason? Did she ever do any harm to you?"

The youngster flushed. "No, sir. I never saw her before until that night. I'm sorry about her trouble. I never made any complaint about her."

Sam pursed his lips. "Then what brings you here today?"

"I'm just curious, I guess. We never meant to . . . it was just a lark, getting a drink. . . ."

Sam noticed the newspapermen looking at them questioningly. This was no place to talk. He gestured quickly to Canfield, and said, "Young fellow, she's in really bad trouble. If you don't want this on your conscience, I've got to talk to you. We can't talk here. Will you meet me later?"

"Yes, sir. Sure."

"Can you meet me for lunch—on me?"

"Yes."

"All right. Meet me at Fisherman's Wharf, at Joe DiMaggio's Restaurant. About twelve-thirty. Can you be there?"

"Yes, sir." They shook hands. The boy seemed sober-faced and sincere. He brushed a lock of hair from his forehead. "I'll be there."

The office was buzzing with activity when Sam got back. Trudy had the usual pile of messages, and he hastily dictated replies and directions. Then he had her make a luncheon reservation for him at DiMaggio's. He told Hank to call Spangler and try to feel him out about what was back of the pressure in the D.A.'s office on the Larkbey case. There was something, no doubt of that now. But what? Then he went out again, hailed a cab, and went to Fisherman's Wharf.

Since its beginning in the Gold Rush days, almost everything about the fishing industry of the Bay Area has changed. The fish caught, the ships, the nets, the gear, the methods of packaging the catch and distributing it have become modernized with the times. But the biggest change, the old-timers say, is in the Wharf itself. There were no markets and restaurants on the early wharves, just plenty of room to spread out the nets and to repair the boats. The fish markets in those days were as simple and uncomplicated as the times. Practically anyone with the nose for it could get into the business of distributing the bounty of the sea. All that was required was a fish cart, a strong pair of legs, and a horn to toot as you progressed through the streets of North Beach. But in time the markets came to the wharves, and then the restaurants, and dinner at the Wharf became the fine local custom it is today.

The chief regret Sam had about Fisherman's Wharf was its gaudiness and cheapness, the junk-laden gift shops, the loud restaurant barkers, and the crowds. Most visitors, he thought gloomily, probably left the Wharf remembering only this. Some probably never saw a boat or discovered why the restaurants were world-famous. There was still something of the real Fisherman's Wharf here if you were willing to look for it. But it meant getting out on the wharves, where the crab boats, drag boats, and trawlers were moored. It meant talking to the fishermen themselves, each with a hundred stories to tell if he were in the mood.

Sam found the restaurant, walked up the staircase, and saw that Canfield was already there, seated next to a window. So far, so good. The boy stood up respectfully as Sam came to the table. At least he had good manners; either that, or he was a smooth, sly one. Sam waved him back down in his seat and joined him, facing him across the table. They were a little apart from the other tables, as Trudy had requested when making the reservation. There was a pleasant view over Fisherman's Wharf and the boats tied up in the marina.

The boy seemed to be ill at ease, and Sam tried to get him to be more relaxed. "It was nice of you to meet me. This is a pleasant place for luncheon, isn't it?"

"Yes, sir."

"If we're going to talk amicably, don't you think we ought to be less formal," Sam said pleasantly. "Do you mind if I call you Jim, or do you prefer James?"

"Jim is fine, sir." The boy seemed to be visibly pleased.

"All right, Jim. My friends call me Sam. I hope that we'll be friends." Sam had a distinct impression that this boy was hardly a paragon of virtue, and hardly likely to become a bosom friend of his, but it didn't hurt to be friendly.

The boy was silent. He was looking out the window. Sam beckoned to a waiter and gave his order for lunch. He would have liked a cocktail or a scotch-and-water before lunch, but ordered fruit juice instead. The thing now was to get the youngster to talk freely. It would be necessary to establish an atmosphere of easy camaraderie. There was one fairly sure way to do that. He launched into an easy flow of talk.

"You know," Sam began, "you and your friends, and this scrape at Belle Larkbey's, remind me of when I was young. I got into plenty of scrapes myself. Don't let the gray hair and stern face deceive you. I was no angel myself." He chuckled and the boy seemed to relax. "It was ever thus, I suppose," Sam went on. "The older generation clucks and complains about the young ones. They like the idea of that song that was popular a few years ago—'Why Can't They Be Like We Were, Perfect in Every Way.' As though *they* were perfect. The hell they were. Did you know, for example, that I myself ran away from home when I was about your age? All because of some argument with my father. And I can't even remember now what we argued about. If some young fellow does that now, some people say he must be a bad apple." He paused, reflectively.

"Why, I can remember one time," Sam hurried on lightly, "when I was driving a car with three or four other young fellows—friends of mine—on a dirt road at night, going like the hammers of Hell. We'd all had a few drinks. And remember, that was during Prohibition, so we'd all violated the laws already, buying liquor from a speakeasy. We came to a sudden fork in the road, with a ditch right in front of us. We found out later that the sign warning of the fork was broken and was lying on the ground back a ways. What's more, the road was up on an embankment, so I couldn't turn off. We were going too fast to make the turn, and it looked like we'd pile up, dead, into the ditch on the other side of the fork. So I yelled, 'Hang on. Here we go,' and spun the car off to the right, down the embankment." He stopped, and saw that the boy was interested and curious to know what had happened. "We rolled over. Must have rolled two or three times. Came to a stop upside down, the car sitting on its roof. It was an old-time, square-rigger of a car, built of heavy-gauge steel. The roof held, and the windows weren't even cracked. Everybody was standing on his ear, but it was practically a miracle—none of us was hurt, not even a scratch. We got out through the windows, all okay. Then we rolled the car back over, onto its wheels. It wasn't even dented. The engine picked right up, when I tried it. We jockeyed the car across a field and back on the road and drove back to town. We were good and sober then, I can tell you. When we got to town, one of the boys wanted to stop at a church, so we did. He was a Catholic, and wanted to light a candle in thanks. I'm not a Catholic, but I lit one too."

The boy was smiling. Sam shook his head from side to side. "If some young fellow did that today, a lot of people would call him a bloody juvenile delinquent. But here I am, a pillar of the community, no less, today."

Young Canfield laughed aloud. Good, Sam thought, now we're getting somewhere. Now, to follow it up a bit more. "Another time, I was in New York with some other young fellows, out on the town. I was a prize fighter—for a living, then, believe it or not—and had had a match in . . . I think it was the old Ridgewood Grove, over in Brooklyn. I won the bout, too. Anyhow, some of the boys wanted to go up to Harlem. One of them was looking for something. Wanted to change his luck, he said. Boy, the damnfool, stupid, nasty things young fellows say and do!"

Jim Canfield was bright-eyed with interest, drinking in every word. Either that, Sam thought, or he was a convincing young actor.

"So there we were, standing on a corner on Lenox Avenue. It was pretty late. One of the boys actually was fool enough to stop a passerby and ask him where to go for some 'fun.' This fellow told him to go to some tenement nearby, around the corner, but to wait a while, while he went ahead of us to tell them to expect us. And we all were crazy enough to do as he said.

"In a little while we went to this tenement address, went in, and climbed the dark, dingy stairs. When we got to the third floor landing we heard people coming in down below, at the street entrance. At the same time, we heard footsteps coming down, from up above, at the roof. The picture was clear, even to idiots such as we were. We were being surrounded—trapped on the stair landing."

Jim seemed to be almost breathlessly waiting for him to go on.

"If we had been heroes—or absolute fools worse than we were—we would have tried to fight our way out. There were four of us, I think. But we were surrounded, above and below, by seven or eight men armed with pistols, knives, et cetera. We stood there like embarrassed sheep, and were quickly and efficiently robbed. Wallets, rings, watches. They took my pocket watch. I had little money, but I hated to lose the watch. Always carry a pocket watch, you see, in my vest pocket. Don't like wrist watches."

"Did they attack you?" Jim asked.

"No. Just wanted our valuables. That was bad enough. We hardly could complain to the police about being held up in those circumstances. I suppose they knew that physical attack would lead to police investigation. Anyhow, they took our valuables and left. We went down the stairs and out onto the street, feeling absolutely humiliated. But we knew that we deserved it."

"That's some story."

"Some idiots!" Sam remarked ruefully. "Just the kind of thing that we'd say is awful if young fellows like you did it today."

"Well, wait 'til I tell you what happened to us," Jim bubbled eagerly. "You'll get a charge out of it. So help me, it'll remind you of your own story."

Their meal was being served, and Sam cursed under his breath at the interruption. But the boy was bright-eyed with eagerness to tell his story. As soon as they were alone again, without touching his food he launched into his story.

"Just listen to this, Mr. Benedict." He took a swallow of water. "There were the three of us, 'out on the town,' the way you put it. We spend a lot of time together, the three of us, summers, when we're home from school. We've known each other for a long time. Ralph Hibbes goes to Stanford. Walter Finchley goes to Yale. And I go to the University of Iowa. We went to see a play, that evening, at a theatre on Geary Street. In fact, the play was *A Case of Libel*. Good, too. Then, afterward, we decided to go scout around and see what we could do. We had these I.D. cards that we got from some guy out near Twin Peaks, so we decided to go to some bar and have a few drinks."

Sam interrupted. "Who was this fellow from whom you got the I.D. cards?"

"I don't know his name. Never saw him before or since. We

met him at a place where a bunch of guys had happened to meet, some time ago early in the summer. He sold us these cards for five bucks each, blank, so we could fill in our own names. I have no idea of who he was or where to find him."

Sam was disappointed. "That's too bad. But you've been using these cards all summer, you say."

"Sure." The boy seemed rather proud of that. "Never had a bit of trouble with them, until this night. Why, we've used them in half a dozen places with never a peep about them."

"Then how did it happen that the cards were questioned this time?"

"I'm coming to that."

"All right. Go ahead." Sam was sorry that he had interrupted.

"So we hailed a taxicab and told the driver to take us to North Beach. He dropped us off near this Larkbey place, so we went in there. It was a nice place, with good atmosphere. You know, dim lights and all that. We ordered drinks and sat there shooting the breeze for a while."

"No trouble with the I.D. cards?" Sam asked.

"No. The bartender asked us for them. I guess we don't look very old. Then this blonde woman came and looked at them and said 'okay.' She's the owner, that Miss or Mrs. Larkbey. The bartender served the drinks to us, after that, and we sat around in a booth. Actually, the waitress—this redhead named Gladys—served them to us in the booth."

"Who's she?" Sam asked casually.

"There were two or three waitresses. It's a fair-sized place, you know. Dark and kind of smoky, but nice and tavern-like. This waitress, Gladys, was very friendly and not bad looking. That's what got Walt. He took a shine to her and they got real palsy-walsy. In fact, that's where the evening started to get real cool. She invited him upstairs."

"What?" Sam was startled. This was a new wrinkle entirely.

"Yeah. She was available," the boy said with a grin. "Seems like there are some rooms upstairs, above the tavern, and Gladys was going to meet him up there."

Sam was alertly listening. "Did Belle Larkbey see any of this? Were the other waitresses 'available' too, do you know?"

"No. I'm pretty sure that this was Gladys' own idea. She

said not to let on or the boss would throw her out. I'm pretty sure this was a private deal by Gladys. Walt was interested, but not I or Ralph. I don't go for tramps. You had a saying in your time, when you were a young fellow—Why buy a cow when milk's so cheap?"

Sam looked hard at the youngster, but kept a stiff smile on his face. That was ugly; not yet twenty, and already the boy sounded like a blasé roué. "So then what happened?"

"Walt went up the side stairway to go upstairs. There's a stairway in the tavern that leads upstairs, you know. Gladys followed him. This Larkbey woman was way in the back and didn't notice, I'm sure. Ralph and I sat around and waited."

"How long?" Sam asked.

"Couldn't have been more than five minutes. Then the holdup started."

Sam sat back in his chair, startled. "Holdup? What holdup?" This was beginning to add up. So the rumors about a holdup were not mere rumors!

"Three men came in. They had guns and they said 'This is a stickup. Everybody sit quiet and nobody'll get hurt.' We sat quiet."

"Where did they come from?"

"Through the front door. They held pistols on us and told everyone to gather together in the middle of the tavern. They said that they were going after the till, not the customers, and if we behaved we wouldn't lose anything. This Larkbey woman argued with them. She said she had lots of friends who looked out for her and if they 'took her,' her friends would go after the robbers. It was real cool—like a movie."

"What about your friend?" Sam asked.

"That was a howl—a panic. One of the creeps with a gun went up the stairway to look around. He interrupted Walt and Gladys before they could get started. Funniest thing I've ever seen. He made them go down the stairs stark naked. Not a stitch on them. I thought I'd crack a rib laughing. This Gladys and Walt were pulling on a dress—her dress—between them. Walt had grabbed the dress and was trying to wrap it around his butt, and she was trying to pull it away from him, to put it on. It was a panic. Then this guy on the stairs pointed his gun at Walt and said 'Ain't you got no manners? Give the lady the dress.' So Walt let go, and she put on the dress. Walt stood near us, smoking a cigarette we gave him and trying to look nonchalant—stark naked. I tell you, it was a real cool scene."

Sam grinned. "Did the stickup men rob you? Were they masked?" It might be possible to find them, he thought.

"Naw." The boy was laughing. "They took the money from the cash register and from a tin box under the bar. It looked like a wad of money. Didn't touch us, although I almost got shot at one point."

"How was that?"

"I had a pack of cigarettes in my shirt pocket and without thinking reached my hand in under my jacket to get them. One of the gunmen pointed his cannon at me, and I froze. He came over and patted my chest and under my arms, looking for a gun or holster—'frisked me,' you'd call it. I told him that I was only getting some cigarettes. He took them out of my pocket, holding the gun at my stomach. I was sweating some. Then he gave me the pack and said something about not making any suspicious moves. Right after that they all left. One of them said not to follow them and not to come out on the street for five minutes. Nobody did."

"Did anyone call the police when they had left?" Sam wanted to know.

"This Larkbey woman told everybody to stay put. Nobody in the tavern called the police, as far as I saw. She was shouting that the drinks were on the house. I think that she didn't want anybody to call the police. But then another funny thing happened. Walt, still naked, grabbed the redhead, Gladys, and started up the steps with her again. He had paid her in advance and wanted his money's worth. She was hanging back, scared I guess, not wanting to go with him. Then the Larkbey gal came roaring up, yelling at Gladys and cursing her something fierce. Walt let go and ran upstairs to get his clothes."

"What did Belle say to this Gladys?"

"She called her a 'damn whore' and lots of other things, and told her to get out and never come back or she'd kill her. Gladys ran and got her coat and handbag and ran out of the place. The bartender was holding the Larkbey woman or I think she would have murdered the redhead right then and there. Boy, was she mad!"

"Then what happened?"

"The bartender and another waitress were handing out free drinks and everyone was pressing around getting free liquor. She even opened a couple of bottles of champagne and was filling glasses for anyone who wanted it. We guzzled champagne for a while, until Walt came downstairs. He had got dressed and joined us again. We kidded him. Everybody was all excited and friendly."

Sam made a stab for some vital bits of information. "But I know the police were there. They padlocked the place. When did that happen?"

"I don't know, Mr. Benedict. Nobody called them, as far as I saw. I guess somebody did, of course. But they came in suddenly, a while later. They questioned everybody, and that's when they spotted the phony I.D. cards, when they asked us for identification. Then they climbed all over the Larkbey gal, about selling liquor to minors. They were busy on the phone— calling in, and all—for a long while, and made us wait there. They didn't let me and Ralph and Walt go for quite a while. I didn't get home until three in the morning. Boy, did I get it from my dad."

"Did he know about it?"

"Somebody had called him, I think, from the police. He knew about it, and about the I.D. cards. He was waiting for me when I got home. Boy, was he turned on. . . ."

"What happened with Belle Larkbey?"

"The police took her along with them. They were going to take the bartender, too, but she said she'd be responsible, and they let him go. They let me and Ralph and Walt go, too."

"I don't want to butt into your family affairs, Jim," said Sam, "but what did your father say to you when you got home?"

"Oh, the usual. What a disappointment I was to him. How he was sick and tired of my getting into trouble. How he was fed up on going to bat for me. And all that kind of stuff."

"What do you mean by 'going to bat for you'? Do you often

92 /

get into jams?" He knew that this kind of question might cause the boy to freeze up, but took the chance.

"He'd been talking to the police and telling them that he'd be responsible for me. That kind of thing. Yes, I've had a run-in or two, before. Doesn't everybody?"

"Like what?"

"Oh, a couple of auto accidents. And last year the university was going to suspend me for doing a dance on top of a Volkswagen parked outside the fieldhouse. It was just a lark, and Dad paid for repainting the VW. But he was plenty annoyed."

"That's all?"

"Oh, maybe one or two other little things. Nothing serious, believe me." The boy was becoming increasingly evasive. No use pressing him too hard. Just one more try, Sam thought, and then let go of him. "Do you happen to know, Jim, if your father has been talking with the newspapers about the prosecution of Belle Larkbey?"

The boy hesitated. "I don't really know, Mr. Benedict. He said something about talking to the editor of one of the newspapers, the morning after, but I'm not sure just what it was. I don't remember what he said. He had lots of other things to say, about me, and he sure said them."

Good enough. So the parental pillar of the community probably had been talking to the newspapers, and probably putting the pressure on Belle. It added up. Better to hang Belle than his own boy, probably, in his way of thinking. Sam could not be certain, but the indications were strong. That would explain the newspaper barrage. It probably also could explain the pressure from the D.A.'s office. Canfield, Senior and the other proud papas were influential enough to get such pressure put on if they wanted it.

He changed the topic to small-talk with the boy, and they ate their lunch.

Hank took his little notebook out of his pocket, settled his bulk in the chair, and began his report on the three boys in the Larkbey case. Sam lit a cigarette, leaned back in his swivel chair, and listened.

"First, you know, of course, that James Madison Canfield Number Two is the head man of the Founders Club nowadays. He carries a lot of weight in this town."

"I know." Sam had once had lunch with Canfield II at the Founders Club, when both of them had been members of a money-raising committee for a milk fund for poor children.

"John D. Hibbes, the father of young Ralph Hibbes, is the president of a chain of stores here and has a big interest in two department stores. All of these stores place a lot of advertising in the local newspapers, of course. I'm not saying that he uses his financial influence in any way he shouldn't. I'm not saying that. But I imagine that the newspapers have a lot of respect for big advertisers. Don't you?"

"I imagine so." But Sam shook his head. "Let's not jump to conclusions."

"Okay. Next, Peter Finchley, daddy of Walter Finchley, is connected with a major steamship line based in San Francisco —for whatever that fact is worth. I'm just mentioning all of this by way of background. What I'm saying is that these kids all come from well-heeled and influential families."

"Good enough. So, what else?"

"Take young Walter Finchley, first. *There* is a charming youngster for you! He was sued on a paternity claim by a girl from San Jose about a year ago. The case was settled out of court and the action was withdrawn. Nice?"

"It's consistent with something else I learned today. I'll tell you about it when you've finished. Go on."

"Young Walter was picked up last December, while home from college during the Christmas vacation, on a charge of simple assault brought by a waitress who works in a beanery near the Embarcadero. The file is not clear, but I suspect it may have been a carnal-assault charge reduced to a lesser charge. There was a *nolle prosequi* on it—dropped—quashed. I tried to locate the waitress, but she doesn't work there any more. She's gone with the wind."

"Very consistent," Sam said. "Looks like this boy needs either psychiatric help or a tremendous paddling."

"Okay. Now, Ralph Hibbes. He's well known in his neighborhood as a motorcycle-club cat. Belongs to the Black Demons

Club—that's a typical black-leather jacket, iron cross, swastika, and general bully-boy gang. They've been pulled in for public nuisance and what-not as far away as L.A., not to mention other towns. He—Ralph—personally, seems to have no police record, but his gang has as smelly a reputation as any of the cycle clubs. Neighborhood talk that he's a bully and a trouble-maker, but nothing definite, yet. I'll keep looking."

"All right."

"And finally, James Madison Canfield Number Three. Two civil suits for negligent operation of a motor vehicle. In one case, severe personal injury to the driver of the plaintiff's car, a man named Harris, a tool-and-die maker. Both cases settled by Canfield's insurance company without trial. Also, in the Harris case, young Canfield was cited for reckless driving and paid a fine."

Sam frowned. "That's not very conclusive of anything, though it certainly is not a point in his favor."

"That isn't all," Hank said. "This kid has been in Juvenile Court twice. Once for possession of marijuana—dismissed with a scolding. Second time, for possession of marijuana and also of LSD. That time there seems to have been an intimation that he was selling the stuff—pushing. I can't figure out why he should do that. He certainly must get enough money from his father. He can't be needing the dough."

"Don't be too sure of that. You know the old saying—'Much wants more.' He has expensive tastes. But what happened on the second pickup?"

"Nothing, as far as I can see. He was released in his father's custody, and the case seems to have been quietly hushed up. I don't think that the boy is an addict, do you?"

"No." Sam was positive. "I had lunch with him. He doesn't have any of the symptoms."

"But it sure would embarrass Canfield Two to have it widely known that his boy is a user, even of pot or acid."

"That it would, Hank."

"Anyhow," Hank continued, "It looks like the proud papas all have good reasons for not wanting publicity for their off-spring."

"More specifically," Sam said, tapping the desk, "they simply can't have the boys nailed for anything if it can be avoided. I have in mind that there is a section in the California statutes about fraudulent use of identification cards. If that provision reads the way I think it does, the boys may be liable to prosecution. Look it up, Hank, and let me know just what the statute says."

"Okay." He made a note.

"Also," Sam added, "Belle has tried to prevent me from getting the real story of what happened. She lied to me. I didn't think Belle would do that. Still, it's understandable. She's been afraid of a much worse charge than selling liquor to minors—a charge that surely would close her place once and for all, and that might mean a jail sentence for her. The irony of it is that she's probably innocent, and is just caught in a situation made by other people. But she probably could never prove that. I can understand why she was afraid to tell me the whole truth." He told Hank the story that Jim Canfield had told him at lunch. When he came to the incident of Walt, Gladys, and the gunman, Hank roared with laughter. Sam grinned too, and finished the story.

"Hell's bells." Hank couldn't stop chuckling. "No wonder everybody's so secretive about what happened. Just about everyone in the picture looks like a fool or a heel. No wonder they all lied about it."

"Now, I want you to check out the details," Sam instructed. "Talk to the bartender again. Find the other waitress or waitresses, and talk to them. See if you can find this Gladys, if you can, and talk to her. Chances are you'll not find her. She probably has left town and will keep running until she puts some distance behind her. But try anyhow. Nose around the precinct house and see if any of the police can add anything, though they didn't see it. Why didn't they report the robbery? Or did they?"

"Okay." Hank was making notes.

"I'll talk to Belle myself," Sam concluded. "Really, I can't feel angry with her, but I'll scorch her ears on general principles."

Belle was all injured innocence, at first, when he got her on the phone. But as Sam made it clear that the Canfield boy had told him the whole story, she broke down.

"For Pete's sake, Sam," she pleaded. "What else could I do? They're only charging me with selling to minors. In a way that's decent of them. They could charge me with being a madam. May that little bitch Gladys rot in Hell. I'll kill her if I ever see her again. So help me, I'll kill her. And that lousy creep of a kid—that Finchley fink—there's a crummy louse for you."

"What about this Gladys? What's her second name, and where does she live?"

She told him, and he jotted down the name and address.

"How did you happen to hire her?"

"With an ad in the Help-Wanted column. She had no experience—as a waitress, that is—but she seemed to be fair looking. You don't need experience to serve drinks, you know."

"Did you ever have an inkling that she was hustling the customers?"

"No, never. Once or twice she'd disappear for half an hour or so. Told me that she was tired and went upstairs to lie down for a while. You know me—the old soft touch. I never thought anything of it. I assumed it was ordinary monthly headache or such. You know how girls are."

"So this business with the Finchley boy was a surprise to you."

"As God is my judge, Sam. You could have knocked me over with a feather. The dirty little tramp." Belle was sputtering with rage. "I threw her out. Now I'm sorry I didn't tear her hair out. The spot she put me on. . . ."

Sam meditated for a few moments. "All right, Belle. I believe you. But don't you ever try to mislead me again. Either you tell me the truth, the whole truth, or you can go whistle as far as I'm concerned."

"Yes, Sam. I will. I will." She was contrite.

"Now," he said, almost to himself, "the question is what do we do about all this."

"Anything you say, Sam." She was a soldier acknowledging his command.

"Well, let me think about it for a while." He was far from

certain, as yet, what tactics would be best. "You keep in touch with me. And don't get smart and try anything without asking me first."

"Yes, Sam. I'll keep in touch and I'll keep my nose clean."

"You do that." He hung up the telephone.

Rubenfeld was surprised when Sam phoned him. "After all," he said, "I've only had one session with Janet Porter. It's much too soon to be able to make any kind of sound diagnosis."

"I understand that," Sam agreed. "All I'm after at the moment from you is a prima-facie impression. I know that it cannot be anything more than a superficial impression, but even that will be useful for now. I'm going to New York and Cleveland to check information with people who knew the Porters there. It will help to have at least a general impression of the psychiatric aspects."

The psychiatrist protested. "Come on now, Sam. What I can tell you at this point means nothing. It may be that Janet Porter is perfectly normal. So far I have found nothing that indicates otherwise—that is, if we are agreed on what 'normal' means."

"Did you give her a physical examination?"

"Yes, I did. Nothing worth reporting. She is a physically average woman for her age. Nothing significant."

"And psychologically . . . ?"

"So far, nothing." Rubenfeld sounded slightly annoyed. "You are asking for it, Sam. If you insist, I'll tell you what I have discovered so far. Nothing. You have nothing. Everything about Mrs. Porter so far means nothing."

"Hearken unto me, my friend." Sam spoke slowly and emphatically. "Nothing never means nothing. Everything has a meaning and a significance if only we can see it whole and in relation to other things connected with it. Nothing never means nothing."

"I won't argue that. That is exactly the point. But, you said it yourself: We must see it whole and relate it to other things. Let me have time enough, and perhaps we can do that. I'll be seeing Mrs. Porter as often as possible. In a week or ten days I'll be able to tell you something meaningful. But not now. Not yet."

"All right." Sam was, perforce, satisfied. "You have told me something, even when you said about Janet Porter that there was nothing. At least I know that if there is any psychiatric problem, it is not obvious and easy to see. That is some help for my purpose right now."

"I'm glad to be of help." Rubenfeld was blandly sarcastic.

Sam ignored the sarcasm. "Keep after it, as much as you can, Irwin. I'd appreciate an intensive series of examinations and tests."

"Of course. When will you be back from your trip?"

"In three or four days. Perhaps you'll have something by then. I ought to have a good deal more background data on Janet Porter when I get back."

"Every little bit helps. Call me and tell me what you discover when you get back. It may be significant."

Sam said "goodby" and hung up the phone.

"Nothing means nothing," he said silently to the disconnected instrument. "Nothing never means nothing."

Trudy closed her book and started to rise when Sam finished dictating. She had been taking dictation for an hour, and it was getting late in the afternoon. Then she made up her mind and spoke up. "Mr. Benedict, I know that I urged you to see Belle Larkbey and to take her case when you already were busy enough with the Porter case and everything else. Hank has told me about the complications in the Larkbey case, and I feel guilty. I know that she can't pay much of a fee and I feel as though I almost forced you to do a lot of work for little or nothing."

Sam waved his hand deprecatingly. "Don't feel guilty. I don't force very easily, anyhow. If I hadn't wanted to take the case, I wouldn't have taken it."

"Still, I know how busy you are. I'm sorry that I stepped out of line."

"You didn't. Not at all. Besides, it's part of my job. A lawyer is supposed to help people who are in trouble. I'm only doing what I'm supposed to do."

"For practically nothing? Hank says that he thinks that she just gets along with her tavern and probably won't be able to pay a proper fee."

"Even so. A lawyer has to do what he ought to do, *pro bono publico,* every once in a while, regardless of the fee. Part of the secret of successful—as well as self-satisfying—practice is to cast bread upon the waters now and then. Somehow it seems to pay, even in terms of money, let alone public duty and personal satisfaction. I believe that if you cast bread upon the waters, it surprisingly often comes back spongecake."

"Or water-logged, stale bread."

"No. Let me give you a for instance. Sit down, Trudy, and I'll tell you about a case that I had, years ago, before you worked here. You'll see what I mean." He lit a cigarette and smiled in reminiscence.

"In the mid-thirties, during the big Depression, a friend of mine named Leonard, practicing in New York City, got a call from a woman he knew. She was in bad trouble, needed help, and couldn't afford to pay any fee at all. She told him that her husband Fred had been arrested by the F.B.I., was charged with fraudulent bankruptcy, and was being held in the Federal House of Detention. It seems that a year before the husband had been out of work and they had been in deep trouble. They had two children, no job, and no income, but were too proud to ask for public welfare. Then her husband had received a letter from a brother from whom he hadn't heard in ten years. This brother, named Harry, had abandoned a wife and child in New York ten years earlier and had disappeared.

"Harry's letter, swearing Ted to secrecy, said that Harry was making a lot of money operating retail stores in California. He needed a reliable assistant, and offered Ted a job at a good salary. Ted scraped together the money for transportation by borrowing, came to California, and started working for his brother. He was put in charge of a store in Redondo Beach near L.A., where Harry had another store. Business was booming in both stores. What Ted didn't know, never having worked in a retail store before and not being suspicious-minded, was that Harry was running a full-scale, fraudulent-bankruptcy operation. Harry would order goods on consignment from manufacturers and sell the goods below cost price by running sales constantly. Each store was set up as a separate corporation. Then Harry would pocket the receipts, not pay the suppliers, and put the store into bankruptcy.

"Harry had been getting away with this swindle for years,

using dummy names for the supposed owners of each store corporation. He also moved from town to town so nobody caught up with him. Now he had become so cocky that he was running several stores—and several phony bankruptcies—at one time. That was why he needed his brother Ted. Harry was living high on the hog by then. He had a mistress who traveled with him, a good-looking crook whom I later called 'Nellie the beautiful blonde.' Ted did as he was told, and later said that he suspected nothing.

"After a while, Ted's wife joined him. Ted was managing a store in Fremont, and Harry had also opened a new store in Oakland. Ted's wife was smarter than he was. She quickly got suspicious about Harry's bookkeeping practices and urged her husband to quit and go back East. Ted finally understood that he was being used as a patsy, and he and his wife went back to New York. Soon after they left, the roof caved in on Harry. The creditors traced the swindles to him and a Federal indictment went out for everyone connected with the racket. Harry and Nellie promptly disappeared.

"My friend Leonard got Ted out on bail, and tried to help the F.B.I. find Harry and Nellie. He figured that Ted had just been a gullible tool for them, and if the creditors could catch the real crooks, they wouldn't care about Ted. That was when he called me and asked me to help. It was clear that there was no fee and a lot of work. Ted and his wife barely had enough to eat, let alone pay legal fees. Ted had got a job as a shoe salesman, and was working for mere subsistence wages.

"I helped out all I could. From my point of view this was a pure bread-cast-on-the-waters case. I finally tracked Harry and Nellie to Corpus Christi, Texas. The F.B.I. arrested both of them there. They were living in a trailer, and Harry was operating a fishing-boat-rental business which he had bought. But there was no money worth talking about, even though the creditors showed hundreds of thousands had been stolen. Harry had only a few hundred in cash and no bank books. The F.B.I. searched Nellie the beautiful blonde and found a collection of valuable diamonds wrapped in an oilskin pouch hidden in her clothing. She put up quite a fight when searched, they told me. The two crooks were brought back here for trial.

"Then Leonard sent Ted to me to represent him at the trial

—for no fee. He wanted him to plead *nolo contendere.* You know that I go on the principle of never plead 'guilty.' But I did as he asked, pleaded 'no contest,' and got a suspended sentence for Ted. Harry and Nellie got ten years in San Quentin. And my fee . . . ? It was a 'thank-you,' that's all."

Trudy heard him out and said, "That's exactly what I mean."

Sam smiled broadly. "But wait. There's a sequel. The bread came back spongecake after all. About a year later my friend Leonard got another phone call from the same woman. She had been in an accident and wanted to file a claim for damages for personal injuries. She had been walking across a street pushing one of the children in a baby carriage. Just as she stepped on a manhole cover, it blew up. She was thrown down and suffered a miscarriage. She was only in the second or third month, so she didn't suffer much pain or discomfort. But it *was* a miscarriage.

"The defendant was the Consolidated Edison Company of New York, a choice target for a personal-injuries suit. And the liability was open-and-shut. This was a perfect *res ipsa loquitur* case—the thing spoke for itself. In fact, the woman was delighted with the miscarriage. If there was one thing she and Ted didn't want then, it was another baby. But from the defense point of view the case was impossible to defend. If it had ever come to trial, any jury would award a whopping big verdict for the plaintiff. The case was settled for a substantial sum and paid within a few weeks. My friend Leonard had almost nothing to do; the easiest case he ever had.

"As for me, I got a check in the mail—out of the blue—for a thousand dollars, from Ted and his wife. They insisted that they owed it to me. That was real money in the thirties, and I had done no work on the personal-injuries case.

"You see what I mean, Trudy. Fate works in unpredictable ways. I never expected to get any fee from those people. Incidentally, they later referred some people to me in another case. You cast your bread on the waters and it comes back spongecake."

CHAPTER

5

Hank put the airline tickets on Sam's desk. "Trudy got your tickets. Flight 309. You'll have to change at O'Hare in Chicago. No nonstop flight to New York at that hour. What with the time difference in New York, the next nonstop flight would get you there in the middle of the night."

"That's all right. How about hotel reservations?" Sam was putting papers into his dispatch case.

"At the Regency. The A.B.A. meetings are at the Waldorf, but you said you wanted to stay at the Regency."

"Right. The hotel where the meetings are held is always crowded and noisy."

"Sal Mellito phoned. Said he'd see you in New York."

"All right. Have you read my speech? What did you think of it?"

"Good, boss. It ought to shake the boys up."

"Anything new in the Larkbey case?"

"Just one small item. I checked with the University of Iowa about Jim Canfield the Third. He was suspended for a week last winter for damaging somebody's car by jumping on its roof. The owner was paid for the damage and the boy was restored to good standing with a warning."

"He told me about that, but he didn't mention the suspension. There isn't any doubt that the boys are young hellions and that their fathers are trying to protect them. Anything from the precinct house or the newspapermen yet?"

"Not yet."

"Anything else on Janet Porter?"

"No. I've had a lot to do on other matters too."

"I know, Hank. But keep after that while I'm gone." He tossed a slim volume on abnormal psychology into his dispatch case. "Maybe I'll have a chance to read that." He put the leather case aside, ready for later. "Sit down, Hank. I want to go over some ideas on the Porter case and see how you react to them."

"As the law stands now," Sam said reflectively, "the courts are still committed to the M'Naghten Rule as to what is and what isn't insanity. Is that a fair statement?"

"Yes, generally," Hank answered. "But not all of them. Not always."

"True enough. But the Durham Rule is still only a small minority rule."

"Yes."

"The M'Naghten Rule is the one almost certain to be applied in a plea of insanity as a defense in a criminal case in California."

"Yes."

"So it behooves us to understand fully the M'Naghten Rule. Whether we go along with it or seek to overturn it, we must understand it as it is."

"Yes."

Sam went on with his train of thought. "We know that even in ancient times our ancestors recognized mental affliction and were rather charitable towards the mentally afflicted. The scriptures tell us that lunatics were allowed 'to dwell among the tombs.' The Egyptians acknowledged that mentally afflicted persons—insane persons—could not comprehend what their duties and obligations to Pharaoh were, and thus could not be held to these duties and obligations. Pagan Greece and Rome deemed insane people to be under the special protection of the gods and had special laws for them."

"All that is history," Hank remarked almost impatiently.

"Then we know," Sam continued, "that in medieval times the lot of the insane became harder. They were viewed as possessed by demons which had to be exorcised. There were even special tribunals of monks devoted to the exorcising of such demons. In some monasteries the 'therapy' for insanity was ten lashes a day as regular 'treatment' of the affliction. In fact, there were codified rules to this effect."

"I didn't know that." Hank was interested.

"Still later, the custom was to imprison lunatics in dark chambers or even in dungeons. Shakespeare mentions this in *Twelfth Night*. In England a place devoted to custody of the insane was the Priory of St. Mary of Bethlehem. Its name was shortened to Bethlem, and then to Bedlam, in common speech. Everybody has heard of Bedlam, and you know what it has come to mean as a word even today." Sam paused.

Hank acknowledged his ignorance. "I know the word, but I didn't know how it originated."

"You know," Sam continued, "that by the seventeenth century insane persons were confined in dark places, kept in chains, and beaten and starved. In the early seventeen hundreds, in the Arnold Case in England, the first legal test of insanity seems to have been stated. That rule said that punishment for commission of crime could not be imposed on a person who was so deprived of reason as to be as unreasoning as a brute wild beast. Later, in the Hadfield Case, the defendant was held to be suffering from delusion when he fired a pistol at King George the Third, even though he knew that he was firing at the King."

"That's new to me. I never studied the history of the rule that thoroughly." Hank looked surprised.

"So then we come to 1843 and the M'Naghten Rule. M'Naghten undoubtedly was suffering from paranoia. He had delusions of persecution. The court said that a defense of insanity must show that the defendant, when he committed the act, was laboring under such a defect of reason—from mental disease— as not to know the nature and quality of the act he was doing, or if he did understand the nature and quality, that he did not know that what he was doing was wrong."

"That seems to me to be a pretty good rule of law." Hank crushed out his cigarette aggressively. "At least it seems practical and workable. The Durham Rule would set no guidelines at all, and every case would depend on what expert-witness opinion turned out to be."

Sam stared at him. "Do you really believe that mental affliction can be boiled down to a one-line rule of law, with even the present state of our knowledge of psychiatry? I will grant that the M'Naghten Rule was very good indeed for 1843, before Sigmund Freud was even born, and long before the time of Jung or modern research into the nature of mental illness. But, for today. . . !"

"I can't see why not." Hank was stubbornly unconvinced.

"Look at it this way. The basic test in M'Naghten is whether or not the person could reason. Is that not so?"

"Yes."

"But even a lunatic can reason. He will pick up a coat and put it on when he is cold. He recognizes people and things and their relation to him. If you insult him, does he not understand, and grow angry? If an automobile runs at him, he has reasoning power enough to get out of its way. No matter how imperfectly, he does reason."

"I suppose so."

"Then, if he can reason, the M'Naghten Rule does not protect him. Lunatic or not, he will be taken and executed—for doing something that he might have been utterly incapable of *not* doing."

"It could happen," Hank admitted.

"Is that not a brutal and archaic rule," Sam argued, "if it can produce such a result? Court after court has admitted that the law has failed to keep abreast of modern progress in psychiatry. Yet they slavishly follow the old, archaic rule. But you know, apparently, of the 1954 decision of the court in the District of Columbia, adopting a new test which says that an accused cannot be convicted if his unlawful act was the result of a mental disease or defect. Mark that word—*defect*. That additional word allows the courts to consider facts which they were not allowed to consider before. That is some progress, but not enough."

Hank was still not convinced. "That will mean that each case will boil down to a battle of the experts. The psychiatrists will try the case, not the court."

"Aren't they better qualified to say who is, or was, insane, than a judge who doesn't know anything about the science and art of psychiatry? And psychiatrists will be used for expert testimony anyhow, won't they?"

"I guess I'm stubborn. I like the simplicity of the old rule. And I like to have courts try cases—not psychiatrists." Hank stuck his jaw out defiantly.

"And you refuse to follow reason, and to change with the times, and to use the knowledge we have?" asked Sam, suavely.

"Psychiatry is still a long way from being an exact science. I think that it usually is simply a complex vocabulary applied to ordinary horse sense—a lot of hot air. I've never seen a psychiatrist who wasn't a little batty himself." The big man was stubbornness incarnate.

"Well. There's no use trying to reason with that kind of thinking." Sam was a bit disgusted. "But let's leave the theorizing. As it stands, I don't want to try to change the California rule if I don't have to. The practical question is what can we do with the Porter case under the law as it now stands—under the M'Naghten Rule?"

"If the old rule is as bad as you say it is, why not try to get it changed?" Hank asked. "We can take it up on appeal, or maybe the trial court will accept a change."

Sam shook his head. "The chances of getting a trial judge to change the law are almost nil. You know that. It's a rare judge who has the fortitude to call a rule bad and to take the chance that his decision will be upheld on appeal. No. Most judges are afraid of one thing above all—afraid of being reversed on appeal. It's much safer to simply follow the rules, and to let the higher courts change them. A lot of judges are fond of clucking and expressing their forward-thinking views, *in dicta,* but they usually follow the safe old rule. They often say that the legislature should change the rule if it's going to be changed."

"But this rule was made by judges, not by the legislature," his assistant insisted.

"Exactly!" Sam's voice was triumphant. "But the judges cling to *stare decisis*—follow the rule. They forget that the greatest quality of the common law is flexibility. They forget that the courts can, and should, change a rule when it ceases to be sound, if the legislature doesn't move to do so."

Hank objected. "You can request the court to charge the jury in a modern way, rather than by simple parrot-like repetition of the M'Naghten Rule."

"I can," Sam admitted. "And the judge can refuse to do so. Then we are right back where we started. Then we'd have to take up the question by appealing from his refusal to charge as requested. That would be a long, slow process, with little probability of success. Meanwhile, what happens to Janet Porter? She becomes a pawn in a legal argument. No, there must be a better way."

"How?"

"Suppose that we do not fight the M'Naghten Rule, poor as it is. Suppose that we try to achieve a just result with the law as it is. Can we do that?"

"I don't see how." The big man was bewildered. "There is no evidence of what the M'Naghten Rule requires—a defect of reason from mental disease that caused her not to know right from wrong, or that caused her not to know what she was doing."

"It is enough, under the Rule," the older lawyer insisted, "if we can show that she did not understand the nature and quality of her act, because of mental affliction. That is probably what we must try to show."

"How?" Hank was doubtful.

"I don't know yet. But there are certain signs in her history that suggest possibilities. She is, for one thing, so absolutely controlled that it suggests an unconscious, or even conscious, awareness of some dark something that must be rigidly suppressed. She is so rigidly self-controlled that it suggests secret fear of something in her own mind. A person can be so inflexibly sane as to suggest suppression of an insane tendency. It is simply unnatural to be so perfectly disciplined. Normal human beings are not perfectly self-controlled. They simply aren't. Normal people have normal amounts of anger and fear and hostility toward various things."

Hank Tabor shook his head. "You're losing me."

Sam explained, patiently. "Janet Porter apparently was dominated by her father, though she may have loved him or she may have hated him. Her relation to her husband is unclear, however, though she says she loved him. I have a hunch about both relationships—a hunch that there was some deep, dark, ugly thing in her mind which exploded one night and killed Kevin Porter. I don't know what it was, yet, but I mean to try to find out."

"And if you find out?"

"Then I'll know how to defend her," Sam concluded. "Because I am going to defend her as hard as Barney Rosvalley is going to prosecute her. Between us we'll get the truth out into the open. When we know the truth, we'll know what should be done about it—and so will the jury."

After lunch Hank came into Sam's office again. He had a question to ask. "About the Porter case—I know that your trip East is intended largely for investigative purposes. I know that you mean to talk with people who knew the Porters in New York and in Ohio. I understand the importance of getting the facts, of course. But I do not understand why you can't get all the facts you need right here. You can talk to these people by phone or get their stories some other way. I think that I ought to go, not you. Why such persistent personal investigation? It kind of deflates me, in a way. Can't you rely on me to do it?" He sounded aggrieved and hurt.

Sam put his hand on Hank's shoulder, his affection unconcealed. "Don't be silly, Hankus. I'd rely on you absolutely, for anything. But there is a peculiar aspect to this investigation. What I'm looking for is not so much hard facts as nuances in the narratives of those facts. I have to know how the people who relate them look and seem to feel about what they say. This is a peculiarly subtle investigation. I think that these people will tell me more with their intonations and expressions than they will with their words."

"I could report that sort of thing," Hank protested.

Sam nodded. "You could, but not as clearly as I can see for myself. I'm the one who will have to try the case, after all. I'm looking for something that probably cannot be spelled out in hard facts. It is something that would be not only concealed, in terms of conduct or actions, but possibly not even comprehended by the actors themselves—by Janet, her father, and Kevin. Do you see what I mean?"

I guess so." Hank didn't sound quite convinced. "But I can see things too."

"It is partly a matter of chance, of course." Sam tried to be conciliatory. "People may remember things and tell me about them or they may not. They may have seen things or they may not. It puts me in mind of an incident during the war—talking about seeing or not seeing. Stay a minute and I'll tell you about it. There is an oblique kind of parallel in it. Sometimes a thing is right in front of you and you don't see it. The seeing it, or not seeing it, of course, makes all the difference.

"This happened to a friend of mine who was a captain in a tank unit in France during World War II. You know that I was in the Cavalry when I was a young fellow, and also was in Tanks and G-2—Intelligence—in World War II. A lot of my friends were, and are, in armored outfits—the modern cavalry. They've told me a lot of incidents, and I've told them some of mine. We old veterans tend to be bores with our reminiscences sometimes, I suppose. But, about this incident. It happened to Mark Schoenberg. He lives in St. Louis now.

"Mark was riding in a jeep, with a non-com driving it, in France in September or October of 1944. They were riding along a winding road when an M.E. 109 appeared. That's a Messerschmitt fighter plane. This plane, all alone, came in low from ahead of them, and began to strafe the jeep. Mark could see the flashes of the four machine guns in its wings and bullets were whipping by them.

"Mark yelled at his driver to take cover. The driver pulled the jeep around off the road and into some bushes. He and Mark dove into a ditch there, just as the Kraut fighter roared past overhead. They lay in the ditch and watched the Kraut bank around in a turn and go back, apparently meaning to come up the road again in another strafing run. The pilot probably wanted to use up his ammunition before going home, because a jeep with two men in it was hardly a major target worth all this attention.

"Just as the plane turned into its low approach, another jeep came along the road from the same direction from which Mark had come. A lieutenant and a driver were in it. They, too, saw the German plane coming, and ran off the road into some bushes hardly forty yards ahead of where Mark was. They, too, dove into the ditch for cover. The pilot of the plane was a poor shot, because once again he roared over them, spraying the road and tearing up the earth but doing no damage.

Then he banked around and went back to make a third run.

"Mark started to pull his pistol out of its holster in order to take a few shots at the plane, but then put it back, figuring that it was pointless to use such a popgun against four machine guns in a plane flying at over four hundred miles an hour. Just at this moment a third jeep appeared on the road, again coming from the direction from which Mark had come. The plane was coming around again for a third pass. But the new jeep stayed right on the road and gave no sign of running for cover.

"When Mark saw the man riding in the jeep, he noticed that this officer's helmet was brightly lacquered, so that it shone. And it had stars on it. Also, the rider was wearing a pearl-handled pistol in an open holster. And he was sitting with his arms folded, in absolute disdain of the approaching fighter plane. There was no doubt who it was. He was General George Patton—old 'Blood and Guts' himself. Every man in the Third Army knew what he looked like, pearl-handled pistol and all.

"Patton's jeep stayed on the road, contemptuous of the German plane, which again passed harmlessly overhead and then disappeared once and for all. But Patton saw the lieutenant and his driver cowering in a ditch. He stopped his jeep near the lieutenant's and called that officer to come to him. Then, while the abashed lieutenant stood at rigid attention, Patton bawled the hell out of him. He said that it was a disgrace for an American officer to hide in a ditch when he should have been shooting back at the damn Nazi plane. Meanwhile, Mark and his driver were trying to bury themselves in the earth, not forty yards away, praying that Patton would not spot them. Fortunately for them, he didn't, though if he had turned his head just a little he would have seen them.

"If Patton gave hell to a lieutenant for not firing back, just imagine what he would have said to a captain. He would have singed Mark's hide for sure. Then the fiery general continued on his way, leaving the embarrassed lieutenant still standing at attention and sweating profusely. Mark escaped a raking-over only because Patton didn't see him, though he was right there. Incidentally, that was the only time that Mark saw the famous Patton, in all the time he served in the Third Army. He believed that Patton was perfectly capable of having him court-

martialed for cowardice in the face of the enemy in this incident. It could have happened, though Mark certainly is no
coward, and has a Purple Heart to prove it if it needs any
proving, as well as other medals for gallantry in action.

"The point of this anecdote, Hank," Sam said slowly and
emphatically, "is that very often there are things to see, if a
man has eyes to see, only if he looks in the right direction. But
if he doesn't happen to look in exactly the right direction, he
probably will not see something that is there plainly to be
seen."

It was still too early to start for the airport. Sam had finished
dictating and had given Trudy all the necessary instructions
for what to do while he was away. He buzzed Hank to come
to his office again. "It seems to me," he said, "that we are con-
centrating too much on the three boys in the Larkbey case.
It is not the boys, per se, who will determine what ought to
be done with this case."

Hank was in a quibbling mood. "If it isn't the boys, who is
it? Is it the wanton waitress? Is it the disappearing desperados?"

"Very nice alliteration." Sam's voice dripped sarcasm. "I'm
talking about the misconduct of young pups, and the reasons
for it. Who really is the wrongdoer when eighteen-year-olds
misbehave regularly and persistently?"

Hank cocked his head, half mockingly. "Delinquent parents?"

Sam grimaced. "That is not as far-fetched as you make it
sound. Yes. It could be delinquent parents."

Hank's voice was triumphant sounding. "That's the inevitable
source when some young punk does something nasty. It could
be, of course, that the juvenile is just a vicious character in
himself."

Sam controlled his impatience. "I'm not one to say that there
are no bad boys, as some social workers like to say. There are
some who are just born vicious. But the problem of juvenile
delinquency is nothing new. It has been a problem since time
began."

Now Hank seemed to be sure that he was right and that
his boss was wrong. "The statistics say that juvenile delinquency
is at an all-time high today, and getting higher."

"Statistics . . ." The word sounded contemptible as Sam pronounced it. "When did we begin to record reliable statistics on crime and especially on juvenile crime? Not very long ago."

"The statistics can't be ignored. I've read report after report. Look at the F.B.I. reports that J. Edgar Hoover has been putting out in recent years. They're bloodcurdling." Righteous indignation showed in Hank's face.

"Are they?" Sam picked up a book on social statistics that was lying on his desk. He opened it to a page where a bookmark protruded. "Listen to this: This is a report by San Francisco Police Chief Patrick Crowley."

"Crowley? He's not the Chief," protested Hank.

"Just listen." Sam read a paragraph that bewailed the terrible increases in crime statistics in San Francisco. It spoke with alarm of the skyrocketing rates of juvenile misbehavior. It called for stringent laws to curb youthful vagrancy and crime. "Do you know the date of this official report of the police department?"

"No."

"It was the statistical report for the year 1870, issued by Police Chief Crowley in 1872."

Hank grinned.

Sam went on. "We have only put a new name—'juvenile delinquency'—on a human problem that always has existed since man began to live in organized societies. That term has been applied, in recent years, to conduct ranging from lack of respect for parents to the ultimate crime of murder. You'd think that juvenile delinquency began when social workers came into existence and began to fight this dread problem."

"You have a point there."

"The point is, let's not become bemused with words or terminology. The problem in the Larkbey case is not the tendency of children to be childish."

"What, then?" Hank asked.

"The problem in this case is the conduct of the parents, rather than of the boys. Both are interwoven, no doubt. But as far as Belle Larkbey is concerned, it seems to me that she is being harassed not by the three boys, nor even by the police, in the last analysis."

"By the D.A.?"

"Only incidentally. It is the boys' parents who seem to be applying the pressure."

"So what can we do about it?"

Sam spoke slowly and emphatically. "We can either stop the pressure or neutralize it."

"How?"

"We can neutralize it by forcing the D.A.'s Office to follow the spirit of the law—to be fair and reasonable, though enforcing the law."

Hank was dubious. He shook his head. "Easy to say."

"True," Sam admitted. "Not so easy to do. But we'll try to do it."

"And . . . ?"

"Concentrate on the main source of the trouble—the parents. Stop the pressure, if possible."

"How?"

"That is the sixty-four-dollar question. But before you can properly handle a problem you must isolate and identify the main elements in it. The main element in the Larkbey case is the pressure by the boys' parents. I think that we have identified the main element in the problem."

"I think you're right," agreed the big man.

"That being so," Sam continued slowly and evenly, "let us concentrate on countering, neutralizing, or stopping that pressure. It sounds pretty theoretical, but that is the practical problem to resolve now. What we need is an instrument—a law, a weapon, what-have-you—for that purpose. Let's look for that."

"I'm willing. Tell me how."

"Remember that California statute about false I.D. cards which I asked you to look up for me?"

"I remember, but I haven't had a chance yet. A hundred things to do."

"Do that while I'm away, Hank. Get me all the dope on it. An annotated summary. Any cases on it that you can find. Shepherdize the cases and bring them up to date. Have it for me in detail when I get back."

"Okay." Hank scribbled in his memo book.

"All right then," Sam concluded, "I'm on my way. Off we go, into the wild blue yonder."

Sam sucked in his breath as the big jet leaped into the air and began to climb steeply upward. As often as he rode in airplanes, the rocket-like ascent of modern jets made him a bit uneasy. Riding in a plane was not his idea of fun. He sometimes said about such trips that he took second place to nobody in being timid about airplane rides and visits to the dentist.

The plane banked sharply as it climbed and made a sweeping turn to the left. The ground became visible to his left as they rose over San Francisco Bay, the city itself pearly white and pink below them. Then they were over the hills and valleys, heading East. It was only minutes later that the pilot's voice sounded on the public-address system telling the passengers about their cruising speed and altitude, and that the big lake to the north on the left side below was Lake Tahoe. Then they were over the dry flats and hills of Nevada. The ground unrolled below them like a vast contour map.

A stewardess stopped at his seat, smiled at him, and asked him what he would like to drink. He ordered a scotch-and-water. Then he opened his dispatch case and looked at the schedule Hank had made out for him: Visits were scheduled with neighbors who knew the Duffield family in Great Neck on Long Island; friends of Janet and Kevin Porter in New York City; associates on the faculty of N.Y.U. Law School; a psychiatrist on Park Avenue; friends and associates of the Porters in Cleveland and Shaker Heights in Ohio; a doctor at Cleveland Clinic who had treated Janet; a faculty man specializing in research on Justices Holmes at Northwestern University Law School in Chicago; and more. All this plus his speech at the Waldorf in the morning and time to visit some conferences and round-tables at the A.B.A. meeting. It would be a busy trip.

The man in the seat next to him touched his arm and introduced himself. "My name is Charlie Kangesser. Aren't you Sam Benedict, the lawyer?"

Sam acknowledged that he was, and they shook hands. Kangesser was a talkative fellow, plainly pleased to meet Sam, and a bit awed by him. It turned out that he was the owner of a novelty company and was on a sales trip to the East. "But I once meant to become a lawyer," he said. "I have a B.A. from U.C.L.A., and had one semester of evening law school in L.A. That was a tough row to hoe. I simply couldn't hold down a job and go to law school too. Some people do it, and my hat is off to them. It was too much for me. Wore me to a frazzle. After one term I knew that I had bitten off more than I could chew, so I withdrew before they threw me out. But I'll have you know that I had a high score on the Legal Aptitude Test. Might have been a good lawyer if I could have made it all the way through."

Sam politely indicated that he was properly impressed. "You seem to be doing well in the novelty business."

"Can't complain. Make a good living and the company is sound and growing. My partner is a good inside man and I'm a good outside man. You can't beat a combination like that. But I've often regretted that I never became a lawyer. I liked the mental challenge and the logic, and the fun of taking a factual situation apart and analyzing it."

"That training is valuable for any kind of work," Sam agreed. "You know that legal training used to be a main type of education for future leaders of public affairs in England. It still is, for that matter."

Kangesser beamed with pleasure. "I can see why, from my short experience with it. I'll never forget a prof we had in Torts, and the way he taught the concept of 'proximate cause' —the key factor in a negligence case. He called it the 'but-for' factor, the fact but for which the injury would not have occurred. How's that for remembering! I still can remember the 'but-for' doctrine of 'proximate cause.'" He was pleased with himself as he recited the rule.

"Not bad at all." Sam smiled.

The salesman happily went on. "The prof gave us an illustrative case that I'll never forget, too. He called it the 'Michigan Pumpkin Case.' Have you ever heard of it?"

"No. Can't say that I have."

"Let me tell you about it. It's a pistol." He launched into his narrative while Sam listened resignedly.

"There was a farmer, long ago, in Michigan," Kangesser related. "This was before the days of modern statutes on child support. That's an important point. There were no statutes to apply. This farmer had a daughter, and he had a hired man. The hired man and the daughter liked each other, got intimate, and began to do what comes naturally to young men and women. They used to meet in the barn and do it there."

Kangesser paused, to make sure that Sam understood what he meant. Then he continued: "Now, the farm was far from any town, and the hired man had no contraceptives. So he used the old technique of withdrawal at the proper time, instead. It worked well enough, and they carried on that way for a long time with mutual satisfaction and no trouble at all. One day, about a year later, the farmer happened to go into the barn unexpectedly, and he saw his daughter and the hired man in the very act. He was furious, of course, and looked around for something with which to strike the hired man. The first thing that came to hand was a large pumpkin, so the farmer picked up the pumpkin and hurled it at the hired man. It struck him in the rump.

"Unfortunately, this was at exactly the wrong moment. The hired man zigged instead of zagging. So, in due time, a child was born to the daughter and the hired man."

Kangesser was grinning from ear to ear. Sam listened patiently as the man went on. "Then the girl brought suit against both the hired man and the farmer, asking the court to order one of them to support the child. The question is: who should support it? Most people say that the hired man should support the child, because he is the natural father. But this is a question in pure, theoretical law, with no statutes to apply. So the court should order the farmer to support the child. The reasoning is this: The girl and the hired man had been doing this for a year with no child being conceived. It was reasonable to assume that if there had been no interference in the usual chain of events, no child would have been born. The one factor that was new or different in the chain of events was the pumpkin; that is, the throwing of the pumpkin by the father. But for his action of throwing the pumpkin there would have been no child. His action was the proximate cause of the birth of the child. Therefore, he should support it." Kangesser smiled triumphantly and waited for Sam's reaction.

"That's quite a case," Sam agreed, noncommitally.

"Sure is. And I'll never forget about the doctrine of 'proximate cause.'"

Sam's mind returned to the Porter Case. That was not a negligence case, of course, but the doctrine of 'proximate cause' applied to that case, too. The trick was to pick out the ultimate, the real, the proximate cause out of heaven-knows-how-many possible causative factors. Ah, that's the rub . . . , he thought. What is the factor that was the proximate cause of homicide?

It was evening in New York City when Sam checked in at the Regency Hotel. The air was warm and sultry with the retained heat of an August day. He thought of the cool, windy, summer-evening weather of San Francisco, and sighed. After showering and changing his clothes he called home. Then he went downstairs and walked to the Plaza Hotel to stop in at the Oak Room for a pre-dinner drink. He had eaten little on the flight from Chicago to New York.

Sipping his usual scotch-and-water at a single table in a corner, he looked around the wood-panelled lounge and tried to imagine Janet and Kevin Porter sitting here. She had mentioned the Oak Room, and the fact that she and Kevin had gone there during their courtship days. He tried to visualize the tightly self-controlled, prim Janet and the scholarly law professor, both younger then, talking and looking into each other's eyes, surprised by the emotional excitement of romance—or love. Which one had it been, he wondered; or had it been both?

He decided to walk down to the Waldorf Hotel instead of taking a taxi. It was a pleasant evening for a stroll. There would be many people he knew at the main center of the meeting. He walked down Fifth Avenue, turned east at the block next to St. Patrick's Cathedral, and picked a pleasant-looking restaurant on Park Avenue for dinner. It was a good, leisurely dinner, and it was dark when he came out on the avenue again.

At the Park Avenue entrance to the Waldorf there was a group of familiar faces, most of them lawyers Sam had know for years—Sal Mellito from San Francisco, Hal Bauerback of New York City, Bill Cooley from Chicago, Gary O'Hare of New York, Bud Raker from Dallas, and Steve Randall from Cleveland. He walked up quietly and said "Hello."

They greeted him with warm welcomes.

"The Master himself. Welcome to Gotham on the subway," boomed big Bill Cooley. "The meeting can come to order. Sam Benedict is here and all's right with the world." They slapped each other's backs affectionately.

Sam turned to Steve Randall. "I'm going to stop off at Cleveland on my way home, Steve, on a matter I have. Maybe we'll travel together."

"Delighted, Sam," the Clevelander answered. "Can I be of help in any way on whatever brings you to my town?"

"Could be," Sam answered. "I'll let you know if it's necessary. But I'll only be there briefly."

"Just call on me if you want anything. You know that. And if I'm not in, anyone in my office will be glad to help. Just ask if you want to."

Hal Bauerback broke in. "Let's adjourn to some nice quiet bar and continue the discussion. We're having a difference of opinion on traffic laws and radar. Come on along, Sam, unless you have something to do." He turned to the others, "How about a short discourse on radar law from the Master?"

They strolled in a group to Madison Avenue, found a quiet spot in a nearby Longchamps lounge, and settled down for an hour of shop talk.

Traffic laws and the legality of radar evidence of speeding were interesting subjects, but after a while, when a lull occurred, Sam took the opportunity to shift the talk to a subject of more immediate interest to him. Here was a group of some of the best trial lawyers in the nation. It would be interesting and valuable to see what they thought about law and practice in psychiatric problems—more particularly, insanity.

"All of you fellows have handled cases involving insanity as a defense in a charge of crime," he began. They all nodded agreement. "Most of the time," he continued, "public and court concern with insanity has concentrated on the exculpatory plea of 'not guilty by reason of insanity.' In other words, we have been concerned chiefly with the question: 'Was the defendant legally insane at the time of the commission of the act?' But there is another twilight zone of legal responsibility—the standard of competence to stand trial. Guttmacher, an authority on the subject, recently had an article in the *American Journal of Psychiatry*. He said that determination of unfitness to stand trial, beforehand, may avoid exposing a defendant to what he called 'the vagaries of jury decisions.' And often, if a defendant is found to be unfit to stand trial, he is committed to a hospital, treated, later found to have recovered, and he is released without trial."

Hal Bauerback, the New Yorker, picked up the new subject. "That sort of thing has been criticized, you know. When psychiatrists make recommendations about competence of an accused person to stand trial, it is said that they are not properly participating in the adversary system of trial procedure. Thus, they act as expert witnesses without submitting to the legal rules of criminal law and procedure. That may be a serious objection."

Steve Randall nodded. "New problems and new knowledge require new procedures. The use of psychiatrists before an adversary-type trial should not be barred simply because our pretrial-and-discovery procedures are not modern enough. For that matter, the conflict between law and psychiatry, or law and medicine, or law and any kind of expert-opinion evidence usually turns on the relevance and role of experts in various capacities in the judicial process. We need the help of the scientific experts. That much is certain."

Hal Bauerback went on with the subject. "Here in New York our procedure seems to work well enough. Usually, two consulting psychiatrists are appointed in a criminal case to evaluate the fitness of the defendant to stand trial. There are a number of state-supported psychiatric hospitals in this state. The law provides that the director of one of these hospitals shall designate two qualified psychiatrists to examine the defendant. Theoretically, they should be from his hospital staff, if available. In actuality, the director usually appoints men engaged in private practice. This is largely because of the shortage of staff men in state hospitals. Also, they tend to prefer psychiatrists who live in the community of the court."

"We have found, in California," Sam said, "that some psychiatrists refuse to give expert advice on questions of competency to stand trial. It apparently is not fashionable in some medical circles to render professional services except in a strictly doctor-patient kind of relationship. Some psychiatrists say that they cannot function in a governmental proceeding. They say that the courts force them to answer questions that are moral or legal rather than medical in nature. They often dislike the whole flavor of the courts and of rules of evidence. In the case of men on state-hospital staffs, of course, they may be asked to work for no fee, as they already are being paid by the state— which does not attract them."

"It's just about the same in New York," Bauerback commented.

"Notice," added Sam, "that the very order of the court which calls for the examination declares that the court already believes that reasonable grounds for assuming incompetency have been found by the court. That hardly will please a psychiatrist, except maybe the defendant's psychiatrist. Then add to that the fact that a crime allegedly has been committed by the 'patient.' A psychiatrist can well argue that a neutral evaluation of the person is impossible under these conditions."

Bauerback nodded agreement. "What's more, when a defendant is taken to a hospital for diagnostic evaluation, other factors come into play. Nurses and interns observe the patient and report to the psychiatrists, who usually interview him two, three, or four times. Other hospital personnel add their observations. Consulting psychologists, social workers, and staff personnel who do the electroencephalograph tests put in their reports and comments. Obviously, conclusions reached in a hospital study may be very different from those reached by defense psychiatrists making their diagnoses of the defendant in a jail cell."

Sam went on. "Also, it is commonplace nowadays for diagnostic interviews to be taped, although use of sedatives and 'truth serums' seems to be disappearing. Tape recordings of the defendant's words in these circumstances raise big questions of doctor-patient privileged communications and of invasions of privacy. Under the recent Supreme Court decisions on rights of an accused person to presence of counsel and other such rights, we have complex questions of constitutional law."

"I saw a statistical survey in some law review, recently," Randall interjected, "which said that there never seem to be any differences of opinion between the state's experts. The survey said that the state's psychiatrists always agree on what will be expressed in their reports, even though in private discussions between themselves they may have disagreed on their findings and conclusions. This is very disturbing. The statutes usually provide that if the psychiatrists disagree, still another psychiatrist may be added to the team. But this rarely seems to be done. Usually one of the team withdraws or a new team is designated when disagreements occur. You can see how easily a tendency will develop to blur the findings in order to reach gentlemanly agreement—with what results to the defendant you can imagine."

"Bear in mind," Sam urged, "that the psychiatrist does not like to give a positive 'yes' or 'no' about the defendant. Psychiatrists, more than most people, know that human thought, mentality, and 'sanity' rarely can be pictured in plain black-or-white terms. They usually file a detailed profile-study of the defendant as the basis for their answer to the legal question asked. They particularly dislike a court's request for a prognostication about the probability of recovery of the defendant from any mental illness diagnosed. And it is clear that many psychiatrists doing this work view themselves as agents for the softening or mitigating of the punishments provided for by the law."

"That's right!" Randall agreed emphatically.

"And finally," Sam concluded, "they view their role as basically humanitarian in nature. Legally they are agents of the court, but some of them do not clearly take that view. They all want to make detailed reports rather than say 'yes' or 'no' to the question of insanity. They are not in agreement as to their obligation to follow the M'Naghten Rule, the Durham Rule, or their professional standard of what is psychotic. Some of them believe that any criminal act is evidence of psychosis. All in all, it is clear that neither psychiatrists nor the courts are satisfied with the present standards set by the law for determining exculpatory insanity or psychosis."

"But we have to live with those standards, such as they are," Randall said.

"We don't have to like them," Sam answered, "and we can try to improve them. We had *better* try."

CHAPTER

His speech to the National Association of Trial Lawyers went well, and Sam enjoyed giving it. His talk was on a technical subject—"Statutory Bases of Discovery and Examination Before Trial"—and it had taken some doing to make it exciting as well as valuable to such a group of experienced trial lawyers. But Sam was good at doing that. He had sometimes toyed with the idea of accepting a position as a law professor. Offers of faculty appointments came to him every once in a while. His first love, however—practice and trial work—always won out, and he had declined all the offers. Still, the occasional lectures that he delivered at Bar Association meetings and at law-school conferences were enjoyable and always went well. If he could have spared the time he would have done more such lecturing. Requests to do so came to him almost every day.

After his speech, he begged off from invitations to go to lunch with several old friends and left the Waldorf meeting halls. Hank had arranged a full-day's schedule for him. The first appointment was with Dr. Ward Kepler. He took a taxicab to the doctor's office at 1000 Park Avenue. He knew that it probably had not been easy for Hank to get this appointment for him on such short notice. Kepler was world-famous as a research psychiatrist.

Kepler was a neat, prim little man with pointed chin and a pointed goatee. His eyes were bright blue and sparkling under arched tufts of dark eyebrows. Kepler already had received what data Sam and Hank had been able to accumulate about Janet Porter, and he even had talked with Rubenfeld about her by long distance telephone earlier that morning. Sam breathed an unspoken message of thanks to Hank for a job well done. His burly assistant was a gem of reliability and helpfulness.

Kepler was blunt and direct, unlike most of the psychiatrists Sam knew. He got right down to business. "From what I know about this woman, you understand of course that I can only theorize in general terms. You understand that there simply is not a fraction enough material here for any kind of proper diagnosis, do you not?"

"Yes," Sam agreed. "All I expect is a theoretical analysis of the possibilities. But I need that."

"Then I will speak in terms of general theoretical possibilities in cases of this general type. That is all. You are agreeable to that?"

"Yes."

Kepler leaned back in his chair, scratched his chin meditatively, and said, "First, there is the possibility of schizophrenic aspects to Mrs. Porter's case. Such a possibility will have to be explored by Dr. Rubenfeld, and will require intensive work and much more data than we have here. I will, therefore, leave that to Dr. Rubenfeld and will not spend more time on it now. The same is true as to paranoid and other psychotic possibilities generally."

"That seems to eliminate most of the possibilities I expected," Sam protested. "What does it leave?"

"Not much," the psychiatrist acknowledged. "But, as I understand Dr. Rubenfeld and Mr. Tabor, what you want from me is a different approach than the standard procedures. Is that correct?"

"Yes."

"Are you aware," Kepler asked affably, "that today many researchers believe that schizophrenia may be a biochemical disorder, rather than a mental ailment which Freudians would attribute to childhood disturbances? In other words, that mental illness often is chemically caused?"

"I have heard such reports," Sam said.

"Then I believe that I have what you are seeking—a radically different approach," the psychiatrist said in a positive tone. "It may well be too radical, and you may not like it. It lies in an area of medical research and psychiatric development that is still highly theoretical. Worse still, from your point of view, it is not yet proved and is not yet accepted in the area of forensic medicine. Indeed, it is hardly known there, as yet."

Sam smiled. "Let me be the judge of that."

"Well, then, I will have to explain the origin and nature of the theory before applying it concretely to your client's case. But I hasten to add that I think that there is a fair possibility that it may apply. Otherwise I would not waste your time, and mine, explaining it. What I have in mind is the possibility of the presence of severe premenstrual tension—so severe as to result in an acute temporary schizophrenic condition periodically."

"Whew," Sam exclaimed. "That does sound radically theoretical."

"Not quite as much as it may seem on first mention. Dr. Rubenfeld reported a history of premenstrual tension in Mrs. Porter, according to her statements. I do believe that those statements are probably accurate. She would hardly have any reason to invent them, unless she was acquainted with the medicolegal literature and had chanced to read something on this subject. I understand that she has had legal training. Is she a specialist in the criminal or forensic-medicine field?"

"No. In legal history and constitutional law."

"Then the likelihood of her being acquainted with the forensic theory as to premenstrual tension is small. And the likelihood of deliberate simulation is remote. In any event, she could not simulate the physical symptoms. Blood-sugar tests and other tests would reveal the falsity of a simulated condition."

Sam looked bewildered. "I'm afraid you're losing me, Doctor."

"I'm sorry. Let us go back and begin at the beginning. You know, of course, that many women suffer recurrently from distress of various kinds, caused by the menstrual cycle. In many women this distress reaches a peak a few days before the onset of the menses. We refer to this peak period of distress as premenstrual tension."

Sam nodded. "I know that."

"Premenstrual tension," Kepler continued, "is a syndrome manifested by deep depression or anxiety. It is associated with such symptoms as intense irritability and nervousness, insomnia, fatigue, emotional instability, painful swelling of the breasts, abdominal bloating, and headaches. In 1931 a Dr. Frank made a study and ascribed somatic and psychic symptoms to heightening of the levels of estrogen—hormone imbalance. Dr. Morton, in about 1950, made an intensive study of the matter. He said that endocrine dysfunctions can influence the psychological balance and produce mental symptoms, and, conversely, emotional disturbances can and often do alter the functions of the endocrine glands. He then concentrated on the physical, glandular, and other—somatic—factors, rather than on emotional disturbance as a cause of premenstrual tension. He made a study of inmates of Westfield State Farm, a state prison and reformatory for women at Bedford Hills, New York. His findings were dramatic. There was a 'premenstrual padded cell' for some inmates."

The psychiatrist saw that Sam was keenly attentive, and he hurried on. "Morton found that sixty-two per cent of crimes of violence committed by women at Westfield prison were committed in the premenstrual week, and seventeen per cent during menstruation. And he found that sugar-tolerance tests revealed a hypoglycemic-type curve in the premenstrual phase, while premenstrual vaginal smears indicated hypoestrogenic stimulation. In simple language, there was a change in blood-sugar levels in these women at the premenstrual time."

Sam, who had been listening closely, became even more alert. "That is interesting. Go on."

Kepler resumed his lecture. "Morton tried medications on these women to control the hypoglycemia—he called it 'spontaneous hypoglycemia'; spontaneous deficiency of sugar in the blood. That would be a kind of reverse diabetes. He found that seventy-nine per cent of the inmates reported improvement when given certain medications plus supplementary high-protein diet. He said that the medication in this study was effective on the symptoms of premenstrual tension rather than on the underlying estrogen-progesterone imbalance. The prison records showed, for women treated for premenstrual tension, a sharp improvement in behavior and attitude, fewer requests for sedatives, less punishment for infraction of rules, and a marked increase in general morale."

"I follow you," Sam said, "but I'm not quite sure of just what you're getting at."

Kepler shook his finger warningly. "Bear in mind that we are talking about your client being one of the group of women subject to acute premenstrual tension. One physician, writing of the etiology of this, said as follows." He picked up a medical journal lying open on his desk and read aloud from it: " 'Whenever the monthly tension reaches its maximum height, the manic activity of the patient beggars description . . . Physical unrest, causeless irritability, hair-trigger temper . . . and depression. . . . Most frequent, however, is the periodic and spectacular alteration of personality, taking in general the form of either recurrent frenzy or catatonic-like depression.' "

He stopped reading, and put the book down. "Of course, such severe symptoms are found only in some women, not in most. The precise cause is still uncertain. But, be the cause spontaneous hypoglycemia, sodium retention by the hormones, defective mineralocorticoid action, or what-have-you, it is regularly repeated each month. It is recurrent at regular periods of time in quite a few women. Do you begin to see how all this might apply to Mrs. Porter and her history of premenstrual tension?"

"Yes." Sam's mind was racing. All kinds of possibilities were beginning to appear.

"In 1952," Kepler continued, "in the *Journal of Nervous and Mental Diseases*, a study revealed that women suffering from the severest form of premenstrual tension have periodic and spectacular alterations of personality, with bizarre manifestations, including psychotic episodes. In one case, for example, an otherwise well-balanced housewife threatened her husband with a knife regularly, at the same time every month. Inmates of mental institutions are more difficult to manage during their premenstrual periods. Other researchers have reported that the mental upheaval at this period can be so great that the patient is temporarily manic. One researcher, Cooke, reported that eighty-four per cent of all crimes of violence in Paris committed by women are perpetrated during the premenstrual and early menstrual cycle. A two-year study by a Dr. Balsam in California of major automobile accidents involving women found premenstrual tension to be a direct causative factor in many cases. Yet, many physicians report that hardly any women who suffer from premenstrual tension recognize the source of their trouble."

"I see exactly what you are suggesting," Sam said, "and I understand the possibilities. But the proof of so novel a premise, in a court of law, is something else again."

"Quite so," Kepler agreed, "but the groundwork has been laid by lawyers as long ago as 1953." He held up a bound book. "This is the *International Record of Medicine,* 1953 issue. At pages 492 to 501 is the report of a symposium on premenstrual tension. One of the articles is by a Professor Oleck—a law professor. It is titled 'Legal Aspects of Premenstrual Tension.'"

Sam scribbled a note of the title and volume in his pocket notebook. He would have Hank get a copy and look for other articles on the subject in the legal journals.

Kepler continued. "This law professor suggested that sometimes the premenstrual medical tests of women who have committed crimes might be adequate to show their probable mental condition at the time when the crimes were committed. He suggested that, since the physical evidence of spontaneous hypoglycemia and other symptoms may be recurrent and periodically regular, they might be shown on charts or graphs. Such graphs might even be projected forward, or back, to see what the condition of the woman will be, or was, on a given date. These data would include blood-sugar tests, electroencephalograms, and other tests, of course. This might have remarkable impact on the rules of evidence. An interesting idea, don't you agree?"

"Fascinating." Sam meant it. "But you say that the causes and tests are not yet reliable enough."

"They already are substantial enough to be distinctly helpful. They will be more so soon, I believe. In fact, there is a medical convention scheduled for this month at Brunswick Hospital on spontaneous hypoglycemia. And, what is really significant—a psychiatric symposium will discuss that subject as its major topic. It became a popular subject in the medical literature and at medical conventions in 1966 and 1967. It is developing rapidly now. Judge Murov, the District Judge in Suffolk County, and others have said that premenstrual tension will have far-reaching legal as well as medical and psychiatric aspects, according to an article I read recently in an O.B. journal."

"It sure is a novel and interesting possibility." Sam got up, walked to a window, and looked out over the streams of traffic on both sides of the center gardens down below on the avenue. "It will take some digesting, and a lot of research. But it certainly looks like a possibility worth exploring."

Before starting for his next appointment, Sam telephoned Hank long distance and started him on the research for the premenstrual-tension angle.

"There's no doubt of one thing," he instructed. "We'd better concentrate on the key question—Janet Porter's intent, or what was in her mind. Since she does not remember, we'll have to get evidence to show her state of mind. We'd better have more than one string to our bow. Hank, get Rubenfeld going."

"Okay. First thing in the morning, I'll call him."

"This trip is worth-while if for this idea alone. I always say, Hank, 'Seek and ye shall find.' At least we have one possibility more for Janet Porter's defense."

Next on Sam's appointment schedule was a visit to a neighbor of the Duffields out in Great Neck, Long Island. Sam could have taken the Long Island Railroad, Port Washington Branch, to the North Shore. It was quicker and simpler to take a taxicab. Also, it gave him an opportunity to relax on the ride along the parkways skirting Long Island Sound. Forty minutes later they were driving through the peninsula town of Great Neck to the imposing Kings Point area on the tip of the peninsula. Stately homes, each set in parklike grounds, bordered the road. They passed the peaceful campus of the United States Merchant Marine Academy and entered a narrow, tree-lined road that followed the curves and inlets of the shore.

The Gerber home was a big, Tudor-type mansion facing the Sound. Its immaculate lawn sloped down to the water's edge. Paul Gerber, a dark-complexioned man of about sixty, met Sam at the door and ushered him into a spacious room overlooking the glittering stretch of water. The room was full of easels, canvases stretched on frames, and finished and partly finished paintings. Most of the paintings were portraits. Sam knew that Gerber was a successful portrait painter who had done pictures of many of the great and near-great of the time.

They sat facing a large picture window that gave a sweeping panoramic view. Sailboats and powerboats moved across the Sound. In the distance, on the other side of the Sound, they could see the coast of Connecticut. It was a peaceful, charming scene. Off to their right, across a hedge of privet almost eight feet tall, they could see the upper part of a large house built in Norman French style.

"That's the old Duffield house," Gerber said, pointing to it. "A family named McMahon lives there now. We don't see much of them, as they are away much of the time. When the Duffields lived there, years ago, I was quite friendly with John Duffield—as much as anyone could get to be friendly with John."

"Was he hard to get along with?" Sam asked.

Gerber shook his head. "Not really. He was a reserved, austere kind of man, but not unfriendly. In fact, he was an important man in the society doings on the North Shore. He liked big formal dinners and receptions. He was an imposing figure in white tie and tails. But he was not the kind of man who made intimate friends."

"How long did you know him?" Sam asked.

"Seven or eight years," Gerber responded. "They already lived here when I moved here. Of course, Duffield was away a good deal. He taught law, you know, at Harvard and Columbia, I believe. That was back some years. His wife had died before Anna and I bought this house. We never knew his wife. John and his daughter Janet lived over there, and the girl was cared for by a governess, you might say. He had three or four different women, successively, running the house for him and taking care of Janet. They were middle-aged women—governess-type, I used to call them."

Sam got up to admire some of the paintings, and they spoke of paintings and art for a few minutes. Then Sam returned to the real purpose of his visit. "What about Janet, the little girl; what was she like?"

Gerber thought for a moment, and then said, "A quiet, subdued little girl. Shy, and not easy to talk to. Actually, I never got to know her very well. Anna and I were already the parents of grown children then, and naturally I didn't have many occasions to chat with Janet at any length. But I felt a little sorry for the child. She seemed to be lonely and unhappy. That was natural enough, what with no mother, and her father away much of the time."

"How did John Duffield and Janet get along, do you think?"

"I can only guess, when you come right down to it. I actually saw them together only now and then. He was a stern and austere father. No doubt of that. But he seemed to be fond of the girl in his stiff, formal way. There was little of the usually warm and close father-daughter relationship, I'm afraid, such as I had with my daughter when she was a child. But maybe I shouldn't say that. It's only an impression. I didn't really know."

"What was her attitude toward him, do you think? I know you can't be sure. Just your impression."

"Shy, I'd say," the painter answered, after thinking for a moment. "She seemed almost in awe of him. Sometimes I thought she was almost afraid of him. That's a terrible thing to say, but you asked me."

"Do you mean physically afraid of him? Did he strike her, or that sort of thing?"

"Oh, no. Maybe he paddled her sometimes. Most parents do. I don't mean that. I mean that there was a sort of formality between them—a kind of politeness that was unnatural between a parent and child. I'm not sure of exactly what I mean, I'm afraid. I remember that Janet was a solitary kind of child. She never played much with the other children of her age around here—not that there were many close by anyhow. Often I'd see her sitting alone, down near the boat dock they have over there." He pointed to the spot. "She'd just sit, all by herself, and stare out over the water, for an hour at a time, until she was called back to the house. It was pathetic, I used to think."

"Was she a sickly child?"

"No. She seemed healthy enough."

"Did she have any emotional problems that you might have noticed? Any misbehavior or indications of emotional instability?"

Gerber snorted. "Lord, no. She was as well-behaved and polite a child as I've ever seen. If anything, she was unusually quiet and well-behaved. A child is expected to make a ruckus or to break something, or have a fight with another child now and then. Not Janet. Never a bit of noise or commotion. Too quiet and too old for her age, she was." He hesitated. "I may be out of line in asking this, Mr. Benedict. Your assistant, on the phone, said something about your visit being about a legal matter involving Janet. I assumed that it concerns John Duffield's estate, or something like that. Is that right?"

Sam shook his head. "No, not exactly."

"May I ask, then, what it is?"

Sam sighed. "I'm sorry to tell you this, Mr. Gerber. Janet is now Mrs. Janet Porter. She married a man from San Francisco. She is being held by the police, charged with his murder."

"Oh!" It was almost a gasp. "Little Janet! Murder!"

"So you see why I am asking all of these questions about her."

"Yes. I see."

"Do my questions make sense to you now?"

"They do." The painter paused, and then added. "But I can't say that it really is as much of a shock as you may think. I'll tell you why. I'll tell you what I really think. I would have been still less shocked and surprised if you had told me, not that Janet murdered her husband, but that she had killed her father."

Sam blinked. "That's quite a thing to say."

The artist faced him almost belligerently. "Now that I know what this is all about, I'll take the gloves off. I was being diplomatic. John and I were friendly, and I don't want to blacken his name. But the truth is that he was a pretty poor father to that girl. She was a sad, miserably unhappy little thing, and he just let her be that. If she grew up warped and mad at the world, he caused it. I used to feel damn sorry for that child, though I never interfered. I had no right. But it was not hard to predict that such an unnatural childhood would produce an unhappy, bitter woman. I'm not surprised. Not one bit surprised."

Sam tried to cool him down. "That was a long time ago, Mr. Gerber. It couldn't have been easy to bring up a child without a mother."

"All the more reason," the painter almost shouted. "All the more reason to be a father to a frightened, lonely child—not a cold and distant overseer, barely tolerating the nuisance of responsibility for a child. I'll put it this way. If she had killed

John Duffield instead of her husband, I not only wouldn't be surprised, I'd probably sympathize with her."

It was early evening when Sam's taxicab deposited him back in Manhattan in front of the tall, red-brick apartment house on lower Fifth Avenue at Ninth Street, where the Morrisons lived. They had been the neighbors of Janet Porter when she was working at New York University, when she first had met Kevin. Hank had told him little about them, other than that Helen Morrison and Janet had been friends and that he had told Mrs. Morrison about Janet's trouble.

It was an expensive-looking apartment house, complete with canopied entrance and a uniformed doorman. Sam went upstairs after being announced from the reception desk in the chapel-like lobby. Helen Morrison met him at the door of her apartment on the twelfth floor, and apologized for the absence of her husband. She was a matronly and friendly woman, with pale, hazel-colored eyes and an earnest face.

"Donald had to go uptown unexpectedly," she said. "There's some trouble with a shipment to a department store in Atlanta, and he has to straighten it out. He's in the dress-manufacturing business, and this is always a hectic time of year for his company, with the kind of line they produce. Anyhow, he hardly knew Janet, except to say 'hello' and 'good evening' now and then. I was the one who saw her fairly often. She lived on this floor, just down the hall, in those days."

The apartment was richly furnished, and it was easy to guess that the Morrisons were interested in the theater. Autographed photos of many celebrated stage and screen stars were scattered everywhere, many inscribed to the Morrisons in personal terms. Sam took the cue and talked about the theater and plays and stars for a few minutes. Mrs. Morrison was delighted by his interest, got him a scotch highball, and chatted warmly about her pet subject. In hardly any time they were on easy and friendly terms. Almost imperceptibly, Sam directed the conversation to the subject of Janet Porter.

"Janet and I used to go to the theater often—many times, to matinees," Mrs. Morrison reminisced. "I think that the first show we saw together was *One Touch of Venus,* with Mary Martin. That was a delightful musical."

"Did Janet have a great interest in the theater?"

"No, not really," she said. "It was mostly just something to do, for her. She lived alone and had almost no friends—I mean no close friends, if you know what I mean. It was a solitary kind of life for a young woman. That's why I used to invite her in for dinner with me now and then, or to go to see a show with me. My husband is away often, you see, and I rather welcomed her company, too."

"Was she working at New York University then?" Sam asked.

"Yes, at the law school. That's down at Washington Square, you know, just a few blocks south of here. She did some kind of research work there. I'm not sure just what it was."

"What kind of person was she?"

"A nice girl, well dressed and well groomed at all times. Nice manners, and pleasant; never very pushy or demonstrative. Quite reserved, but amiable. She may have seemed very stand-offish to most people, but we were good friends. I believe that she talked with me and confided in me far more than she did with other people. At least that's the way I think it was. And Kevin, too, a little."

"Was she a happy or gay person, would you say?"

"Quite the contrary. No. She was very sober and serious most all the time. Even at a comedy, where everyone would laugh aloud, the most she'd do was smile a little. She did have a sense of humor, though. Don't misunderstand me. Sometimes she'd say the drollest things, in her dry kind of humor. But she was not the gay or casual kind of girl."

Sam sipped his drink, and then asked, "What do you think of her now, now that you know what she is accused of doing?"

She looked at him soberly. "That is quite a question, but I'll answer you. I think that it is just unbelievable. It simply must be a mistake. Janet could no more kill Kevin than I could. She just is not that kind of person. The last thing in the world she would do would be something as violent and irrational as that."

"You seem very sure."

"I am. I know Janet, and I knew Kevin Porter. Those two

loved each other if ever two people loved each other. You don't kill what you love—never."

Sam grimaced as he thought of the many bitter examples he had seen of just the opposite of what she so firmly declared. To himself he murmured, "Don't you, though!" Then, aloud, he asked, "How do you know, for certain, that they loved each other so deeply?"

She tilted her head, and looked at him for a moment. Then she said, "I know, for certain. Let me tell you about how they met and how they got married. It's a true romance if ever I saw one.

"Kevin Porter was a fine-looking man," she said, "in his thirties and unmarried when he met Janet Duffield. He was tall, prematurely gray-haired, and rather handsome. But he was a reserved, introspective kind of person. He never talked a great deal. He and Janet were much alike in that respect. Both were quiet, restrained kind of people. Kevin was a young law professor at some university in Ohio, and was in New York to attend some kind of law convention being held at N.Y.U. That was when he met Janet. There was a party being held there one evening, and Janet was there. That's when they first saw each other.

"Kevin said," she explained, "that the first time he saw Janet was altogether extraordinary. She was standing on the other side of the room, and there was a circle of young men around her. She was unusually vivacious, apparently, and she was relating something to these young men and they all were laughing. There was a ceiling spotlight right above Janet's head, and under the light her brown hair was full of glowing reds and golds. He was reminded of the old song, 'Jeannie With the Light Brown Hair,' and he thought her the most charming girl he had ever seen. Kevin told me that what happened to him then was something he never had experienced before in all his life. He said that it was like the kind of thing the movies and stage like to show—love at first sight. He never had believed in that sort of thing, until it happened to him. He said, almost embarrassed to tell it, 'zing went the strings of my heart. I heard bells ringing, and there was music in the air.' At that moment, before she had even seen him or knew that he existed, his mind was made up—this was the girl he was going to marry. He moved closer and joined the circle around her, and was relieved to see that there was no wedding ring on her finger.

"Someone introduced them and he chatted with her, together with the others, for a while. She was excited about some legal project they were talking about and was full of wit and sparkle that evening. She had no idea, though, that the sober, visiting law teacher was smitten with her. She probably would not have believed it anyway, at that time. After a while, when they were a bit apart from the others for a minute, Kevin asked her to go out to dinner with him the next day. She declined, saying that she had a previous dinner engagement, which was not true. The fact is she was completely surprised and was getting back into her shell, suspicious of such direct admiration. He asked about seeing her at another time, and she put him off again. He could get nowhere with her, which confirmed his belief that she was very popular and would be hard to win. Then the others grouped around and Kevin withdrew from the circle, sure that he was being rejected.

"Kevin said," Mrs. Morrison continued, "that he went back to his hotel in a confused state of mind—a mixture of fascination, rapture, and misery. He could hardly sleep that night. He saw Janet's face on the ceiling over his bed as though he were a lovesick boy. He was really smitten. Next day he made inquiries and learned all he could about her. When he found out that she was John Duffield's daughter and held in great respect at N.Y.U., his misery grew worse. Everyone spoke well of her, and he took their professional respect to be awe of her glamorous attractiveness. Next morning, at another meeting at N.Y.U., he saw her again. She, meanwhile, had forgotten about him. Once again there was a circle of men around her. She was telling them something and they all seemed highly amused.

"It seems that she occasionally did research work as a free-lancer for some magazines. She had done some such job for a company up on Madison Avenue. In doing this kind of work, she used to carry around with her a portable photocopying machine which she used for copying material from books in libraries. She had left this portable, worth about seventy dollars when new, at the magazine office, intending to pick it up that morning. When she called for it the receptionist at the office had refused to return it to her, saying that it was not hers. It was not worth very much, being old, but she was incensed about it. Her annoyance made her face flushed and her eyes sparkling. Kevin thought that she looked adorable. He told her that he would get it back for her. She was surprised by his offer of help, and away he went—Sir Galahad to the rescue."

Sam looked amused as Mrs. Morrison went on with her story. "Well," she said, "he rushed downtown to the law office on Wall Street where he worked for a number of years before leaving to become a law teacher. He got permission from one of the firm's partners to use the office and a secretary—offering to reimburse them for it if they would take his check—which they did. Then he settled down to getting out all the papers needed in order to get a court order to get back the little photocopy machine. I remember that Kevin described the procedure as rather involved; out of all proportion to the value of the thing he wanted to recover. It was called a Writ of Replevin, and required the preparation and typing-up of several legal documents—an affidavit, an order for a judge to sign, a bond to make good the value if the order should turn out to be unjustified, and other things. It took most of the day to prepare. Kevin told me all about the details some time later.

"Anyhow, Kevin took the order to the courthouse on Foley Square to get it signed by a judge. The judge thought that he was crazy to go to all this bother for such a trifling thing, when a claim for damages would have been much simpler. But the judge signed the order. This also meant a trip to a bonding company to get a bond for the proceedings. Keven paid for the bond himself.

"After he got the bond and order all ready, he had to go and pay another fee to get a man from the Sheriff's Office to serve the papers. This man must have been sure that Kevin was out of his mind, but he went along with Kevin uptown to the magazine's office. They went into the office in a blaze of legal authority, just before the office closed for the day, and served the Writ of Replevin on the amazed office manager.

"The funny thing was," she related, "that the magazine's manager explained that it had all been a mistake on the part of the receptionist. The portable photocopy machine did indeed belong to Miss Duffield. It was all a silly mistake, and they were dreadfully sorry and apologized. He was glad to hand over the battered little contraption, and no court order was really necessary after all.

"Kevin insisted on having the Order served, and the machine repossessed by the power and authority of formal legal procedure, not just by being politely handed over. He wanted the thing seized, not just returned. Then, leaving the people in the office gaping, he triumphantly marched out with the cause of the uproar—a worn, old, portable photocopy box in a worn, old carrying case. He could have bought several of them for what he had spent to get this one back. He hurried to Janet's apartment, got the doorman to go with him and let him in, and left it for her inside her door with a note from him explaining that he had rescued it for her. Later that evening, he telephoned her. She was astonished and impressed. She hardly could refuse to have dinner with him under the circumstances. That was how Janet and Kevin got acquainted."

Sam smiled at his mental picture of the dour law professor smitten with love and the plain-Jane girl besieged by this eager suitor. "Then what happened?" he asked.

Mrs. Morrison's voice grew tender. "It was the sweetest thing I ever saw. He was at her doorstep constantly, and she was walking on air. They were together constantly for the few days he was here, and she positively blossomed. It was the first time in her life that she ever had been courted and adored. She just loved it. Maybe she loved the idea of being loved, and in love, more than she loved Kevin himself. But she said that she grew to love him quickly. How could she do otherwise, when he adored her so?"

"Didn't Porter have to go back to Ohio?"

"Yes, he did. But then he was here again almost every weekend. They were together every weekend running around town and having a whirlwind romance. Then, one day they came and told me that they had been quietly married, and Janet was leaving. They left that same day. I made the arrangements for Janet's furniture to be shipped to Cleveland. Before I knew it they were gone."

"Did you correspond with them?" Sam inquired.

"Yes, for a while. Then the letters petered out. They moved to San Francisco. I never saw them again after the day when they got married."

"Tell me," Sam asked. "Was Janet ever sick? Did you ever know her to be emotionally ill?"

"No . . ." Mrs. Morrison seemed uncertain. "Sometimes she didn't feel well—like any woman, but not sick really, and certainly never mentally ill. That's what you mean, isn't it."

"Yes."

"Never mentally ill. Never," she said with finality.

It had been a tender and lovely period in Janet's life, Sam thought, but it didn't seem to suggest anything that would help in her defense—not anything that he could see at the moment, anyhow. He thanked Mrs. Morrison for her concern and her effort to help, and left.

Up early the next morning, Sam went for a pleasant stroll down Fifth Avenue. He stopped at Dunhill's shop at Radio City, bought some cigarettes, and then went on to a shop that specialized in fine, made-to-order shirts. He had himself measured for several white-linen shirts and ordered them sent to his home, plus a dozen rich silk neckties in his invariably preferred dark-blue colors, and three tastefully wrought sets of silver cufflinks. Then he took a taxicab down to Washington Square to the Georgian mass of the New York University Law School building.

Professor Lucian Phillips, a man with a long, narrow, puritanically severe face, was the man in charge of the law school's research staff. He was expecting Sam. He already had on his desk the employment record of Janet Duffield.

"It was a rather unusual thing for us," he explained in his precise, stiffly correct manner. "Normally we would not employ a person who was not academically unimpeachable as to credentials. Miss Duffield not only held no law degree, but she even lacked a baccalaureate degree. Of course, she was not a member of the Bar. In all my years at this university I never have seen another such waiver of academic requirements."

"Then how do you explain it?" Sam asked pleasantly.

"Patently, this young woman had 'friends at court,' so to speak. The dean and the faculty-recruitment committee approved her employment and the waiver of academic credentials, and I was outvoted." Apparently the affront to his academic authority still rankled. "She was the daughter of the highly reputable Professor John Duffield, and she did have considerable competence in legal research, I must say," he admitted grudgingly. "She was employed as a research assistant. Her salary was quite nominal," he added, as an afterthought.

"It would seem that she didn't need the money."

"So it would seem."

"What kind of research did she do?"

"Chiefly in the area of legal history. She was quite good on the history of the Colonial courts, but most of her work was in the history of the Supreme Court and of the justices of that court."

"For whom did she do this research?"

"Primarily for men working in the field of constitutional law," the dour professor replied, "and also for general historical material in papers or books on other subjects. She was what you might call a 'utility outfielder.' . . ." He smiled with self-satisfaction at his use of a colloquialism. "We have a great deal of research work done here, especially in the preparation of masters' theses and doctoral dissertations. This is perhaps the major center of graduate legal training in the country." He was sententious. "More future law professors are trained here than at any other university in the world. Miss Duffield assisted both faculty members and graduate-degree candidates."

"What kind of person was she? I mean personally, as an individual rather than as a scholar?" Sam asked.

"Competent enough." Then, as he understood the question's real meaning, the professor added stiffly, "Her personality—or rather her personal character and characteristics—are not recorded."

"I mean, what did you think of her?"

Phillips was becoming testy. "I didn't think anything about her, Mr. Benedict, as long as she was competent and did her assigned work properly—which she did, according to this record."

Sam took a stab at a slim possibility. "Would your records show anything about absenteeism of such an employee, Professor?"

"They would indeed." That was a more proper question, to his mind, obviously. He picked out a card from the open file. "We do not require research workers to punch a time clock, and we do not take issue with occasional absences. But we do keep records of such absences." He studied the card, his eyebrows rising as he read it. "This is interesting. I had not paid much attention to it before. Miss Duffield apparently took a day or two off almost every month. Quite regularly, it would seem; a day or two absent every month."

"Would the card show the dates?"

"Yes, of course."

Sam was alertly interested. Regular monthly absences. That tied in with the theory of premenstrual tension. It was far from conclusive evidence, but it was evidence.

"Could I have a photocopy of that card?" he asked.

Phillips looked surprised. "I suppose so."

"Please have it photostated or Xeroxed, or however you do it here. I'll be glad to pay for it."

"No need to pay for it. I'll have one made for you." Phillips buzzed his intercom and gave the card to be photocopied to a student assistant who came in in response to his call. When the student returned with the card and the photocopy of it a few minutes later, Phillips gave the copy to Sam who pocketed it and rose to go. He had another professor to see at N.Y.U., before he left.

Professor Alvarez, the other man with whom he had an appointment, insisted that Sam accompany him to lunch. They walked across the Square past students, nursemaids with baby carriages, and seedy Greenwich Village residents sitting on the benches scattered about. It was hot. The August sun was cooking the concrete sidewalks and stone-faced buildings of Manhattan. Sam was glad to reach the air-conditioned coolness of the little restaurant to which Alvarez led him.

Alvarez, a hearty, jovial man with a pleasant smile and bright dark eyes, had known Janet Duffield when she had worked at N.Y.U. She had assisted him in his research on a book about the impact of the Puerto Rican immigrants on the city and their transposition from the Spanish-derived Civil Law to the Anglo-American Common Law. He had been active in the effort to get Spanish literacy recognized as sufficient for voting-literacy purposes for the Puerto Rican immigrants.

"I'm a man of the people," he announced as they started on their lunch. "I intend to always be that. But that doesn't mean that I can't understand people from other backgrounds and with other cultural heritages. Take Janet Duffield, for instance. She was a good research assistant. She and this Porter fellow she married were altogether different from me. Yet, I understood them—the poor bastards."

"Why do you say 'poor bastards'?" Sam was taken aback.

"I say poor bastards because I mean poor bastards. They were a couple of prime examples of the worst results of the Puritan ethic and life guided by the Puritan ethic. They were the Puritan ethic incarnate. That's a poor term, for what I mean, though. *Carne* means 'meat' in Spanish. They were dry, bloodless people, just the opposite of meaty, earthy people like me. They were people who denied their own nature as hot-blooded, predatory mammals."

"Do you believe that's what people are?"

"Hell, yes. A species of predator, meant to live and to hunt and to fight and to love vigorously—savagely."

"You say that—a *law* professor?"

"Sure." Alvarez was emphatic. "Law is the rules of the pack, to prevent them from fighting among themselves too ferociously. That's what it is in the last analysis."

"How does all this apply to Janet and Kevin Porter?"

"It applies. I knew Janet, and I met Kevin Porter a few times. They reminded me of the famous Grant Wood painting called 'American Gothic.' You know the picture. It shows a farmer and his wife—their faces gaunt and self-righteous, staring straight ahead—prim and sour and dour, tight-lipped, humorless and sure that they are the elect of the earth. But behind the self-righteousness is a hidden doubt. Deep inside they are not quite convinced of their eternal Calvinistic righteousness. They suppress their appetites and lusts and aggressions—or sublimate them into hymn-singing scorn of healthy, outgoing, laughing people like me."

"Janet and Kevin did that?"

"Sure they did. Oh, not consciously, not aware of what they were doing. They always were correct and respectful and decorous. After all, I was an established man. But they believed, inside, that they were of finer clay. I knew that they believed that, even if they themselves didn't know it. Little did they know that I thought myself a far better human being than either of them."

Sam objected. "I thought that Janet was a rather gentle soul under her shy exterior."

"I'm not saying that she isn't, in spite of what she did. Your Mr. Tabor said that she killed Kevin Porter and was found in a state of amnesia. That adds up like two and two adds up to four. Her quiet, solitary suppression of normal emotions just burst through the dike—that's all. You can't live like an emotionless machine without having something break. My metaphors may be mixed up, but you see what I mean, don't you?"

"I think I do," Sam agreed.

"And take this Porter fellow. He was like that, too, only he got clobbered before his dike broke. He was a sour lemon, for my money, absolutely certain that he was born to be a prophet. He was thoroughly and completely uninterested in what other people thought and felt. He must have been a hell of a man to be married to. Oh, I know they say 'de mortuis nil nisi bonum,' but that's a lot of hogwash."

"But you never knew him very well."

"Well enough to recognize the type."

"Type?" Sam looked at him quizzically. "You classify people into types?"

"Sure I do. Everybody does, only I admit it."

"And what types were Janet and Kevin Porter?"

"American Gothic. Both of them were American Gothic."

After lunch, while walking back toward Washington Square, Sam asked Alvarez, "How can you speak of Kevin Porter as a self-appointed prophet when he was a student of constitutional law? The two things just don't seem to go together."

Alvarez answered quickly and positively. "In the few conversations I had with him, he was always absolutely rigid and inflexible—sure that he was right and everyone else was wrong. For instance, he believed that Oliver Wendell Holmes, Jr., the Supreme Court justice, was the absolute paragon of American liberal legal thought. Do you agree with that?"

"Hardly. I think that Holmes' liberalism was greatly exaggerated and that he placed property rights over inherent human rights."

Alvarez grinned triumphantly. "Porter was certain that property rights *are* superior and that Holmes was absolutely correct. He revered Holmes. He even echoed the old bromide about women's place being in the kitchen and the natural right of the male to dominate the female—the fundamental inferiority of females, and all that kind of bilge. I tell you, he was reactionary conservatism embodied. The odd thing was that Janet loathed Holmes. Wouldn't even discuss him."

"But wasn't Porter courting Janet when you knew him? Wasn't all that sort of thing contrary to what I'm told was a sweet and romantic courtship?"

"Sure, he was courting her then. Oh, he was in love, all right —as much as that kind of man can be in love and be a giving rather than a taking creature. But it was contrary to his real nature—a temporary aberration that would last only until he got what he wanted. I believe that it was absolutely out of character, for him. It couldn't last. And you see—it didn't."

Sam looked at Alvarez with respect. His puckish, ribald view of the world did not blind him to realities. He might be just exactly right in his estimate of Kevin Porter. "And Janet?" he asked.

"She was less out of character than he was. But she was yearning for exactly what she thought Kevin Porter was offering her—love and warmth and beauty of life. She thought that that's what she was getting. But it wasn't. You can see now that it wasn't. She let down the bars to the chamber of her secret soul, for the only time in her life, probably."

Sam walked along in silence. Alvarez might have intuitively recognized what it had taken him hard study and search to see.

"You know," Alvarez said, "that odd romance of those two reminds me of the popular song—'It Was Just One of Those Things.' . . ."

The 21 Club on 52nd Street was the place where Sam usually had most of his meals when he was in New York City. Its name continued to be synonymous with elegance and luxurious cuisine, and as Sam's taxi pulled up before it he was looking forward to a truly fine dinner. Bob Simms, a law professor at Harvard, was to meet him there. Simms was an old friend, and had known John Duffield at Harvard. Bob was waiting for him inside, and they settled down to a leisurely dinner. Bob knew nothing of the Porter case, and Sam told him about it before asking what he could tell about John Duffield in return.

Simms could tell him something, though not as much as he had hoped. "John Duffield was a starchy, rather remote kind of man," he said. "He was a brilliant scholar; no doubt of that. But he was not a man that others like, in spite of his fondness for big social soirees. He had a marked tendency to dominate and direct other people. In a word, he was arrogant. I knew him as well as anyone on the law faculty did, but I never liked him much. The students, who had a nickname for everyone, called him 'Domineering Duffield.' That is a revealing appraisal."

"Did you know his daughter then?" Sam asked.

"I knew her only enough to say 'hello.' She used to be at Langdell Hall quite often, accompanying John. She would wait for him in his office while he was in class. You'd see her tagging along behind him, looking pale and unhappy, as he strode down the hall. He never seemed to have her at his side, but barged along as though unaware that she was there. Then he would turn and look sternly at her without a word, as though annoyed, and resume his pace. She hardly could keep up with him, which seemed to frighten her and irritate him."

"Not what you would call a picture of a loving father and daughter," Sam remarked.

"Not by a long shot. It rather made me think of an old-time lord of the manor, and his little slavey timidly following behind, waiting to be summoned and given some task to perform."

"Can you be more specific," Sam asked. "Is there any illustrative event that you can tell me about?"

"One little incident between John and his daughter particularly sticks in my mind. It seems to me that it illustrated their relationship, as far as my view of it goes. It happened in John's office one day, and I chanced to come in just in time to witness it. The girl was sitting at the table, with a mass of books and journals open before her. But she was holding a magazine in her hands, and reading it. It was either a copy of *Life* or of *Look* magazine. I'm not sure which it was, now, but it definitely was one or the other. John walked into his office just before I did. I guess that he was returning from his class, as I was from mine. I wanted to borrow a certain book from him. He saw what his daughter was reading and anger was visible on his face. Without saying a word he strode up to her side. She looked up, surprised. Then I saw on her face a look that I can only describe as a look of fear. He snatched the magazine from her hands and ripped it in half. Then, still without a word, he threw the pieces into a wastebasket. After that, he turned to me, as unconcerned as you please, and asked me what he could do for me.

"I hardly could take my eyes from the girl. She sat there, rigid—absolutely petrified—without uttering a sound. Her face was completely expressionless. John didn't even look at her. He gave me the book for which I had come. I was embarrassed, thanked him quickly, and left. Perhaps I should have said something to him, but I didn't. What could I say, right in front of her? From that day forward, my already cool regard for John turned into almost active dislike. Any man who could treat his own daughter with such callous indifference for her feelings was not one I'd like to have as a friend. That girl was afraid of her own father. What a terrible thing!"

Sam sat quietly, thinking of Janet Porter and the sad and fearful childhood that had made her what she was. Then he asked, "Duffield worked mainly in the area of constitutional law, didn't he?"

"Yes."

"Any particular aspect of it?"

Bob nodded. "The Supreme Court and most particularly the Court under the influence of Justice Holmes. He was the leading scholar on the opinions and writings of Holmes. He revered Holmes; viewed him as far and away the greatest justice ever to sit on the Supreme Court Bench. He spoke of him constantly, and wrote about him. He even looked somewhat like him, being tall and white-haired. He had a white moustache, too, though not the handlebar-kind that Holmes affected."

"I've been told," Sam pursued, "that she used to help him with his research and writing. Would you happen to know anything about that?"

"I heard that, too, when she was here regularly. It even used to occur to me that she was here often during the day, when she should have been at her own school. Gossip had it that she was educated by private tutors, and by John himself. But that might have been just gossip. I do know, though, that I occasionally saw her in his office reading what seemed to be legal works and reports, and obviously making notes about what she was studying. It very likely was work she was doing for John, but I do not know that definitely as a fact."

"In his writing—articles or studies or reports—did he ever give her credit as his assistant? Many men do that, as a courtesy, at least with a footnote credit."

"Not as far as I can recall," Bob said, with a definite shake of his head. "You can check up on that yourself, as far as his published articles are concerned."

"I have," Sam said dryly, "but haven't found such a footnote. But then, for a man who was such a famous scholar, he published very few articles, as far as I or my assistant have been able to discover."

"No, he didn't. He worked mainly on a big project he had that would be a study of the Supreme Court and of Holmes. This was to be published as his autobiography, built around his observations and studies, but mainly consisting of his analyses and comments on the opinions of Holmes in various cases. This project I'm sure about, because he listed it regularly in the customary annual university listings of 'Research Projects Under Way.' He died before completing it, though. I heard somewhere that Janet was completing it."

"That probably is so." Sam remembered the sheaf of notes on Holmes' opinions that he had seen in the library of the Porter mansion.

"Anyhow," Bob Simms commented, "if I were Janet I'd have been tempted to throw the whole project into a wastebasket when John died—or burn it."

"I wish she had," Sam added fervently. "I wish she had."

CHAPTER

7

From Cleveland-Hopkins Airport to downtown Cleveland the limousine and taxi route runs through a sprawling complex of factories, steel mills, and refineries. Sam, riding downtown from the airport, was much interested in the industrial scene—so different from San Francisco. The city had an atmosphere of its own which contrasted sharply with the debonair quality of San Francisco and the febrile sophistication of New York. Cleveland was the epitome of the modern manufacturing center— plain almost to the point of drabness, and bluntly dedicated to work and production. Yet, Sam knew that its suburbs were among the handsomest and wealthiest in the world.

He checked into the Sheraton-Cleveland Hotel, went up to his room, showered, and put on fresh clothing. Then he stood at the window for a few minutes looking down at the traffic in Public Square, the city's center. The old Soldiers and Sailors Monument, almost beautiful in its Victorian angular ugliness, stood in one quarter of the Square like a symbol of the city's soul—traditional, with the structure and values of the century past. It was a clear, cool day, typical of the climate that the vast stretch of Lake Erie bestowed on this city in summer and fall. He remembered, having been here once in December, the gray, windy days that that same lake bestowed in the wintertime.

This is the key place, he thought, where the drama of Janet and Kevin Porter took its inexorable turn toward the ultimate tragedy. They came here full of love and hope. But when they left and settled in San Francisco, the warm togetherness was gone, and they lived like strangers sharing a house. Why? What happened here, to start them on the road to tragedy?

He went downstairs, crossed Public Square, and headed up Ontario Street towards the big, pillared County Court House, its granite façade topped by six giant, brooding statues of ancient great men of the law. He knew that Cleveland-Marshall Law School stood almost next to the big courthouse building. Hank had scheduled a visit for him.

The law-school building was big and square, too. Its façade of modern gray, black, and aluminum was plain and business-like, in the tradition of the city. The name set above its ground-floor expanse of glass was studded out from the wall in black, iron letters—*Cleveland-Marshall Law School.* A severe, stern building, he thought, and went in.

In the reception office a secretary came to him at the information counter and told him that the dean and associate dean were not in. They were away, at the American Bar Association meeting in New York, and would not be back for two or three days more. He asked for Professor Robinson, with whom Hank had made an appointment for Sam. Robinson was in, and expecting him. He went up to the professor's office. It was neatly furnished with a modernistic desk and leather chairs, its walls flat-panelled in light walnut wood. Impressionist paintings hung on the walls, opposite large, built-in bookshelves jammed with law books.

Robinson was in his shirt sleeves. It was quiet in the row of faculty offices. All the other doors were closed. The hum of air conditioning came softly from a vent in the acoustical-tile ceiling. The room was bright with fluorescent light from big fixtures set into the ceiling behind translucent glass sheets. This again was a no-nonsense, efficient, working office.

The professor was a small, wiry man. He greeted Sam warmly. "I've heard and read a lot about you. Very glad to know you."

"I gather that you have been with this law school for a long time," Sam said. "Full professor for quite a while, haven't you been?"

"Yes. Over twenty years. And five years at the University of

Oklahoma before that. I guess you'd call me an old-timer at this game."

"You were here, then, when Kevin Porter joined your faculty —and when he left—weren't you?"

Robinson nodded. "Oh, yes. I knew Kevin well. Dreadful thing that happened to him. And Janet. A dreadful, shocking thing."

"I'm here investigating that whole business, you understand. I'd like to ask you a lot of questions about them. Is that all right?"

"Of course. Go right ahead."

"First, how did Kevin Porter happen to come here originally?"

Robinson smiled. "To explain that I'll have to explain the system—if you can call it that—of how law schools obtain law teachers."

"All right. Please do."

"In the old days," Robinson began, "when a law school needed a teacher, the dean simply found one and hired him. Of course, the president of the university or some other potentate, or a prominent alumnus or benefactor of the institution might suggest someone. Mainly, it was a straight-forward matter of personal friendships or influence. Sometimes, if the school could afford it, the dean would invite some well-known law teacher from another school. But mostly the administration ran the show as it pleased. Then an Association of American Law Schools was formed. Some people still call it the 'law-teachers union.' It is dedicated to the improvement of legal education and of law schools in this country. It definitely has raised the standards of legal education and of law-school operation. Throughout its history, and especially in recent years, it has introduced rules and standards to improve the quality and position of law teachers. Now, for example, the faculty as a group has much to say about who shall be hired and who shall not be hired. Of course, this is still not true in some authoritarian institutions, but it is getting to be so even in those places. In addition, the Standards of the American Bar Association, which is the accrediting authority for law schools, especially the new Standards of 1968, have a similar effect.

"Here in Ohio, there is a League of Ohio Law Schools, similar to the A.A.L.S., with similar rules and standards. There are other, equivalent groups elsewhere. And on top of that, the American Association of University Professors—the A.A.U.P.—has done much the same for colleges and universities generally. The net effect of all this is to place a large degree of authority as to faculty recruitment, promotion, tenure, et cetera, in the hands of the faculty. Some say that the effect is to make law faculties into self-perpetuating groups of vested interests."

Sam broke in. "That's all very interesting, but . . ."

"Bear with me," Robinson went on. "You'll see the point in a minute. So this law school, like most others, appoints or elects a faculty-recruitment committee to pick new faculty members. The dean gets letters and calls regularly from people—mostly lawyers who are fed up with the tensions of practice—who want teaching positions. Also, several times a year the A.A.L.S. sends around batches of résumés of people who apply to them to be listed in their 'Faculty Appointments Register.' Then, every year between Christmas and New Year's Day, at the Annual Meeting of the A.A.L.S. in some different city, the 'Slave Market' is held. There, at a meeting ostensibly dedicated to professional, technical conferences and discussions, most of the deans and faculty-recruitment committees spend most of their time in their suites interviewing candidates for jobs. Much of their time is also spent eating and drinking, too—especially drinking. The liquor consumption at a law-professors' meeting will compare well with that at a plumbers' convention. We got Kevin Porter at a 'Slave Market' meeting one year. You see! Would you have understood if I had told you just that last sentence?"

"I see," Sam said, smiling.

"Kevin registered with the A.A.L.S. 'Faculty Appointments Register,' " Robinson continued. "He was with some law firm in New York at that time. We got his résumé in a batch of about a hundred men's records sent to all law schools by the Executive Director of the A.A.L.S. We were interested in his academic and other qualifications and invited him—and a dozen others—to meet us at the Christmas conventicn for an interview. He did, and we interviewed him. Kevin had excellent qualifications. Degrees from good colleges and law schools, near the top of his class in law school; he had Law Review Board experience in school, and several years of practice experience with a good law firm. He had no teaching experience, of course, but that's not unusual. He did not have delusions about what faculty rank he should have. Also important, he was available at our salary scale, which is not the highest in the country. In fact, he didn't seem to care much about what his salary would be. That's a big item here, because we can't compete with the salary scales of the big, rich schools like Harvard or Michigan or Berkeley."

"I've wondered," said Sam, "why a man with Kevin's qualifications didn't get a job with one of the big schools. I mean no reflection on your school, Professor, but you see what I mean, don't you?"

"No offense at all," Robinson said warmly. "We are a small school when compared with California or N.Y.U., though we believe that our quality is very high. Also, we are mainly a regional school rather than a national school. And chance—combinations of events—enters into the picture. Kevin was a constitutional-law man. That year we needed a specialist in constitutional law, and perhaps the other schools didn't. Or maybe they wanted an old hand rather than a beginner at teaching. Another thing must be remembered. The smaller, lower-paying law schools are used as hunting grounds by the bigger, richer ones. Something like the bush leagues and the major leagues for sources of talent and experience, you might say. Not that we're 'bush-league' in the baseball sense. We are very proud of this school. But we are raided regularly by larger and richer schools for our younger men after they have had a few years teaching experience here. And Kevin may well have had in mind the wisdom of getting some experience at a regional school before moving on to a national school. Kevin always was a man with his eye on the main chance. He only stayed here for two years, you know."

"How did he work out?"

Robinson hesitated for a moment, and then answered. "Good enough. He was a fine scholar and a competent teacher. We hired him in the rank of instructor—the bottom of the totem pole. In his second year he was promoted to assistant professor. Oh, he was competent, all right."

"But . . . ?" Sam queried. "There seems to be a 'but' in what you are saying."

"Yes, there is a 'but.'" Robinson seemed to be uncomfortable. "He was a cold fish, not easy to get along with. He was amiable enough at first. But then he seemed to become more and more remote—more and more difficult to live with."

"In what way?"

"We are a small group on this faculty—less than twenty on the full-time faculty in the law school. We have to live together closely, both at work and socially. When Kevin first joined us we welcomed him warmly. He was a bachelor then, and everyone went out of his way to be friendly and hospitable to him. His reaction was polite but distant. Then he met and married Janet, as a result of an institute he attended in New York. He married her soon after meeting her and brought her to Cleveland. When they first arrived here he was quite friendly for a while, and so was she. It seemed that things would be friendlier between Kevin and the other men."

"And then . . . ?"

"Then, in a little while, he became cold and stand-offish again—even more so than he had been before. The honeymoon didn't last long, it seems. He went back into his shell."

"Did you know her well?"

"Oh, yes." Robinson spoke in matter-of-fact tones. "We had them to dinner at our house two or three times. She was a pleasant creature, though not outgoing in nature at first. Then she seemed to become more and more remote as time went by. We'd see them every now and then at various campus faculty gatherings, too. You know—the Christmas Reception for the faculty, faculty-wives' teas, and that sort of thing."

Sam pressed the point. "You seem to be suggesting a conflict between Kevin and the faculty. How did he clash with the faculty, as you seem to suggest he did?"

"Oh, there never was any 'clash,' as you put it," Robinson protested. "He simply didn't join in. He attended faculty meetings and did his work, but he always seemed to be 'in' the faculty and yet not 'of' it. It's hard to explain. For example, in faculty discussions he said almost nothing. When it came to volunteering help to someone or for something, he just never did. When several men would go out to lunch or dinner together and relax and joke, if Kevin joined them at all—which he seldom did—he would be humorless and formal as if they were holding a faculty meeting."

"And Janet?"

"She seemed to be anxious to join in with the girls—the faculty wives—when she first arrived. They helped her to find a house, buy furniture, and all that sort of thing at first. But in a while she seemed to withdraw, too, and to stay away from the others. Do you know that she and Kevin never had any of the gang over to their house? Never. Not once after they bought the house and settled down in it."

"You mean that they were both antisocial by nature?" Sam asked.

"It was more than that." Robinson groped for the right words. "They seemed to live in a private world. I mean each of them, separately. He had his own private world, and she had her own private world. Nobody was admitted. I do believe that they did not even admit each other to their private worlds. That is a strange and maybe a bad thing for me to say, but I believe that it is true."

"Tell me about Janet's legal research work, if you can," Sam requested. "I understand that she did research work here, too, as she had done at New York University."

"Not quite like she did there, as I understand it. Our graduate program is small compared with N.Y.U. And our faculty research work is on a smaller scale, too. This is a smaller operation altogether. Our library is not as big as theirs, for example. We have a system of student research assistants for the faculty and relatively smaller need for outside people to assist in research work. She did help some of the men on some projects, but it was not a full-time everyday sort of job."

"So she had time on her hands here."

"Probably so," Robinson agreed. "I'd see her working in the library now and then, but not continually. Then two or three weeks would pass and I wouldn't see her here at all. She must have had quite a number of idle periods of time."

"Do you have any idea what she did with her free time?"

"No. Maybe she worked on her father's notes for a book. Somebody told me once that she was doing something like that, apart from the work she did here."

"Did she have friends in Cleveland, other than the law-school faculty people, would you happen to know?"

"I don't know." Robinson shrugged. "I suppose so. She and Kevin lived in Shaker Heights. No doubt her neighbors there would know better than I. The office downstairs will tell you their old address if you don't have it."

"I have it."

"You know," Robinson said, "The plain truth of it is that we all were glad—almost relieved—when Kevin Porter told us that he'd had an offer from Berkeley and was going to move to California. He was a good teacher and a good scholar, and yet we were glad to see him go."

"I appreciate your frankness." Sam thanked him. "You have been very helpful. I'm obliged to you."

"I wish the circumstances were other than they are," Robinson concluded almost sadly. "But this whole business reminds me of the ancient Greek philosophy which said that a man's character is his fate. It seems that Kevin Porter's character was his fate."

Sam looked at him wonderingly before going out the door. "That's a curious comment, Professor. Somebody else whom you don't know made almost the same observation about him a few days ago."

After lunch in the English Oak Room restaurant in the Terminal Tower Building at Public Square, Sam took a cab out to Cleveland Clinic. He was interested in this big complex of buildings that was one of the three or four greatest medical research centers in the world. It was typical of the Porters, he thought, to go to the Cleveland Clinic and not to just some facility near where they lived for medical services. Only the best—that was their natural way of life as far as comforts and services were concerned. But the way they managed their own lives was quite the contrary.

He found the wing in which Dr. Stewart Tatum's office was and waited in Tatum's office while the doctor's secretary called him. Stewart Tatum greeted him with professional courtesy which changed to less reticent cooperation when he saw the authorization note signed by Janet Porter. "Dr. Rubenfeld called me from San Francisco and explained why you were coming here to see me. Even so, the problem of doctor-patient privileged communications was in my mind. I could not be sure that I had any right to reveal anything to you about the Porters, even in so serious a court case, without some kind of waiver of the patient's right to my silence. Your authorization is something of a relief from a dilemma."

Sam nodded understandingly. "The fact is that I am not even sure of what I want to find out. This is an exploratory visit. I want to find out what there is to find out about Janet and Kevin Porter, insofar as you can help me. It may literally be a matter of life-and-death to Mrs. Porter."

Tatum was sober and earnest. "Tell me where to begin. Basically, my records are my chief source of recollection. Will they do for a beginning?"

"Yes."

The doctor silently read papers from a Manila file envelope labeled "Porter." Then he explained, "Mrs. Porter came here for consultation regarding complaints of general malaise. That is, she was persistently and frequently not quite ill, but not quite well. 'Feeling poorly' was the term people used to apply to that. We put her through the usual physical-checkup series. Nothing significant appeared from the routine examinations."

"You mean that she was normal and healthy."

"Not exactly. Only that she was not suffering from any organic disease or major malfunction. But there's more . . ."

"Yes? Go on."

"She complained of periodic trouble related to the menstrual cycle."

"You mean 'premenstrual tension.' . . ."

The doctor looked up with surprise. "Quite so. You know what this is, then, I would surmise."

"Yes, more or less," Sam said.

Tatum was sober and professional in his manner. "In any event, she had the periodic symptoms associated with what laymen refer to as recurrent premenstrual tension. Rather severe, too, as I recall."

"Did you do any tests in that connection?"

"Yes. Blood tests, vaginal smears, and so on. We found the classic symptomology and data—hypoglycemia and water retention in the tissues, and so on."

"Could I have copies of the test records?"

Tatum looked surprised. "I suppose so, if you want them."

"I'd be obliged if you would have photocopies made and sent to me as soon as possible."

"We'll send them tomorrow." Tatum jotted down a note.

"Did you treat her for premenstrual tension?"

"Yes, I did. But success in such treatment is not assured. We didn't have much success with Mrs. Porter, I'm sorry to say. The etiology of that condition is not yet fully understood."

"Do you mean that she continued to complain?"

"Yes."

"And was psychiatric treatment involved?"

"No. I view the problem as primarily somatic in nature. In any event, Mrs. Porter stopped coming in for study or treatment after a little while. Our procedures never were completed. If she had continued to come in, and to follow the prescribed regimen, I might have been able to help her much more. Like so many other patients, after a while she dropped out, admittedly did not take the medication prescribed, and ceased to be taken seriously as a continuing patient. It is disheartening sometimes."

Sam told him what he had learned about premenstrual tension and its possible causative nature in cases of temporary psychosis. Tatum was frankly skeptical. "You're mixing two different questions," he objected. "Law is law and medicine is medicine. They affect each other sometimes, of course. But you can't take a legal theory and then conveniently search out medical evidence to support it."

"That is precisely what I have in mind to do," Sam said, emphatically. "Scientific facts are facts before they are recognized as such by the medical profession. The bacteria of disease were alive and doing their damage long before the medical men recognized their existence. The fact that the doctors had not said that they were real did not mean that they weren't real."

"But until the physicians found them you didn't know of them either."

"Other people—philosophers—had guessed at their existence."

"Are *you* guessing?" Tatum sounded sarcastic.

Sam bridled. "No. I'm reasoning from what facts are available, as the philosophers did."

"Premenstrual tension as a cause of psychosis is not yet a fact—not yet proved."

"There already is a body of evidence to support a causative hypothesis, and that's enough for my purposes. The absolute proof required by scientists is not the same thing as the relative weight of evidence required by the law for trial purposes. We are trying to settle a problem between two people, in a manner of speaking, between the defendant and the prosecutor, for *law* purposes, not for the purpose of establishing scientific absolutes. We don't need absolute certainty. Reasonable probability may be good enough for legal purposes."

"I see what you mean," Tatum conceded. "With that limitation, then, the evidence as to Mrs. Porter indeed may be helpful to you."

"It surely may."

"Then, granting that the purpose is the legal one only, I would agree that the evidence of premenstrual tension may be enough to suggest a possible cause of psychosis. I will agree to that."

That's a great deal to have admitted, Sam thought, as he got up to go, especially from a hard-headed scientist with the prestige of Cleveland Clinic behind him.

Before going on to his next appointment Sam stopped at a public phone booth in the lobby of the Clinic and telephoned his office. Hank was there and took the call. Sam wanted to know how Rubenfeld was progressing with the psychiatric examination of Janet Porter.

"He's been spending a lot of time with her," Hank reported. "He also called in Dr. Carruthers for a consulting opinion."

"All right," Sam said, "though I'm not as confident of Carruthers as I used to be. Did you ask Rosvalley about the state's psychiatrists?"

"Yes."

"Any resistance from Rosvalley?"

"No. Not a peep."

"I take it that he has state psychiatrists examining her too."

"Oh, sure. She's getting quite a workout."

"Of course, we will use their findings, too, if they are useful to us. Maybe we can use some of Rosvalley's data that his investigators dig up?"

"That's not so easy."

"It can be done. Sometimes by informal discovery procedures through cooperation with the Prosecutor's Office. I think that Barney Rosvalley will be cooperative if you ask him."

"You'll run into the 'Attorney's Work Product Rule.' . . ." Hank objected. "You can't force opposing counsel to allow discovery of data that he sweated to accumulate."

"Yes, you can in California, both in civil and in criminal cases. It's a matter in the discretion of the courts everywhere. California favors broad discovery rights for defendants. The courts do not want trials to be games of skill or deception. They want them to be procedures for getting at the truth."

"That's fine as a generalization. But what legal authority can I cite?"

"I don't recall the exact citations, of course. But I can remember off-hand a few cases that you ought to look up. Use them if you have to. The whole 'work-product' limitation idea is well described in Hickman versus Taylor, a 1947 case in the United States Supreme Court."

"I know about that case."

Sam went on, citing several case decisions for Hank to check on in the California case reports, as well as statutes for him to look up. "Look up the law in all its technical rules, Hank," Sam instructed, "and have it ready in case Rosvalley fights us on this. But get the information without a court fight if you can. Let's not get into involved technical proceedings unless it is to our advantage to do so. Try the cooperation approach to the D.A.'s Office first. I think that Rosvalley will go along with it. He's a fundamentally fair prosecutor."

"Okay, boss."

"Anything new on the Larkbey case?"

"Not a thing. She's still closed up."

"We'll finish that one as soon as I get back. I think that I have the solution. Did you look up that statute on false I.D. cards as I asked you to?"

"Yes, I have it."

"Was I right? Is it a misdemeanor?" Sam asked.

"Yes, it is."

"All right, then." Sam was pleased and confident. "We'll nail their ears to the wall when I get back."

En route to Shaker Heights in a taxicab, Sam saw the proof of the impression he had that Cleveland lay in a bowl facing Lake Erie, surrounded by a ring of hills and plateaus. They rode up a fairly steep slope as they left the city limits and mounted to "The Heights" of the suburbs. It was distinctly cooler in the elevated area. Looking out the back window as they reached the plateau, he could see the vast expanse of the city spread out below, fading into the distance to the north and west. They drove past increasingly fine and expensive-looking homes on increasingly larger green-velvet lawns set with ornamental shrubbery and multitudes of trees. Every street and avenue here was lined with trees. No wonder Cleveland was called "The Forest City." The hills were mere shadows of the steep heights of San Francisco, but they were pleasant. The greenery was thick and heavy, though not as brilliantly colorful as the semitropical vegetation of California. It was more like New England, and very lovely. Sam could understand why the Porters had chosen this area for their home while they were in Ohio.

Before going to the Ventriss home for his scheduled appointment, Sam decided to stop for dinner. The cabby drove him to Shaker Square where, the cabby said, there was a good restaurant. The Square was really a big circle, its center consisting of grass-and-flower islands studded with large trees and surrounded by a handsomely planned ring of fine shops. All were Colonial in architecture—Georgian dull-red brick with white trim and ornamentation. Traffic ran quietly, though thickly, in the circle's driveways. Railroad tracks showed where the Rapid Transit line entered a grassy channel leading toward the city's downtown center. It was a charming shopping area, old but beautifully maintained. A big Colonial building set behind a row of tall, white pillars was Stouffer's—the restaurant which the cab driver had suggested.

Sam had a leisurely dinner of excellent quality. The interior of the restaurant—high and sparkling under crystal chandeliers —was very pleasant, too. He decided that he liked the Shaker Heights area, even before going on to the residential streets. The people, too, were well dressed and friendly looking.

After dinner he took another cab to the Ventriss house. It was bright early-evening. A garrulous driver drove him up Van Aken Boulevard, where a forty-yard-wide center area of grass was bordered by the two automobile lanes. Railroad tracks in the parkway's center aroused his curiosity. Fine mansions bordered the Boulevard and the tracks seemed incongruous. He asked the driver about them.

"This is a funny town," the driver explained. "The 'best people' live right on the railroad tracks in Shaker Heights. There are two spurs, one on Van Aken Boulevard and one on Shaker Boulevard. The Rapid runs along both to Shaker Square, and from there on, one line down to the city. You can catch the Rapid every few minutes during rush hours and be downtown in no time. Shaker Heights was the first suburban development ever built in this country, they say. The Van Sweringens planned it and built it back in the late twenties or early thirties. It was a new idea then—living in the suburbs. You had to be rich to afford a house here, and the zoning and building laws are tough. It still is supposed to be the richest town in the country —highest average income and all that, best schools, and so on. Most of the big executives and professional people in the Cleveland area live in Shaker Heights. No blowing off about how rich or important they are. You won't see many Cadillacs. Plain cars and no hot air. Pretty regular folks, even though they may be loaded. They keep the town up, too.

"Lately—in the past few years, for instance—one corner of Shaker, the Ludlow area, has become integrated. They set up a bureau or something to keep it from becoming all Negro. It has stayed balanced, and the Negro people who moved in are executives and professional people, too. It's a nice town, and they're keeping it that way. In Cleveland, when you've made it you move to Shaker."

"Very interesting," Sam commented, and thought, no wonder the Porters had lived in Shaker Heights.

Chadbourne Road, where the Ventriss home was situated,

was a fine street lined with immaculately kept houses set far back from a narrow sidewalk behind a sweep of lawns. Huge shade trees lined both sides of the street, their branches meeting over the center of the roadway to form a green arch stretching block after block. All of the houses were of Colonial, Tudor, or English Cottage styles. All were of about equal height and all had "Shaker Windows" of small panes of glass, though no two houses were alike otherwise.

The Ventriss house was a half-timbered, Tudor type, a style of architecture no longer in fashion for the new "ticky-tacky" development area of California, Sam thought with regret. Next to it, on one side, was a small, red-brick, Georgian-styled house, and on the other side a gleaming white home of the style he thought was called Dutch Colonial. In one of these two, he knew, Kevin and Janet Porter had started their married life in the rosy glow of new love and marriage. Children were playing on the lawns in front of two or three houses down the block.

Paula Ventriss met Sam at the door and called back over her shoulder, "Steve, Mr. Benedict is here." Then she said to Sam, "I'm sure you must be Sam Benedict. We've read so much about you, and your gray hair and white, pointed pocket handkerchief tell me that you must be."

Sam smiled. "I had no idea that you'd ever have heard of me, or that I'd been 'typed' by my handkerchief."

"Oh, yes." Mrs. Ventriss blushed slightly. "I'm afraid I've embarrassed you. Please forgive me. Do come in."

Inside, in a comfortable sitting room full of casually overstuffed and rumpled chairs and couches, Steve Ventriss was waiting, his hand outstretched. "Glad to know you, Mr. Benedict. Have you had dinner yet?"

Sam assured him that he had.

"So have we. Please call me Steve, if you don't mind," Ventriss said, "and this is Paula. Sit down, won't you. Would you care for a drink?"

Sam asked for a scotch-and-water, and sat down to wait for it. The room was delightfully cool and sunny with the long rays of evening light—homey and comfortable and inviting. Nice house, nice people, he thought. Steve Ventriss came back with Sam's drink and one for Paula and for himself, and they settled down to chat.

"You don't sound like Midwesterners," Sam observed. "Neither of you seems to have the flat 'A' sound in your speech."

"We're originally from Philadelphia," Steve explained. "We moved to Ohio about fourteen years ago and settled in Shaker because it was supposed to have a superb school system. We have two daughters. One is a junior at the University of Michigan. She's away now, working as a counselor in a summer camp. The other is a senior at the high school, and wants to go to Radcliffe. The schools here are just great—about eight or more National Merit Scholarship winners every year in the high school, for instance."

"Yes." Sam wanted to get to the subject of his visit. "What do you do for a living, if I may ask?"

"I'm a research engineer with T.R.W."

"You were living here when the Porters moved in next door, weren't you?"

Steve looked at his wife for a moment, before answering. "Yes. They bought the red-brick house next door. We thought that they were going to stay here—buying the house, and all. But they only lived here about a year and a half."

"Did you know them very well?" Sam inquired.

"Fairly well," Steve acknowledged. "We were neighbors, you know. When they first moved in, Pauly and I dropped in to welcome them to the neighborhood and to get acquainted. They seemed to be nice people and we were rather friendly at first. Later on we didn't see too much of them, and it got to be a sort of 'Hi, good evening' and 'Be good' kind of thing— not very close."

"Why was that?"

Steve hesitated, and then continued. "Well, when they first arrived they seemed to be a cheerful, friendly couple. They had no kids and they were pretty mature people for newlyweds, but nice. We went to hear the Cleveland Orchestra at Severance Hall a few times together, and saw some plays at the Hanna Theatre and The Playhouse, and all that kind of thing. Mostly we visited of an evening for a drink and to shoot the breeze. It looked like we'd become close friends."

"Yes," Sam prompted.

"They were cultivated people. She liked to go to museums, to lectures, and concerts and things. She wasn't a very talkative kind of person, but pleasant enough. He was rather friendly, too, at first. He said he was anxious for Janet to get to know people and not be a stranger. Pauly took her around and introduced her to a number of her friends. But it didn't work out the way we thought it would."

"How so?" The man seemed to be avoiding something, Sam thought. He seemed not to want to talk frankly about the Porters.

"Well, you know how it is," Steve said lamely. "People don't always turn out to be the way you thought they'd be. We saw less and less of each other after the first few weeks."

Sam decided that he'd better take the bull by the horns. "I don't want to press you, Steve, but it's important to me to learn as much as I can about Kevin and Janet. This is a murder case, you know. Being polite and discreet and avoiding 'gossip' about them won't help at all."

Steve was thoughtful. "I hate to throw stones at people. You understand, don't you? The truth is that after the first few weeks Kevin got to be rather distasteful to me. It got to be uncomfortable to visit with him and Janet. Embarrassing, too."

"Why?" Sam kept pressing him.

"Well, his way with Janet, mainly. He'd talk down to her, right in front of us, something awful. He'd sneer at things she'd say, or ignore her as though she were a piece of furniture. Sometimes he'd order her around right in front of us. He was plain cruel."

"Didn't she assert herself—talk back to him?"

"No. She just seemed to shrivel up when he'd do that. I felt sorry for her and annoyed with him, but I knew better than to butt in. Pauly disliked it, too, even more than I did."

"Do you think that she was physically afraid of him?" Sam asked.

"No." Steve was positive. "I don't think that. He was not the kind of man who'd hit a woman, I think. No. His way was different; more subtle. He'd lacerate her with a snide remark or treat her as if she was some kind of moron or flunky. That kind of thing."

"And she never fought back?"

"Never, as far as I know. We used to wonder how she held it all in. Pauly said that she'd knock my head off if I ever treated her like that. Pauly said that if I did that to her she'd be in tears, or shoot me—one or the other."

"So you think she had reason to fear—maybe even hate—him?"

"She sure did," Steve said stolidly.

"Enough to justify killing him?" Sam asked carefully.

"Now that's something else again. I didn't say that."

"But she had reason to hate him?" Sam pursued.

"Yes. I'd say she had reason to hate him."

All the while that Sam was conversing with her husband, Paula Ventriss had sat quietly listening. She had not made any remark at all. Sam turned to her, now. "Mrs. Ventriss, you must have seen more of Janet than your husband did, I imagine."

"Yes. We did see quite a bit of each other at first," she agreed.

"What did you think of her, personally?"

"She was a sweet thing. She really was, and awfully anxious to be nice and to make friends. She just didn't know how, poor thing."

"What do you mean by 'didn't know how'?"

"She was rather shy. Sometimes she seemed pretty unworldly, for a person as intelligent as that. She was no good at all at chit-chat—you know, woman-talk. She'd just sit and listen and say very little. Being a good listener is fine, but being absolutely uncommunicative is not. You had to pull the words out of her to get her to say anything. And she was so serious all the time. She seemed to carry the weight of the world on her shoulders."

"Was she at home much?"

"Not after the first few weeks after they moved in. She'd go somewhere, usually, every day. She told me that she worked downtown at the law school, in the library."

"Was she ill, or anything like that, very often?" Sam asked.

"No. Not that I know of."

Sam sat back and sipped his drink. "Did you think that Kevin was nasty to her, too?"

Paula Ventriss nodded. "My, yes! At least after a little while."

"Did she ever confide in you about how she and Kevin got along?"

She shook her head. "No. She never said a word about that. We never got to be that close friends."

"Did you ever see him abuse her?"

"It depends on what you mean by 'abuse.' I never saw him strike her, if that's what you mean. I did see him act nasty with her."

"Can you give me an example?"

"More than one," she said. "For instance, there was the time when we were having a snack at their house after going to see a play downtown one night. Janet served some cheese and crackers and tea or coffee—instant coffee or tea, you know. Well, Kevin got all upset because she was making instant tea or coffee. He wanted *brewed* coffee. He got all worked up about it and ranted and raved about the incompetence of modern women. He told her that it was little enough that he expected of her but, 'by Jove'—believe it or not, he said 'by Jove' —he expected her to do her job properly.

"Then he didn't like the cheese she had served," she went on, "and got unpleasant about that, too. He was in a temper about nothing. Then he said something that I didn't quite understand, about some law-case notes that she had done for him. They were inaccurate, he said, and that it was pretty sad if he couldn't rely on her research assistance. He said something about her misleading him on some legal quotation so that he was embarrassed before his students. He was polite and sarcastic and ice-cold—ugly in a very civilized way. He worked himself into a positive cold rage about it. All this time she just stood there looking at him. She was very pale and her face was rigid. Then he said—and I'll never forget it—'No wonder your father never finished his book with that kind of research assistance. You must have been as much help to him as you are to me.' Steve and I excused ourselves, and left. It was the cruelest, unkindest thing I ever saw. The poor thing. . . ."

After a while, Sam thanked them and asked them to call a cab for him. The picture was becoming clear now, about Janet, her father, and her husband. She had exchanged one harsh taskmaster for another when her father had died. Her husband, from whom she had hoped to get love and kindness, had reverted to his natural habits and was her cold, domineering, demanding father all over again.

When he got back to his hotel room at the Sheraton, Sam decided to spend a quiet evening alone. It had been a busy day and he was tired. He had friends in Cleveland and might have phoned them, but he decided not to do so. He called home for his usual "check-in." All was well there.

He sat in a comfortable arm chair after turning on the FM radio, and looked out at the lights of the city. The story about Kevin Porter in Shaker Heights stuck in his mind. People like that seemed to think that they were a special elite—*Ubermenschen*, the Germans called them, supermen. He grimaced. It was like the ugliness of the Nazi philosophy. He remembered especially the brutal SS men. There always had been and probably always would be such men, he reflected. With or without uniforms or swastikas or other symbols, such men believed that others existed only to serve them. Had Kevin Porter been that kind of a man, or had John Duffield?

Once, some years ago, he had defended a man who was accused of having beaten up another man and who was charged with assault and battery. The victim had been one of a small group of neo-Nazis, complete with jackboots, riding breeches, heavy-buckled belt, swastika armband, and Storm Trooper cap. Someone in the group had pushed his client—a man named Steinfeld—at an outdoor rally and Steinfeld had struck back. In fact, Steinfeld had walloped the would-be Storm Trooper thoroughly. He had been about to take on another neo-Nazi when the police had arrived and stopped the brawl. Sam had gotten Larry Steinfeld acquitted on the basis of provocation and self-defense. Larry was of the Jewish faith, had been a veteran of World War II, and had served in combat in Europe. He had told Sam just what he thought of Nazi supermen. His hatred of the Nazis, and of anything and everything German, was almost a monomania in itself. To Larry Steinfeld the sight of anything German was distasteful, and the very suggestion of anything Nazi stirred him to a fighting fury.

It was curious and sad, thought Sam, how one irrationality

produced another. Nazism, born of hate, gave birth to hate and was destroyed by hate. It was a vicious circle, hate spawning hate, endlessly; evil spawning evil, endlessly. John Duffield in his way had done an evil thing, and so had Kevin Porter—to Janet. It was far from the utter bestiality of Nazism, of course, but it was an evil thing, too, on a small scale. And see what it had produced: homicide, by a woman who was basically decent and good. The things that human beings do to each other in their selfishness and foolishness! Sam thought back to his own encounter with the utter evil of Nazism years ago, in Buchenwald, Germany. He had seen much of war and bestiality in his time, but Sam never would forget Buchenwald.

Buchenwald Concentration Camp was a big, sprawling collection of long, one-story huts, set in an open compound on the top and slope of a ridge. Double lines of tall, barbed-wire fences surrounded it. All about were thick groves of pine forest. From a little distance it suggested, to an American, a big civilian conservation camp such as were to be seen back in the States. It was a pretty, forested place that resembled a summer-resort area. Not far away was the city of Weimar, clean and handsome in its Mitteleuropa *way. This was a German university town, and had been the peaceful setting of the short-lived Weimar Republic Government, for a while, between World Wars I and II.*

The war was nearly over in early spring of 1945, when Sam's outfit came to Weimar. Resistance by the German army had dwindled to a few scattered skirmishes by die-hard Nazis. The Americans—battle-hardened, tough as nails, and supremely self-confident—brushed aside the resisting German groups almost contemptuously. Ironically, the American G.I.s, whom the Nazis had said would be decadent weaklings, had become the very epitome of the skilled and irresistible fighting men that the Germans had thought they themselves were.

Sam watched the lines of hard-bitten, leathery infantrymen move into and around Weimar. In the city the Germans stared dully at the conquerors. Batches of bedraggled German soldiers,

herded by pairs of G.I.s or sometimes by a lone American in-
fantryman, moved toward the west bound for prisoner-of-war
camps. Bewildered slave laborers from all over Europe, suddenly freed by the onrushing Yanks, wandered aimlessly looking for the Allied food-and-shelter depots. From the freed
"volunteer" workers the Americans heard of Buchenwald,
nearby. A rifle company was sent to take it, and Sam went along.

With long-practiced sureness, the olive-drab lines of rifle-
men swept through the woods, enveloped the silent camp, cut
through the barbed-wire fences, and filtered down the alleys
between the long rows of huts. Sam accompanied one rifle
squad into the compound. Pistol in hand, he looked for SS men.
There were none to be seen. From a watchtower in one corner
of the compound a Spandau machine gun burst into startling
sound. Then there were the familiar ripping noises of German
burp guns—"br-r-r-rp-p." Some of the SS men had delayed too
long in the camp. Almost in seconds the deeper "bub-bub-bub"
of American automatic rifles drowned out the sounds of the
German Schmeizers. Sam could hear the thudding of M-1 rifles
and the chatter of tommyguns. He saw a coal-scuttle-helmeted
figure topple lifelessly from the watchtower. The sounds disappeared down the slope into the thick woods and open fields
below as the Yanks pursued the fleeing defenders of Buchenwald. Then all was quiet. The camp had been taken.

Sam walked to the closed double doors of one long hut.
Three G.I.'s, rifles at the ready, moved behind him cautiously.
He lifted his foot and kicked hard at the door with his heel.
The door flew back, open. Inside all was darkness and silence.
A sickening odor poured out of the interior.

Sam stepped up the one step at the door and darted inside,
pistol pointed before him. Then he stopped and peered into
the half-darkness. There was a narrow center aisle that ran the
length of the hut. On both sides, floor to ceiling, were rows of
shelves, hardly two feet above each other, made of raw planks.
They stretched back from the center aisle to the walls on right
and left. Raw stench permeated everything. In the dim, murky

interior things moved in crowded, huddled masses on each shelf. Eyes stared dully at him from the layers of shelves in the darkness.

Then realization burst on him. These were men—hundreds of them—crammed into the shelves in ghastly masses. All were dressed in thin, blue-and-white-striped, pajama-like uniforms. All were puny, emaciated, almost skeleton-thin. Their faces and heads were big and bony above their shrivelled bodies. Some of the figures on the shelves were rigid with the unmistakable stillness of death. Horror and nausea swept in waves over Sam. He turned to the G.I.s. "Get these people out of here!" he commanded. "Get them out into the compound. See if we have some rations around. They're starving to death." Then he walked back, out of the charnel house, stiff-legged. He was afraid that he was going to vomit.

Down the slope, near a corner of the big compound, there was a brick building with a tall chimney. Sam walked toward that building. He passed a pile of human corpses—stacked like cordwood—all skin and bones. The huts were being opened by grim-faced soldiers as he walked by. Other Americans were seeing, in the huts, what Sam had seen. Pajama-clad, scarecrow-like figures were pouring out into the lanes between the huts. Here and there were helmeted Americans, their rifles and carbines slung over their shoulders, their faces ghastly with shock and revulsion and fury. He heard one sergeant spit out an order to several soldiers: "You, you and you . . . come with me. . . . We're going to take a walk in the woods. Maybe we'll find some Nay-zighs. They can't have got very far." The G.I.s trotted off after the non-com. One soldier was putting a fresh clip into his carbine. There was a look of death in his eyes. God help any Nazi they find, Sam thought.

The brick building was open and he looked inside. It contained big ovens, like bread-bakery ovens, with doors wide enough to admit a human body and metal stretcher tables. "Crematorium," he heard one prisoner say. Outside it, there was a wooden structure like a heavy soccer-field goal post. At intervals on the thick crossbar were set big hooks—like meat hooks. His mind reeled at what this probably had been used for. Off in the woods he heard occasional rifle shots—American, from the sound of them.

There was a well-kept building nearby which looked like an administration center and Sam went to it. Sure enough, a sign outside it read Hauptquartier. He was glad that he could read German. Inside he saw desks, filing cabinets, and the usual drab but precise fittings of a military administration office. All were in good order, though a few papers were scattered about. He went from room to room finding them all much alike. The administrators had left in haste, but it was clear that this had been an orderly, efficiently run installation. Very efficient, the Germans, at everything they do—including assembly-line murder, Sam thought. There was a picture of Hitler on one wall and above it, the garish Nazi banner—a red, white, and black flag with the hooked cross in the center. He gazed at it for a moment, loathing and hate welling up hotly in his chest. His pistol, still held in his right hand, felt heavy.

A door creaked in the next room. Sam was suddenly alert, listening. He moved quietly to the door and called out, "Who's there? Anyone inside there?" No answer. He opened the door carefully with his left hand, his body to one side pressed against the wall. Slowly and carefully he moved his head and peered into the room. He could see desks and chairs and nobody there. He walked into the room, pistol held near his waist, its muzzle pointed forward.

As he stepped forward, he thought he saw a flicker of movement to his left. Had he imagined it, or had the closet door there moved? He faced the door of the closet. It was partly ajar.

Sam spoke clearly and loudly: "Come out of there if you're in that closet. Komm' 'raus. 'Raus. Hände hoch! Come out with your hands up!"

Like an explosion the door burst open. A man's figure, all in black, appeared in the doorway. There was no mistaking the uniform and silver, double-lightning marks on the collar—an SS officer. He had a pistol pointing at Sam.

The two reports sounded like one shot—startlingly loud in the empty room. There was a thud in the wall behind Sam's shoulder where the Luger bullet struck. Then the SS man was leaning stiffly forward and falling, almost slowly, out of the closet. The gun was still in his hand.

Sam squeezed the trigger again to make sure. The black figure lurched under the impact of the .45 slug and collapsed in a heap on the floor in front of the closet. It lay still. The Luger was on the floor just beyond the doorsill.

Sam walked forward cautiously and kicked the Luger to one side. The Nazi looked very dead, his face flat on the floor on one side as though he were asleep with his eyes open.

Sam picked up the Luger with his left hand. He would keep this one. It would hang on the wall of his den when he got home. Just this one. He pushed the SS captain with his toe. Inert. The Nazi was dead.

It was a queer feeling, Sam thought; not like the fierce excitement of combat. He felt numb and drained. This was very different from battle. He was glad of this one—not happy, but satisfied, somehow. He had killed a man, and the killing somehow had a rightness about it.

Sam awoke suddenly. He was in his hotel room and had dozed off. The FM radio was playing softly a familiar Latin ballad he liked: *Acércate Mas*—"Come Closer To Me." It was getting late and tomorrow would be another busy day. But the dream was still fresh in his mind.

Did Janet Porter feel something—or nothing—when she killed Kevin? he wondered. Did she hate him? Did she think that what she had done was just, was right? Had Kevin been evil?

He started to get ready for bed. There are many degrees of evil, he thought, and degrees of good. Nothing is all black and nothing is all white. Almost everything is gray. Even that dead SS captain may have been sweet and good to his wife and children. To them he may have been goodness incarnate. To me, he was evil incarnate. What had Kevin Porter been to Janet? He was a good man in many ways. Did she see only the evil—so that she killed him?

CHAPTER

From Cleveland to Chicago's O'Hare field was less than an hour by jet. It was a breakfast flight with barely enough time to finish the meal before the plane began to descend for the landing. Sam had ticketed his baggage through on the later flight he was to take to San Francisco. There was ample time to keep his appointment at Northwestern University Law School. He caught a taxicab and directed the driver to 357 East Chicago Avenue.

It was still early when the cab let him out in front of the cloistered-looking, collegiate, Gothic-style Law School building. Professor Whiting was not in yet, though he was expected at any moment. Sam strolled around the building to pass the time. He came to a large black column set prominently in one of the hallways. It was about three feet thick at the base, tapering upward over six feet to a rounded top. Cuneiform letters were carved densely all over its surface, and at the top, on one face, there was a bas-relief scene. It showed a standing figure in front of a figure seated on a throne, both men with long, curly beards and both dressed in robes of the ancient Near East. The scene, Sam knew, depicted King Hammurabi of Babylonia receiving the laws from the sun god Shamash.

This was the copy of the famous black-diorite stele of the Code of Hammurabi, the most ancient, complete written code of laws known to history. Janet Porter had mentioned seeing it when she had accompanied her father here. It had left an impression on her mind. The mystery of ages of the past seemed to hover over the brooding monument.

Sam could not read the cuneiform writing, but he recalled

some of its ancient lines from memorizing translations of it. One law, particularly, came to his mind:

> If anyone has taken a wife and sickness has seized her, and if his face is set toward taking another wife, he may take (her), but his wife whom the sickness has seized, he may not repudiate her; she shall live in the house he has built, and as long as she lives he shall support her.
>
> If that woman does not desire to live in the house of her husband, he shall give her the marriage portion she brought from her father's house, and she shall go.

That was a wise and humane law, Sam thought. The laws of today were hardly better, and often worse. How much better it would have been for Janet when she did "not desire to live in the house of her husband," if she had decided to take "the marriage portion she brought from her father's house, and . . . go."

Professor Whiting was all apologies when he finally came to his office half an hour late for his appointment. Traffic, he explained, as he shook hands vigorously with Sam. He lived near the Northwestern University campus, north of the city in Evanston. He was a big, bald-headed man with heavy, fleshy jowls and rather thick lips.

Sam had been concerned about the delay. He had planned to stay only a half-hour or so altogether lest he miss his flight at O'Hare. He got right down to the business that had brought him here. "I understand," he said, "that you are one of the two or three top experts on constitutional law, and know pretty much everyone worth mentioning who works in that field or has contributed to it. I will much appreciate your help in the problem I have."

"You flatter me," Whiting said modestly. "I do know most of the people who are important in the field, however."

"Specifically," Sam asked, "are you, or were you, acquainted with these people and their work in constitutional law—John Duffield, late of Harvard; Kevin Porter, late of the University of California at Berkeley; and Janet Porter, wife of Kevin Porter?"

Whiting nodded vigorously, his jowls shaking. "'Yes' to all three, but not equally so. John Duffield and I did some work together in the past. We collaborated on an article for the *Iowa Law Review* once. I knew him fairly well. Kevin Porter is a promising scholar in the field. I've met him two or three times and expect that he'll be one of the best quite soon now. His work is sound and promising. As to Mrs. Porter, I only met her once, years ago, when she was working with her father. She was a good assistant to him, I recall, knowledgeable in the subject but not an authority in her own right then. So far as I know, she hasn't published anything nor is she a member of any law faculty. I know that she married Professor Porter after her father died."

"Can you tell me about John Duffield and his main field of interest?"

"Yes." Whiting beamed with self-assurance. "He was primarily an analytical legal historian, I'd say. The Supreme Court and its justices were his main interests."

"Which justices particularly, do you think?"

"No doubt whatsoever about that. Holmes was his abiding interest. Almost everything John did either began with Holmes, ended with him, or revolved about him. John was bemused with Holmes, in my opinion. Too much so, I thought. Why, he even tried to look like him."

"What do you mean 'tried to look like him'?" Sam was alertly interested.

Whiting smiled. "He actually tried to emulate him in clothing and appearance. A bit much, I'd say, dressing in that Victorian manner. He once tried to get his moustache to grow wide, like Holmes', but it didn't work and he had to settle for a broad, white brush but without the long, drooping ends. That was carrying admiration too far, I'd say."

"Did he always dress like Holmes?"

"Not always, but most of the time, apparently, from what I saw of him and what others remarked about him."

"And what about Professor Kevin Porter? What was his main field?"

"Another legal historian," Whiting said, "and interested mainly in the Supreme Court's influence on the development of corporation law. Curiously, he, too, is much interested in Holmes and in Holmes' opinions on corporate and business law. He views Holmes as the great liberal of constitutional interpretation of corporate and commercial law."

"Would you say that he was an *aficionado* of Holmes, as Duffield seemed to be?"

Whiting shook his head. "Not quite the same. Duffield was altogether wrapped up in Oliver Wendell Holmes, Junior—almost totally so. Porter is keenly interested in him, but not to the extent that John was."

"In your own opinion, do you place as much emphasis on Holmes as they?"

"No. I believe that Marshall was the one who set the model, of course. Taney impresses me too. So do Brandeis and Cardozo. I think that Warren ultimately will be recognized as one of the major figures of the court."

"And do you think that Holmes was the great liberal that Porter thought him to be—or the conservative that Duffield did?"

"Neither," Whiting equivocated. "For his time he was moderately liberal. By the wisdom of hindsight he was a moderate rather than a liberal."

"A 'moderate,' you say." Sam showed a flash of annoyance. "Is that because Holmes was so successful at being pictured as a liberal? Do you recall the Dunne case in 1932?"

Whiting looked surprised. "Yes, a question of multiple counts in a single indictment, and conviction if any one count was sustained by the proof."

"Not exactly," Sam disagreed. "I would call it trying a man twice for the same crime. Dunne was charged with keeping liquor for sale, possessing liquor unlawfully, and selling it. He was convicted of keeping liquor for sale, but not of unlawful possession nor of sale. Holmes' opinion upheld that incredible verdict. He said that 'Consistency in the verdict is not necessary.' Apparently he never heard of the rule of 'included offenses.' Dunne was convicted of 'keeping liquor for sale' but not of 'possessing' it. That is nonsense. How can anyone keep something for sale without possessing it?"

Whiting looked confused. "You have a point there."

"If Holmes had had his way," Sam continued, "we would have junked the Bill of Rights, double jeopardy would be legal, and we might be living in a police state, today. Was that wise, sound law, or was it time-serving compliance with the mode of 1932?"

"It's very questionable." Whiting flushed with uncertainty.

Sam pressed his argument. "And didn't this bold 'dissenter' go along with the majority opinion ten times as often as he dissented? Was this the great liberal?"

Whiting looked at him with evident respect. "You are quite a constitutional lawyer, Mr. Benedict, as well as a famous trial lawyer."

"This was the paragon who inspired John Duffield and Kevin Porter," Sam concluded angrily. "This was the man they set up as the model for all men."

Before taking a taxicab back to the airport, Sam stopped for a few minutes in the law-school library. He took down a large Bible that had a lengthy concordance, and a copy of the works of Hippocrates, the ancient Greek physician-philosopher. Then, settling hurriedly at a table with the books spread open before him, Sam made some notes:

Leviticus (18:19) speaks of woman's menstrual period as her time of "uncleanness."

Leviticus (20:18) also says that it is a kind of "sickness."

Ezekiel (18:6) warned that men should not "come near to a menstruous woman."

Jeremiah's *Lamentations* (1:17) spoke of the desolate, chaotic melancholy of his era as very like "a menstruous woman."

Hippocrates (*Oeuvres Complètes*, trans. into French by E. Littre, V, pp. 553, 702; and VII, pp. 275, 505) spoke of mental disturbances in women just before the menstrual period.

Sam had time to note a few more points, relating to mental disease—(he was thinking of premenstrual tension)—that might apply to Janet Porter:

Justice Somerville, in the Alabama case of *Parsons vs. State,* back in 1886, recognized:

"It will not do for the courts to dogmatically deny the possible existence of (such) a disease, or its pathological and physical effects, because this is a matter of evidence, not of law, or judicial cognizance. Its existence and effect on the mind and conduct of the patient is a question of fact to be proved, just as much as the possible existence of cholera or yellow fever formerly was before these diseases became the subject of common knowledge. . . . The courts could with just as much propriety, years ago, have denied the existence of the Copernican system of the universe, or the efficacy of steam and electricity as a motive power. These are scientific facts, first discovered by experts before becoming matters of common knowledge. So, in like manner, must be every unknown scientific fact in whatever profession or department of knowledge."

The three-hour flight back to California was a fine opportunity to rest and relax, and after lunch Sam took a nap. He knew that the time change on the flight west would add two hours to the length of the day for him.

When he arrived at his office, Trudy greeted him with relief and joy. Things had piled up, as they always did when he was away for a few days. The stacks of mail and messages on his desk were a foot high. After calling home, he spent the first two hours turning out a barrage of dictation and quick telephone calls. Hank came in as soon as Sam had finished with the first rush of catching up, and Sam sat him down and told him in outline what he had learned during his trip.

"You can begin to see," Sam concluded, "the direction of the defense of Janet Porter. It has two main aspects. One, the strong possibility of physical proof of a condition of premenstrual tension, severe enough to cause temporary insanity and the explosion of a psychosis which possibly killed her husband. That will depend on the analysis of the findings of Dr. Rubenfeld, plus the records that I got in New York and Cleveland. The second aspect is the strong possibility of a psychotic condition caused by her father and her husband successively and cumulatively. That, I believe, is somehow closely connected with their fascination by Oliver Wendell Holmes, Jr. Neither theory is ideal, of course, but that's all we have."

"Pretty wild, I'd say, in both cases." Hank was very doubtful. "Hard to prove, if not impossible. And on top of everything, you'd have to make new law with your theory of causation by premenstrual tension."

"It's a long way from ideal," Sam conceded, "but that is about our only hope."

"It will take a hell of a lot of proving. In fact, both approaches seem to be to be impossible to prove. They both are so theoretical and radical that they scare me."

"Got any better ideas?"

"No," Hank conceded.

"Then, we'll go along that way, until something better pops up. I don't think that anything will pop up. Meanwhile, find out the prospects for getting a trial date that will suit my theories. It should be right at the peak of her premenstrual-tension cycle. I'll get the possible dates in her cycle from Rubenfeld, in a series, a month apart. We want her to be in a state of extreme tension at that time, cruel as it sounds to say that."

"I'll start getting the dope on the calendar and the possible available dates in the next few weeks."

"Do that," Sam said, "but don't settle on any date until I've talked with Rubenfeld. I also want to talk to Janet again first."

Hank nodded. "Okay."

"And what's new on the Larkbey case since I've been away?" Sam asked.

"Nothing, really. Belle has been calling and calling. She wants the padlock order lifted."

"I know. I'll tell you what I want you to do," Sam said slowly. "Set up a conference, for tomorrow if possible, with the fathers of the three boys. Hold it here at the office or at some neutral meeting point if necessary. That case has to be brought to a head promptly."

"Okay."

"Do you have a memo on the false-I.D.-card statute?" Sam asked.

"Yes. It's right on your desk." He pointed to it.

"All right. I'll look at it in a while. Right now, please call Rubenfeld and tell him that I want to see him at about eight this evening. Ask him to meet me at Alexis' Restaurant on California Street and to bring his report on Janet Porter, and also Carruthers' report if he has it already. I'd like some French food and I like the gypsy music there. Have Trudy make a reservation for us, please."

"Okay."

Sam got up to go. "I'm going to talk to Janet at the Hall of Justice. We're going to get things moving pretty fast now."

Janet Porter greeted him unemotionally, as though he were a tradesman calling to discuss a bill. She seemed none the worse for her ordeal with the psychiatrists during the last few days.

"I've been traveling in the East, as you know," Sam began. "I've been visiting with old friends and associates of yours in Great Neck, New York City, Cleveland, and Shaker Heights. Also with an old friend of your father's—Professor Whiting, in Chicago." He mentioned the names of some of the other people he had seen.

She showed no particular interest in any of them except her neighbors of Shaker Heights. "How are Paula and Steve?"

"Well," he reported. "They send their regards to you. But I'm here for only a few minutes. There are a number of things that I want to ask you. They are quite personal questions, but I must ask them. Do you mind?"

"After the questions I've been asked by the doctors lately, I doubt that anything would shock me."

He smiled. "All right. First, you've told me that your relationship with your father was cool and almost secretarial in nature. Is that so?"

She nodded.

"Did you ever quarrel with him in any serious way?"

"No one ever quarreled with him," she said evenly. "You either did as he said or you got away from him, if you could."

"Did you ever move away from his home?"

"Not until after he died. How could I? Where would I go?"

"Did he ever abuse you physically?"

"No. Never."

"Mentally?"

"Yes. Often."

"How?"

"He always talked to me as though I were a servant."

"Did you ever remonstrate with him about that?"

She shook her head. "No."

"Why not?"

"It would have been a waste of effort," she answered, her voice controlled and precise.

"Did you like your father?"

"No."

"Did you hate him?"

"No."

"What was your feeling toward him?"

Her lips tightened. "No feeling. I just wanted him to let me be by myself."

"But you worked with him, didn't you?"

"For him, not with him."

Sam tried another tack. "You worked on Supreme Court history."

She nodded.

"In terms of the justices and their opinions and writings?"

Her face was expressionless. "Yes."

"Such men as Marshall and Butler and Cardozo?"

"Yes."

"And Holmes?" He waited expectantly. She did not answer. He repeated, "And Holmes?"

No answer, again. Her face seemed frozen, and the pupils of her eyes seemed to be contracting visibly.

He almost shouted, "And Holmes?"

She stiffened, and turned her face away.

"All right," he said. It was consistent with his theory, he thought. This was the critical, trigger word or idea with Janet Porter. The phobia was there, all right. "Let's talk about something else. Your relationship with Kevin was a good one, was it not, when you first were married?"

"Oh, yes; when we first were married." She relaxed, and turned to face him again.

"You had a normal, healthy relationship with him when you got married."

"Yes."

"Including sex?"

She hesitated momentarily, and then answered. "Yes."

"But that happy relationship did not last long, did it?"

She looked at him silently for a few seconds before answering. "No."

"In fact, within a few weeks after your marriage it had ceased to be what you had hoped for?"

"Yes."

"It became cool and distant, didn't it?"

"Yes."

"Why?"

"I don't know. He just changed."

"Changed? How?"

"He became uninterested in me. He became busy with his work."

"Didn't you help him with his work?"

"Yes."

"As you have helped your father?"

"Yes."

"Did he appreciate and praise your work?"

"No."

"Not ever?"

"Never."

"Did he abuse you physically?"

"No."

"Mentally?"

"Yes."

"As your father had done?"

"Yes."

"He treated you like a secretary?"

"Yes."

"Weren't there intervals of husband-and-wife relationship? Didn't you sleep together?"

"Yes, at first."

"Didn't that continue? You were married for years."

"Yes, but less and less often as time went by."

"You mean that he gradually stopped approaching you?"

"Yes."

"Completely?"

"No. Now and then he would need sex, and then he'd show interest in me briefly. It was soon over and forgotten by him for another interval of time. He 'used' me for that, too."

"Didn't you talk to him about that?"

"No."

"Why not?"

"He didn't want to discuss it."

"And he treated you like a secretary?" Sam repeated.

"Yes."

"And you helped him with his work on constitutional history?"

"Yes."

"And the Supreme Court?"

"Yes."

"And the justices?"

"Yes."

"Like Taney and Hughes and Brandeis?"

"Yes."

"And Holmes?"

Silence. She was staring at him. Her eyes were contracting again.

"And Holmes?" he repeated.

No answer, and her head turned away again. In the midst of pity for her Sam felt a surge of triumph. He was right. By God, he was right about this.

"One more question," he said, "and I'll go. The doctors tell me that you suffer from premenstrual tension. Is that so?"

She relaxed again. "Yes."

"Is it very troublesome to you?"

"Yes, rather."

"Is it regular and severe?"

"Yes."

"Does it affect your nerves or emotions?"

"Yes."

"How?"

"Nervousness, jitteriness, tension."

"Does it ever cause you to faint or black out?"

"No."

"Never?"

"Never," she repeated.

"Never—as far as you can recall, that is, isn't it?"

"Not as far as I know. I surely would know, would I not?"

"Would you?" Sam asked, needing no answer. "Would you?"

Alexis', on California Street on Nob Hill, was the restaurant where Irwin Rubenfeld was to meet Sam. Irwin was not there yet when Sam arrived, so Sam waited in the cocktail lounge sipping a scotch-and-water and listening to the melancholy Gypsy music. He particularly liked the Russian Gypsy songs that predated World War I—echoes of a world that was gone forever. Balalaikas, gypsy singers, accordians, good scotch, and a pleasant atmosphere—it was schmaltz, but he liked it.

Irwin came in, and they went to their table for dinner. Both of them enjoyed the continental French food and Alexis' excellent wine list. Over a bottle of fine Graves wine they talked about Janet Porter.

"Tell me," Sam asked, "in summary, what you and Carruthers have found in your study of Janet Porter."

"Well, now." The psychiatrist was cautious. "You will bear in mind that this was a hasty study. Anything that we say can only be tentative, at best."

Sam nodded. "I understand that."

"She is a highly intelligent woman, with an IQ in the order of 135 to 140. Not genius, but quite intelligent."

"Yes."

"She seems to be normal physically. Nothing specially worth noting in that respect."

"What of the premenstrual tension?"

"That is present, of course. But remember, that is not a unique phenomenon. Many women will show that on investigation. It is not truly abnormal."

"Never?"

Rubenfeld shook his head thoughtfully. "No. I didn't say that. I mean that unless it is quite severe we would classify premenstrual tension in the area of normal variations, for statistical purposes."

Sam leaned forward. "Stop quibbling with me, please. Tell me whether or not your findings indicate severe premenstrual tension."

The psychiatrist answered slowly. "Well, yes. But remember that it would require months of study to reach firm conclusions about that."

Sam pressed him. "Give me whatever answer you can give me. Is her premenstrual tension severe enough to indicate a firm possibility, or probability, of temporary confusion to a psychotic degree? Of lack of the mental capacity to form the *intent* to kill her husband at the time?"

Rubenfeld shrugged. "A firm possibility—yes. A probability —too soon to tell."

"Would you say a reasonable probability?"

"A reasonable probability—yes."

Sam sat back. "Good enough, for my purposes. Can you demonstrate the physical bases of that finding? I mean blood-sugar variations, spontaneous hypoglycemia, and that sort of thing—with concrete figures or statistics as evidence?"

"Yes, to some extent, but not nearly enough to withstand attack."

"You'll have one month more for tests; one more menstrual cycle, before trial. That will have to suffice."

"I'll do the best I can." Rubenfeld shrugged his shoulders again. "If that's what you must have. But why can't you delay and give me more time?"

Sam was positive. "Because of the reasons I've already mentioned. Also, I have some valuable concrete evidence of her prior history from New York University and from Cleveland Clinic." He gave Irwin the copies of the N.Y.U. employment absences record and the Cleveland Clinic report, and told the psychiatrist of his talks with Janet's old friends and neighbors. It took a while to give him all the information. Rubenfeld made notes as Sam went on with his narrative. "This should be of substantial help to you," Sam concluded.

"Invaluable." Rubenfeld was delighted. "Very, very helpful, particularly these dates and medical findings."

"You can tie them into your studies, can't you?"

"Oh yes. It will take a bit of computing, but they undoubtedly will be of great help."

"You can use them in stating the bases of your conclusions, I'm sure."

"Yes, I can."

"What kind of mental effects did you find?"

"Some indications of schizophrenia."

"Positive?" Sam asked quizzically.

"Not positive. Just indications. Quite some, however."

Sam pressed his questions. "Good enough to sustain defense of lack of mental capacity to form the intent?"

Hesitantly, his friend replied. "In terms of a psychiatrist's definition—yes. In terms of a court's definition—I don't know."

"All right. Leave the legal definition to me." Sam smiled. "All I ask of you is the psychiatrist's definition. Give me a written report on the premenstrual-tension aspect, please, as soon as you can."

"You'll have my interim report in a few days."

"Good. So much for premenstrual tension. The history of Janet in relation to her father and to her husband seems to me to be another, separate basis for a possible finding of emotional crisis. Did you find that to be so?" Sam asked.

"Yes." Rubenfeld seemed more positive in his tone than when they had been discussing the premenstrual-tension theory.

"You sound more positive, about this."

"Yes, I am." Rubenfeld agreed. "Even without the information that you've just given me, I had concluded that the emotional stress she suffered was enough to cause an explosion. With that additional data, I have little doubt of it."

"This is the Freudian, rather than the biochemical approach," Sam commented. "Do you prefer that?"

"Quite the contrary. I prefer concrete, objective, physical data, of course. But the science of psychiatry still lacks a sizable enough body of such data. Therefore, we do the best we can, in terms of what you call the Freudian or emotional approach."

"And what did you find in that aspect of your study?" Sam asked.

"Mrs. Porter has suffered severe emotional stresses, amounting to emotional trauma, repeatedly over a long period of time, since her early childhood. The result was not hard to foresee. Indeed, it is almost surprising that she did not end up in a mental institution long before now."

"You mean that she definitely is insane?"

"There you go again, Sam," Rubenfeld said, showing a trace of exasperation. "You lawyers simply will not talk the right language in psychiatric matters. No, she is not 'insane,' in your sense of the word. She is suffering from no physical disease of the brain. But she is emotionally disturbed. Disturbed, I said."

"What does that mean?" Sam was a bit exasperated too.

"It means that she needs help. That's what it means."

"What kind of help?"

"Medical help. Psychiatric therapy."

"You're losing me."

Rubenfeld explained stolidly. "She is perfectly capable of functioning in life. But she is not a well woman. There are suggestions of schizophrenia."

"Damn it." Sam was impatient. "I know that. The question is, is she insane now—in the legal sense of the word?"

"Under the M'Naghten Rule?"

"Yes. Under the M'Naghten Rule."

The psychiatrist shook his head. "The answer is 'No,' under that rule."

"And under the Durham Rule?"

"Under the Durham Rule the answer is 'Yes.' . . ."

"That's great, just great." Disgust was in Sam's every word. "Let's put it another way. Is she fit to stand trial, now, today?"

"Yes, under the M'Naghten Rule."

"Was she 'disturbed,' as you say, when she killed her husband?"

"Almost certainly."

"Could she become irrational—dangerous—again, in the future?"

"Quite possibly," Rubenfeld acknowledged.

"What do you think of my theory that Oliver Wendell Holmes, Jr.—his name or image—is the trigger term or concept that set her off, or might do so again?"

Rubenfeld frowned. "Possible. But how can you prove anything as conjectural as that?"

"That, my friend, is the sixty-four dollar question. I know it. I'm sure of it. But how do I prove it?"

"That," said Rubenfeld, "is your problem, Counselor."

"Have you ever seen any suggestion that the California courts may be ready to accept the doctrine of irresistible impulse?"

"Not in my experience," the psychiatrist replied, "and I've testified as an expert witness in many trials."

"*People versus Hubert*," Sam mused, "119 California 216, 51 Pacific 329. I know the citation by heart. California rejects the theory of irresistible impulse. Damn it!"

Rubenfeld laughed. "You lawyer fellows made the law, not we psychiatrists."

Sam grinned wryly. "Yes. And we're stuck with it."

In the morning Sam took a ride to Berkeley again. There were still a few questions that needed answering about Kevin and Janet Porter's work and other activities at the University of California Law School. Hank had made an appointment for Sam with one of the older professors, a man named Pardee, who turned out to be a red-faced, loud-voiced man.

Professor Pardee clearly nursed an outspoken dislike of Kevin Porter. "Right from the day when he arrived here," Pardee said, "Porter had the idea that he was a specially privileged character." Then Pardee explained angrily, "He obviously was influential in social circles, judging by the frequency of mention of him in newspaper society pages. That meant little to us here on the faculty. But he used to take time off for personal social functions with a free and easy hand. He'd postpone classes and meetings as though the schedule of the school were secondary to his personal affairs. How the dean let him get away with it, I'll never know. And on top of that he was arrogant. He'd talk to the older professors and to some of our most distinguished men as though he were their superior. He had a talent for talking down to people."

"You didn't care for him, I gather," Sam said, with barely a hint of sarcasm in his voice.

Pardee almost shouted his answer. "Not one bit. I was against giving him tenure and told him so to his face. I never was convinced that he was anything more than a pompous plodder."

Sam's eyebrows rose and he sounded surprised. "Why do you say he was a 'plodder'?"

Pardee was positive in his tone. "He never contributed one

single original thought at faculty meetings, and his classes were routine drills in the main cases in his casebook, without range or depth, according to what his students told me. His writings were regurgitations of what other people had written as far as I could see. Only four or five articles—none really important —published in the years he was here, and in second- or third-rate law reviews at that."

"Are you a student of legal history and constitutional history?" Sam asked.

"No. I can't play football either," Pardee snorted, "but I know when the game is well played or badly played."

"What is your field?"

"Bankruptcy and creditors' rights. There's quite a bit of Federal law involved in that, incidentally."

"Did you know Mrs. Porter?"

"Only to say 'hello' to. I saw her here once in a while, working in the library. Charming woman, I'd say, though rather reserved."

"She worked with her husband on his articles, didn't she?"

Pardee nodded. "So I understand. That's not unusual, you know. My wife used to type my material for me, years ago."

"Was Mrs. Porter connected with the university in any formal or academic capacity?"

"Not that I know of."

"Did you see much of her or of Kevin at social functions or gatherings?"

"Nope. Rarely go to them myself," the temperamental professor said disdainfully. "Waste of time."

"Did you ever have a personal run-in with Porter?"

"Yes, I did," he admitted.

"Would you mind telling me about it? It may be illuminating to me, you understand."

Pardee was perfectly willing. "Don't mind a bit. It happened not long after he came to Berkeley, at a faculty meeting. At that time every three faculty men shared the typing services of one secretary. Porter and I and another man shared one girl's time. Alphabetic order, you know—'P' for Porter and 'P' for Pardee. Anyhow, I was working on a book. Porter objected, at the faculty meeting, to what he said was my monopolization of the girl's time. At a *faculty* meeting, mind you. He didn't talk to me about it first, nor even to the dean. That was a damned nasty, impertinent thing to do. Embarrassed me, you know. Then, as though that weren't bad enough, I explained that I was finishing a book, doing a lot of research, and, do you know what he said?"

"No," Sam prompted.

"Porter said with a broad sneer, 'What research?' His meaning was clear. He was implying that my work was based on poor research, or no research at all. I tell you, I was fit to be tied. I nearly exploded. The impertinent, arrogant . . . !" Pardee was scarlet-faced as he spoke.

"Didn't the dean intervene?"

The professor was scornful. "Oh, yes, he tried to make peace and to prevent a scene, but he didn't do anything positive. I said that I would not submit to such impertinence from a junior member of the faculty. The dean suggested that Porter apologive to me, but he never did."

"Was that the end of the incident?"

"No, it wasn't; there was more. Some time later I was the chairman of the curriculum committee for that year. We were discussing some theoretically possible revisions of curriculum, such as changing Constitutional Law from a four-semester-hour course to three-semester hours, increasing Torts from five hours to six hours, and that kind of thing. We had reached no conclusions as to what we would recommend. Next thing I know, I get a call from the dean telling me that Porter had formally accused me of unprofessional conduct—to wit, harrassing him and maliciously trying to cut down his course in Constitutional Law. It was a shocking and damaging kind of accusation, all based on nothing. Someone must have mentioned to him what the committee had talked about.

"Well, the dean didn't take it seriously, especially after getting the facts from the committee members. There was no more said about it, and the charge was quietly forgotten by everybody. But *I* didn't forget it, and probably never will. In all my years as a law professor nothing as nasty as that ever has happened to me. Would *you* just ignore it and forget it?"

Sam threw up his hands defensively. "I don't know."

Pardee had no doubts. "Well, it soured me on Porter, I can tell you. He never retracted that charge and never apologized for it, though the dean asked him to apologize to me. That tells you something about what kind of man Kevin Porter was, doesn't it?"

"Yes. It does," Sam agreed.

Porter was full of triumphant wrath. "Damn right it does."

Before leaving Boalt Hall, Sam stopped at the Dean's Office and asked if the receptionist could tell him which secretary had been assigned to work for Professor Porter this summer. She could. It was a Miss Kay Podrida. Sam went to the administrative office where the faculty secretaries worked and found Miss Podrida—a lovely girl, trim and raven-haired.

"I understand that you assisted Professor Porter as well as some other faculty men in typing up their notes, articles, and other things. Is that correct?" he asked.

The girl nodded. "Yes, it is."

"How long have you worked for Professor Porter?"

"Almost three years now."

"What kind of work?"

"The usual things. Letters and correspondence, course materials, and some research materials for articles he was writing."

"Did you help him on his latest project for the Wallenstein Foundation Grant in constitutional history?"

"Yes. He was very busy with that all this summer."

"What kind of materials was he working on particularly? Do you recall?"

"Yes. Mostly they were brief biographical sketches of various judges and collections of opinions of those judges, with Professor Porter's comments and notes mixed in with them."

Sam looked at her for a moment, and then asked casually, "Do you recall the names of these judges?"

"Oh, there were a lot of them. Professor Porter started at the beginning, by dates. I remember there were James Wilson, John Jay, William Cushing, John Blair, John Rutledge, and so on. I've learned a lot of Supreme Court history this summer." She seemed pleased with her knowledge.

"Where were you on this project, and Professor Porter, by dates in the past week or two?"

"Pretty far along," she said. "We were in the early nineteen-hundreds."

"Do you recall the names of the justices you were working on?"

She frowned with concentration for a moment before answering. "Yes. Joseph McKenna, Oliver Wendell Holmes, and William Rufus Day. That was the last one, Day. I just finished that one a few days ago. What a tragedy! Professor Porter never got to see the last one all typed up."

"Then which one was the last one that he saw?" Sam almost held his breath. He remembered the batch of papers in the Manila folder that he had seen on top of Janet Porter's desk at her home.

"Oliver Wendell Holmes," she answered. "Professor Porter took the typed-up notes home with him the day he was killed. That was the last time I saw him."

"Bingo!" Sam almost shouted. He was right. Those papers on Janet Porter's desk were Kevin Porter's notes on Justice Oliver Wendell Holmes. That innocent sheaf of papers was the percussion cap that had set off the dynamite in Janet Porter. The jigsaw puzzle was complete. The last missing piece had been found and it fitted into place perfectly.

"You're sure now? Oliver Wendell Holmes; and he took them home that afternoon?" he repeated.

"Of course, I'm sure." Her voice sounded injured. "I have the notes in my shorthand pad."

"Young lady, if I weren't a happily married man, I'd kiss you." He grinned at her, vastly pleased.

She looked at him as though he had gone mad.

"Sit down, Hank," Sam said when he reached his office. "I want to try out some thoughts on you about the Porter case."

Hank settled down resignedly to listen.

"I see Janet Porter as the product of three major causative forces," Sam began. "First, a childhood and young womanhood dominated by a selfish, unloving father who used her as a convenient implement for his own purposes. His main purpose was achievement of fame as a scholar-analyst of Supreme

Court history. In his pursuit of this purpose he became ob-
sessed with the personality and thinking of Oliver Wendell
Holmes, Jr. To Janet, after a while, her father's oppression
became epitomized in Holmes. She saw her father, and Holmes,
as almost interchangeable symbols of her fear and misery.
There is little doubt that her emotional response to all this was
first uncomprehending confusion, then fear and resentment, and
finally repressed hatred."

"That's a lot of assumptions," Hank objected.

"Of course, none of this can be conclusive. But the evidence
is strong. Let's go on. Bear with me."

Hank lifted one shoulder in mild protest but said nothing.

"Now," Sam went on enthusiastically, "as she grows into
womanhood, another stress is added to her already tense existence. She becomes a victim of recurrent premenstrual tension of a severe nature. A harsh biochemical stress is added
to the already bad emotional stress on her mental equilib-
rium. This is fortuitous, as life often is, but the effects are
cumulative. Mark that, continued cumulative pressures. Yet,
there is no visible breakdown of which we know. She is a
woman of strong character and keen intelligence.

"At this point she is alone, away from her father much of
the time, working. She is beginning to make her own life and
to achieve a superficial emotional balance. Then along comes
Kevin Porter and woos and wins her. She opens her soul to
this wonderful new life. They go to Cleveland and she is
truly happy for the first time in her existence."

"But," Hank protested, "that was all phony."

"Of course," Sam agreed. "In a matter of weeks the falsity
became clear. Kevin Porter's assumed temporary loving-kind-
ness was replaced by his true characteristics. She found that
she had married her father, all over again. She was cast from
the heights of hope to the depths of confusion and fear all
over again."

He paused for a moment, and then said, "Now, what follows . . . ? They move to San Francisco, and she finds herself
living a life almost identical with the one she thought she had
escaped. Meanwhile, the physical stress keeps adding its weight

as the months and years go by. Her numb resignation conceals, even from herself, the same misery and fear she had known before. Then, as if by a plan of a malicious fate, her husband begins working at the same kind of labor that she identifies with her father. He pushes her, as her father had, to help him in this same hated labor. This past summer must have been a crescendo of horror to her mind."

Hank nodded thoughtfully as Sam rushed on with his thoughts.

"The climax comes on that fatal evening. She has been working all evening on the hated notes of her father, about the Supreme Court justices. She is lonely, oppressed, physically torn by the peak stress of her own private 'curse'—on the ragged edge of mental retreat and breakdown. To this inflammable mixture of mental and physical chemicals comes Kevin Porter. He looks like her father in the half-light away from her desk lamp. He speaks like her father, coming suddenly into the hushed room. And then he casts before her frightened eyes the physical embodiment of all her hate and fear—a batch of notes about Holmes for her to labor on thanklessly again.

"To her mind, so near the breaking point, this is the very *bête noir* itself—the black beast, or more likely, the white-haired beast—which embodies the misery and loathing of her life. It is the final catalyst that converts the chemistry of her mind into an explosive. She explodes mindlessly. She seizes the first object at hand—the statue on the desk—and strikes out at the demon who is tormenting her: the white-haired devil she sees standing there. Then, her mind rejecting all of it, she sinks like a whipped animal to the floor. She is mindless, sightless—insane. . . ."

Hank stared at him soberly. "That is a terrible story to hear, or to tell. I believe it. I think that you're correct. But will a jury believe it?"

Sam sighed. "That remains to be seen. I believe it and the fact that you are convinced is encouraging. Whether or not a jury will believe it, only time can tell. Put it on for trial, Hank, and let us see what we shall see."

His assistant nodded without saying a word.

"A sad and terrible madness," Sam murmured, half to himself. "A singular fury of a tormented soul."

The four men met in a conference room at the plush Founders Club of San Francisco. Hank had succeeded in getting all of them to attend—the fathers of the three youths involved in the Larkbey case. It was the veiled threat, not Hank's sweetly persuasive voice, that had brought them. Their uneasiness and resentment were almost tangible in the air around the long, mahogany conference table. Carleton D. Hibbes was heavy-set and paunchy, James Madison Canfield II was lean and saturnine, and Wilton G. Finchley was a fashion-plate of elegant male attire. Embarrassment and annoyance radiated from all three of them.

When Sam came into the room, Hank got up out of the chair at the head of the table and moved to another seat at the side of the room. Sam sat down at the head of the table. The scene looked rather like a small-corporation, board-of-directors meeting, minus secretaries.

"Gentlemen," Sam said softly but very distinctly, "this is unpleasant for all of us, I know. Unfortunately, it is necessary. You have left me no choice."

The three fathers looked at each other worriedly.

"Belle Larkbey sold alcoholic beverages to your sons. Mistake or not, honest error or not, she did that. That is a misdemeanor, punishable by a small fine. She ought to pay the fine, and she will pay it."

Their worried looks eased a little.

"But—and mark this—the law calls for a *fine* in such cases, and nothing more. It does not call for punishment by being deprived of the right to earn a living. It does not call for public pillorying in the press. It does not call for brutal harassment."

Their worried looks returned again.

"I will put it to you plainly, gentlemen," Sam said evenly. "I know why Belle Larkbey has been harassed. And you know it."

Their eyes flickered at each other.

"Your three sons," Sam continued, "are candidates for juvenile court and penal treatment. You know it, and I know it. If their conduct becomes a subject of the public prints, they may well wind up in jail, and you—each of you—on the front pages."

The three men shifted uneaily in their seats.

"Belle Larkbey is being made the patsy for your sons' misbehavior. She is being used, callously, brutally, as the red herring to draw attention away from your noble sons. The newspaper campaign, and the padlock order, and the whole ugly business, were arranged—I say it again, arranged—by one of you or all of you."

Finchley shook his head as though to deny it, but Sam cut him off. "I don't give one damn whether it is one of you or all of you. But I came here to tell you something very plain and clear. It is going to stop, today. I said *today*. The padlock order will be quashed, today. The newspaper campaign will be called off, today."

They looked at him defiantly.

"Otherwise . . ." Sam paused. "Otherwise . . . your sons will be prosecuted criminally."

They almost gasped.

"I kid you not, gentlemen," Sam said sweetly. "Under California statutes, the *use* of false I.D. cards is criminal. Your sons violated the law by knowingly using false I.D. cards. Any citizen is entitled, under the statute, to file criminal charges against a person who violates this statute. If you don't believe me, consult your own attorneys."

They stared at him, anger and uncertainty and apprehension in their faces.

Sam stood up. "I am a citizen, gentlemen. I can file such charges. And I will, unless . . ."

Hank stood up, too. Sam beckoned to him. "Come on, Hank." They walked to the door.

Sam turned, and pointed his finger at the three silent men around the table. "You can make your phone calls and the matter will be ended peaceably, today. I will check on it before five o'clock this afternoon. Or, first thing tomorrow morning I will file three charges. Take your choice."

Sam and Hank walked out.

It was half-past four when Hank came bursting into Sam's office, grinning from ear to ear. "I just got a call from the D.A.'s

Office. It was about the Larkbey case. They have a proposal."

"Yes. What is it?" Sam could guess what it was.

"If they reduce the charge against Belle Larkbey to a simple misdemeanor sale to minors and drop the padlock order, will you agree that she pay the fine and the case be closed?"

Sam smiled sarcastically. "I shouldn't even agree to the fine. She was honestly misled."

Hank was aghast. "Good grief! That's all you said you wanted."

Sam grinned and nodded. "That's what I said. Good enough. Tell them it's a deal. Pay the fine and close it out, Hank."

"Okay."

"Call the papers, too, and find out if they have called off their dogs. Ask Bud Kennedy. He'll tell you."

"Right."

"And call Belle. Tell her she can open for business again."

"Roger, dodger." Hank was beaming.

"I don't like using this kind of tactics. But . . . it worked. Belle ought to be happy. She'll be gushing all over me."

"She sure will, and should," Hank agreed vigorously. "Congratulations, boss."

Sam waved him on his way. "Big deal. . . ."

It was always the same, he thought as Hank left. Always the feeling of anticlimax. In the thick of working out a case, or fighting it out, the victory always seemed vastly alluring and sure to be a great joy. Then, the victory won, it was just another job done. The expected exhilaration was brief, or there was none at all. So, you go on to the next case content—or almost content—with the finished one, but not exhilarated. He buzzed Trudy. "Remind me tomorrow to make up a bill for the fee in the Larkbey case."

CHAPTER

"This juror is perfectly acceptable to the State." Barney Ros-valley waved his hand at Sam as though to say, "Let's see you get rid of this one." The prospective juror sat bolt upright, his lips thin and compressed, head tilted back challengingly, and his pale hazel eyes staring at something on the ceiling.

Sam started to get up from his chair at the Defense Counsel's Table. "What do we have about this fellow?" he asked Hank in a whisper.

Hank leafed through his list of notes about the prospective jurors. It was routine in their office to get a jury list from the court before every trial, and to find out what they could about each person on it. For major trials like this one, Sam had a special investigator study each juror in particular depth. The bare statistical reports in *Polk's City Directory* were not enough.

"James C. Liggett," Hank read. "Minor functionary in the License Bureau. Active in patriotic clubs. Bachelor. Lives at the Viet Nam War Veterans Society building."

"Oh boy!" Sam knew that he wanted no part of this fellow sitting in judgment on Janet Porter. He walked closer to the man. "Mr. Liggett, I believe you said that you work in the License Bureau, and have been there for ten years, did you not?"

The man nodded positively. "Yes."

"Do you know any of the attorneys here on this case?"

"No."

"Mr. Liggett, do you have any feeling against the defendant here just because she is charged with a crime?"

"No." His voice was very positive.

"As you sit here now, do you have any feeling that the defendant probably is gulty or else she would not be charged by the Prosecutor?"

"I have confidence in our government officials," Liggett answered. "I don't think they'd charge anyone if they didn't have cause."

"Oh? You think that the chances are that if the Prosecutor files a charge against some person, there probably is strong evidence that that person did what is charged?"

"Sure." The witness's voice registered annoyance. "Otherwise he wouldn't bring the charge."

"You are aware, are you not, Mr. Liggett, that in a criminal case the Prosecution must prove guilt beyond a reasonable doubt?"

"Sure."

"And you don't think that rule is merely a matter of words or formality, do you?"

"No. Of course not."

"But do you think that the Prosecutor can do that, or he wouldn't have brought the charge?"

"Sure."

"But do you agree that the defendant is not obliged to prove her innocence, and that the Prosecution must prove her guilt?"

"Yes."

"But you think that the Prosecution probably can do that in most such cases, or they wouldn't have brought up the charge?"

"Yes."

Sam looked at the man reflectively for a moment, and then continued. "Thank you. Now, Mr. Liggett, having worked for ten years in the License Bureau, you have great respect for public authorities, do you not?"

"Of course."

"Including the Public Prosecutor?"

"Sure."

"More so than you have for the ordinary, private defense lawyer?"

"Not always. Most of the time, though."

"Thank you. Now, the fact that the defendant is wealthy would make no difference to you, would it?"

"Not if she's innocent."

"I see. You believe that the law should be applied strictly to everyone?"

"Yes."

"And punishment for a violation of the law should be severe?"

"Yes." Liggett's voice sounded deep and stern.

"What is your salary at the License Bureau, Mr. Liggett?"

"Forty-eight hundred a year."

"That's not very much. But this does not affect your fairness to a wealthy defendant, does it?"

"No."

"And the fact that she is a woman makes no difference, does it?"

"No. Some women are pretty good, too."

Sam arched his eyebrows. "What do you mean, 'pretty good, too'?"

"Oh, some women have sense and can do a fair job."

"Some women? Not all?"

"No. Most of them ought to stay home and raise kids."

"I see." Sam paused, and walked a few steps back from the witness stand. "Have you read about this case in the newspapers?"

"A little," the man admitted.

"You know, then, what the papers said happened in this case?"

"Sure."

"But that wouldn't affect your judgment at this trial, would it?"

"No."

"Even though you think that you already have a fair idea of what happened between Mrs. Porter and her husband?"

"Not a bit."

"You meant it would not affect your judgment?"

"No."

"In fact, the information you got from the newspapers would help you reach a verdict?"

"Sure."

"I see. You are a bachelor, Mr. Liggett, aren't you?"

"Yes."

"Don't care for marriage, eh?"

"Them as wants to can get married." There seemed to be a faint sneer in his tone.

"But you would understand the problems of married people, wouldn't you?"

"Sure."

"And I see that you live at a veteran's club—the Viet Nam Vets Society—don't you?"

"Yes."

"A men's club?"

"Yes."

"You don't associate much with women, I suppose?"

"Oh, now and then."

"Don't care much for women, though, generally, eh?"

"Not much."

"I see. Thank you, Mr. Liggett." Sam beckoned to Barney Rosvalley and moved close to the Judge's Bench. At the Bench he spoke softly so that Liggett could not hear him. "If Your Honor please, I challenge for cause. This man is prejudiced in favor of authority—the Prosecution—as against the Defense. He is prejudiced against women by his own admission. He is prejudiced against wealthy defendants. He is prejudiced against married people, such as the defendant. He admits that he already has formed an opinion on the case, from reading the newspapers. He is totally unqualified to sit as a juror in this case. I ask that he be excused."

Judge Alberts leaned over towards Rosvalley. "Any argument, Mr. Prosecutor?" The judge was a heavy-set man with a deeply lined face and a high, round forehead topped by hair that was still dark, though getting thin. Years of experience with human frailties and follies had etched his face, but his voice was gentle and kind-sounding.

Barney half smiled. "Mr. Benedict is assuming a great deal about this man."

Sam smiled, too. "Would you like to have the examination read back, Mr. Rosvalley?"

"No, I suppose not."

The judge nodded. "I think that you are quite correct, Mr. Benedict." He turned to Liggett and raised his voice: "You are excused, sir. Please go to the other room. You will be assigned to another panel."

It was such a sparkling early September day that it seemed a pity to be indoors and working, Sam thought. Much as he loved the excitement of the jury-selection process, he wished for a moment that he were elsewhere, perhaps riding some pretty trail in the hills on a good mount.

He pulled his mind back to the *voir dire* proceedings. Another name had been taken from the jury drum table, and Rosvalley was starting his examination.

The trial date was perfect, Sam reflected, right at the peak of Janet's premenstrual-tension cycle, according to the charts drawn by Rubenfeld. He had noticed how brittle she seemed to be that morning. Hank had done a good job of maneuvering for the trial date. Judge Alberts was one of the best in the Superior Court, not hidebound by *stare decisis* and not afraid to look at new developments in law and science.

The prospective juror being questioned by Rosvalley seemed to be quite acceptable from Sam's point of view. He was a fairly young man, of athletic build, and of open and straightforward manner. His name was Fouchette, and he was a salesman for a hardware distributing company.

Sam added up the pros and cons in his mind about Mr. Fouchette. First, Fouchette was a young man. That meant that he would not yet have had time to freeze his thinking into a conservative mold. He would still be relatively willing to learn and to listen to new ideas—such as the new concept of premenstrual tension and the desirability of the newer psychiatric approach to mental illness.

Fouchette was athletic-looking. That meant that he was the outdoor type, probably. That type tends to be fairly openminded, Sam thought, and willing to take either side. Yet, if that kind of juror is really convinced of something, he will stubbornly support it. Sam knew that if he could convince him, he would espouse Janet's cause to the bitter end.

Next, the man was a salesman, and that was always desirable. Salesmen see all kinds of people and all kinds of places. They usually are worldly wise and they know the meaning of misfortune and of the pressure of circumstances. They know what suffering means and what it can do to people. Usually salesmen tend to be tolerant and understanding. Janet certainly needed understanding and compassion, Sam thought ruefully.

Fouchette was very different from Liggett, he thought. Liggett had been the typical minor-official, super-patriot type, the kind of man who takes the words of the Prosecutor as the words of God. Such a man was likely to have spent years in slavish obedience to his superiors of one grade of authority or another, and such a man would come to identify strongly with the established order of authority. To such a man's mind, the fact that Janet was being charged with a crime, and tried for it, would be almost enough in itself to prove guilt. Janet would have gotten short shrift from a man like Liggett, Sam was sure.

Fouchette was the opposite type of juror, in Sam's opinion. Ah, there's the rub, Sam thought; probably, but not *certainly*. Always there was the chance that his estimate might be wrong. There might be something in this particular man that would contradict all of the years of study and experience. After all, you can't lump people into categories or types, because they won't stay there. Always there are the exceptions and the odd differences. Even so, Sam knew that the best thing to do was to play the percentages. Fouchette seemed to be an ideal juror from Janet Porter's point of view.

When Rosvalley finished, Sam stood up, smiled at Fouchette, and said, "The Defense finds Mr. Fouchette well qualified to serve on this jury. We are glad to accept him."

Fouchette looked gratified.

"I think he'll be a good one," Sam whispered to Hank.

There was just one more person Sam wanted to see before Janet's trial got under way. Betty Smithfield had been away, out of the country on a trip with her husband, during the month of August. Now they were back in San Francisco, and Hank had arranged a luncheon meeting with Mrs. Smithfield for Sam. He was to meet her at the St. Francis Hotel, in the lobby. She would know Sam by his peaked pocket handkerchief and silvery hair, Hank told her.

"You take the next one," Sam instructed his assistant. "His name is Rittmeister. He's of German or Scandinavian descent, so he may be ultraconservative and bull-headed. That kind of guy often tends to believe in absolute and every-time strict law enforcement—whatever the law may be. He may be dead set on strict punishment of anyone who runs afoul of the law, no matter why or how. He may well be all in favor of the Prosecution, with his mind made up to convict before the trial begins. This is all 'may be,' of course. Anyhow, watch him carefully. Question him thoroughly, and challenge him for cause if there is cause. If necessary—if you feel that you ought to, and yet can't prove cause—challenge him peremptorily. But don't use up one of our peremptory challenges if you don't have to. I'm going over to the St. Francis to meet Mrs. Smithfield for lunch. See you before we resume after the lunch recess."

"Okay, boss." Hank said, delighted to be entrusted with an important piece of trial work.

Betty Smithfield was a small, dainty woman, with reddish-blond hair and bright, friendly eyes. Sam liked her her at first sight. She exuded friendly charm and good humor, almost bubbling with energy and the joy of living. "We heard of what happened when we got home," she said. "What a pity! Janet is such a nice, sweet girl."

"You know her well, I take it," Sam said.

"Not very well, actually. John, my husband, knew Kevin rather well. They were on some Bar Association committee together, and that's how we became acquainted. John is a lawyer, you know. He has mentioned your name, Mr. Benedict, a number of times. He thinks highly of you."

"I know John," Sam said. "Please say 'hello' to him for me. He is one of the best insurance lawyers in the profession, and a fine gentleman."

"Why, thank you." She bent her head in an exaggerated bow.

"Please call me Sam," he said, smiling.

She smiled back at him. "Of course, Sam. And my name is Betty."

They sat quietly, smiling at each other and liking each other.

Then Sam coughed as though a little embarrassed and continued the conversation. "Then you got to know Janet . . . ?" He paused, expectantly.

"Yes. We met at social gatherings once in a while. We and our husbands went out to dinner together occasionally until a year or two ago. I invited Janet to a luncheon or tea at our house, and that sort of thing. So we got to be fairly friendly, though not what you'd call intimate friends. Janet is a quiet kind of girl, you know."

"I know," Sam agreed. "And Kevin?"

"That's hard for me to say. I never got to know him well. Actually, I saw him only a few times, and then only when he was with Janet."

"What did you think of him?"

She hesitated. It would be hard for a woman like this to say anything but good things about anybody. "Please be frank," he urged. "Janet's situation is much too serious to be glossed over with polite amenities."

"I suppose that's true." She lost her bubbling enthusiasm for a minute. "John always said that Kevin was a stuffed shirt. But Janet is such a sweet girl."

Sam pressed her. "You still haven't answered my question."

"I know I haven't," she said, her voice sounding troubled. "How can I answer you?" She reflected for a few moments. "I know. I'll tell you about our last date with the Porters. It was only a few weeks ago."

"Will that tell me anything about them, and what you thought of him?"

"I think it will." she said confidently. "Oh, yes, it will.

"We met the Porters at Banessi's, on Broadway, for dinner," she began. "John loves antipasto and cannelloni and all kinds of Italian food. He's beginning to get a tummy and really shouldn't. ... Well, before we ordered dinner, Janet said that she felt like having some sour Italian red wine. You know, Chianti. Well, Kevin sneered at her low taste. In fact, he said, 'You have rather poor taste in wines, my dear.' Lordly as you please! Then, as though she had no voice in the matter, he ordered a bottle of fine, imported Chablis. As far as he was concerned, he made the decisions for both of them even as to ordering wine with dinner."

Sam listened with interest as she went on.

"When she told the waiter what she wanted for dinner, he did the same thing again. As soon as she got through giving her order to the waiter, up pipes Kevin again and says to the waiter, 'She doesn't really want that. I'll tell you what we'll have—both of us.' Then he proceeds to order for both of them without a word to her about what she wanted. And he didn't order one of the things she had ordered! John and I were quite uncomfortable about all this. John tried to make a joke of it, but Janet was hurt, as anyone could see, though she didn't say anything. The evening was rather strained, after that."

"I imagine that that would be embarrassing to you," Sam remarked gently.

She nodded emphatically. "It really was. I wanted to go home right after dinner, but we had made a reservation to see the show at the Hungry i, and I didn't want to spoil the evening entirely. John and Kevin talked about some committee business and I tried to make like a chatterbox with Janet, but she seemed miles away. Poor dear, my heart ached for her. After dinner we went to the Hungry i. There was a rather good show featuring some fellow in a baggy frock coat and battered top hat who was supposed to be a parody of a Continental savant. He was very funny in fact. John and I howled. He was as droll a man as you can imagine. But all through the show Kevin sat there sneering and making smart-alecky remarks about the show and about people in the audience. He didn't applaud at all and seemed not a bit amused or entertained. Everyone else applauded and laughed and had a fine time—except Janet, of course. She just sat there, as though her mind were a million miles away. As soon as the show was over I said that I was tired and wanted to go home. The truth is, I had made up my mind never to go out with the Porters—I mean Kevin—not ever again. He was unbearable. We said 'goodnight' and went home."

"I guess that tells me what you thought of him," Sam agreed.

"But that poor, sweet, sad girl . . . ," Betty added. "I'm not surprised. Really, I'm not surprised."

"This one is going to be hard to figure out," Sam said, looking perplexed.

"Why? He looks okay to me." Hank seemed surprised.

"His name—Harry Cohen—tells us that he is probably of the Jewish faith. Jews can be tough jurors in hearing crimes of violence. They usually detest violence, and that's no wonder when you look at their cultural background."

"Is this really a 'crime of violence'?" Hank objected.

Sam frowned at his big assistant. "Bludgeoning a man to death? Come on, Hank. I'm surprised at you."

"But Jews usually revere justice and fairness," Hank protested.

"True enough. But just look at this fellow. He's big and burly and tough-looking. I wouldn't want to tangle with him. *He* could be pretty violent if he wanted to be, I think."

"So . . . ?"

"So, he's a problem. Will he abhor violence and be harsh toward anyone accused of it? Or will he, personally, be objective and tolerant about it in this case?" Sam rubbed his chin doubtfully. "This will have to be a detailed, full-length examination. Then we'll see." He stood up and walked toward the prospective juror as Barney Rosvalley finished with him.

"This man is acceptable to the State as a juror in this case," Rosvalley said, obviously well satisfied with Harry Cohen.

Sam walked up to the stand and smiled pleasantly. "So you are a roofer by trade, Mr. Cohen," he began "You build roofs on new houses, install shingles, repair leaks, and that sort of thing, is that right?"

Cohen nodded. "Yes. I also work on gutters and drains, do tinsmithing, caulking . . . you know, general roofing work."

"Do you own your own business?"

"No. I work for the Flaherty Roofing Company."

"Do you know the defendant or any of the attorneys in this case?"

"No, sir."

"Do you have any feeling against the defendant just because she is charged with the commission of a crime in this case?"

"No."

"Do you have any feeling that, because the Prosecutor has filed charges against the defendant, she probably is guilty?"

"Oh, no," Cohen said positively.

"In other words, Mr. Cohen, you believe that unless the Prosecution offers enough evidence to prove the defendant guilty beyond a reasonable doubt, you will not return a verdict in favor of conviction. Is that correct?"

"Yes, sir."

Sam continued. "You understand that the legal requirement of guilt 'beyond a reasonable doubt' is not merely a matter of words or of formalities?"

"I understand that."

Sam emphasized the question. "Will you require the Prosecutor to prove his case beyond a reasonable doubt?"

"Yes."

"And if he fails to do so, you won't hesitate to do your duty by bringing in a verdict in favor of the defendant, will you?"

"That's right."

"You understand, don't you," Sam continued, "that it is the task of the Prosecutor to prove the defendant guilty and it is not the duty of the defendant to prove that she is innocent?"

"I understand that."

"In other words, Mr. Cohen, the burden of proof is on the Prosecutor, and you will require him to assume that burden, will you not?"

"Yes, I will."

Sam looked upward, towards the ceiling, as he asked the next question. "Tell me, Mr. Cohen, do you have any strong opinions about mental illness? Do you hate or fear the idea of insanity, for instance; are you sympathetic toward insane people, or what?"

Barney Rosvalley interrupted. "I must object to that, Mr. Benedict. The question is vague and confusing. Also, it seems to me to be instructing the witness before any evidence is in."

Sam raised his eyebrows. "Do you object to the venireman's knowing the nature of the defendant's defense?"

"No. I think the question is confusing." Rosvalley seemed not quite sure of himself.

"Thank you, Mr. Rosvalley," Sam said, his voice sarcastic. "If the Prosecutor cannot understand the question I certainly will rephrase it." He turned back to Cohen. "Tell us, please, Mr. Cohen. Are you prejudiced against insane people, or sympathetic toward them?"

"Sympathetic." The tone of the answer was positive.

"Is that all right, Mr. Rosvalley?" Sam's annoyance with the interruption was plain in his sarcastic tone.

"No objection." Barney was sorry he had interrupted. The jury candidate was looking at him with what seemed to be mild resentment.

"Shall we go on then?" Sam returned to Cohen. "You know our position in this case. You know that our defense is 'not guilty' and that it is based on the reason of insanity. In law that means that a person who is insane cannot be convicted for a crime committed while he is insane. Now, Mr. Cohen, if the Court should instruct you that insanity where shown by the evidence is a good defense, will you follow and apply that law?"

"Yes."

"You realize, of course, that whether or not a person was, or is, insane is a question of fact, above all, do you not?"

"Yes sir."

"And you realize, too, that insanity is a complex question of fact, not a simple thing easy to recognize, do you not?"

"Yes."

Sam stood silent for a moment. Then he explained carefully, "In this case, Mr. Cohen, the Prosecutor has the privilege of putting on witnesses first. After he gets through, if we desire to do so, we can put on our witnesses. Of course, while the Prosecutor is putting on his witnesses we can't be putting ours on. Will you keep in mind that we will later put on witnesses to refute what the Prosecutor says? Will you try to keep an open mind, and not jump to conclusions, until you have heard the witnesses for the defense?"

"Yes, I think I can do that."

"You will give full consideration to any defense which the Court allows us to offer?"

"Yes."

Sam moved closer to the juror. "Are you familiar with this case from the newspaper accounts?" he asked.

Cohen shook his head. "No, sir. I never read the crime or 'love-nest-raided' stories."

"You know nothing about it."

"I noticed the headlines when it happened. That's all."

Sam changed the subject suddenly. "Mr. Cohen, have you ever been involved in a criminal case before, either as a party or a witness?"

"No, never."

"Will the fact that the defendant comes from a wealthy family have any effect on your ability to return a just verdict?"

"I should say not." Cohen sounded offended.

"Mr. Cohen, you understand—do you not—that you do not have to believe a thing is so just because someone says it is so, if what the witness says does not seem to be correct when viewed in the light of your own experience in life?"

"I understand that," Cohen said. "I don't just swallow what anyone says."

Sam smiled. "In other words, just because you take solemn oath to serve as a juror in this case, that does not mean that you are going to leave all of your own life experience and wisdom outside the courtroom, does it?"

"No, I won't."

"You are a married man, are you not?"

"Yes, I am."

"Does your wife ever become sick or indisposed?"

Cohen looked surprised. "Why, sure; once in a while."

"Do you feel that that is wrong or improper on her part?"

Cohen stared at him as though Sam had gone mad. "Of course not! Why should it be improper?"

Sam nodded. "So you understand that the fact that a woman may fall ill, or suffer—as in what we call 'women's troubles'—is no sin and no crime. You understand that?"

"Sure. She can't be blamed for getting sick."

"And even if a woman becomes seriously ill with 'women's troubles,' she should not be condemned for that?"

"Of course not." Cohen sounded aggrieved.

Sam pressed the point. "Even if her sickness becomes very serious and troublesome?"

"Sure."

"All right, then," Sam said. "Now, you will see the Prosecutor and myself object to certain evidence or testimony. You understand, do you not, that we object because we feel that the evidence or testimony is improper under the rules, and it is our duty to object?"

"I understand that."

"The Judge will uphold or deny our objections. If he upholds an objection, that means that he agrees that the evidence is against the rules. If he overrules an objection, that means that he thinks the evidence is okay and is proper under the rules. Either way, it does not mean that he thinks the evidence is significant or not important. You understand that, do you not?"

"I do," Cohen said positively.

"So," Sam continued, "if either of us objects to evidence or testimony during the trial, you will understand, will you not, that we are only trying to see that the rules are followed, and you won't hold it against us, will you?"

"No, I won't."

"Now, Mr. Cohen, suppose that some witness is put on the stand, of whom you happen to know. He may have a title or be a public official. Will you test the evidence he offers, and examine his testimony in your own mind by the same tests that you apply to other people and their testimony?"

"Yes, I will."

"You understand, do you not, that even people we know, or about whom we know, may be mistaken sometimes?"

"Yes."

"Nobody is perfect and nobody is always absolutely right?"

"That's right," Cohen said firmly.

"Even famous or distinguished people?"

"That's right."

"And so you will view the evidence itself as more important than the person who happens to give it?"

"Yes."

Sam folded his arms and looked the prospective juror full in the eyes. "Mr. Cohen, is there any reason you know, about which I have not asked you any questions, which you feel would make you prejudiced in this case? I do not want to pry into your private life and that is why I put this question entirely up to you to answer."

"No reason," Cohen answered without hesitation.

"You feel that you can give both sides an unbiased, square deal, don't you?"

"Yes, I can."

"Mr. Cohen, I think that you can, too." Sam turned to Rosvalley. "We are glad to accept Mr. Cohen."

The package was small, about six inches by eight inches in

size, and two inches thick. It was gift-wrapped with a wide, blue-silk ribbon and bow on it. It felt heavy, as Sam unwrapped it. Inside was a big, blue-plush jewel box. He opened it. Inside the box, set into a soft, satin-padded white cushion, there was a massive padlock. The padlock was an ordinary hasp and flat-body type of the kind used to fasten gates or barn doors. But it was shining silver in color—nickel plated. A heavy key lay alongside it, and the key was nickel plated too. Inscribed on the face of the padlock, engraved deeply around the keyhole, were the words:

To SAM BENEDICT, THE MASTER
BEST LAWYER IN THE WORLD
FROM
BELLE LARKBEY

Sam smiled with amusement and delight. "I'm a real sucker for this kind of thing," he remarked to the grinning Hank. "You may laugh, but I love this kind of a 'thank-you' note. It means more to me sometimes than any fee." He strode to the massive cabinet that served as a bar in his office. The top of the polished cabinet was covered with other mementos and tributes, many of them engraved with sentiments similar to the one on the glistening padlock. He pushed aside some other objects to make room, and placed the lock on top of the bar.

"She's a character, that Belle," he said as Hank, grinning broadly, watched him with twinkling eyes.

Then Sam walked toward the window, his pleased expression sobering. He stood at the window, thinking. Jury selection had been completed, and the trial proper would begin next morning. "We've got a pretty good jury," he said. "As good as we were entitled to expect."

"Not bad," Hank agreed. "I'm a little worried, though, about that fellow Patterson. He's unemployed and living from hand to mouth. You yourself have said more than once that you should never accept a poor person as a juror on the trial of a wealthy person, and vice versa."

Sam nodded. "True enough. But remember that he is an actor by profession. He's unemployed and poor but, above all, he is an actor. Actors are almost always desirable jurors. They have seen plenty of good and bad in life, and they understand trouble and suffering. They usually are tolerant and compassionate. The same is true of artists and writers. And he's an older man. Older men are usually more understanding, more charitable and forgiving, than younger men."

"I could name you some actors who are just the opposite of charitable and compassionate," Hank responded sourly.

"Of course, there are always exceptions. Like anyone else, when an actor becomes a great success and rich, the tendency is for him to become conservative and harshly self-righteous. But that kind of self-righteousness is the product of age and money more often than it is of being an actor."

"And what about the Negro woman, Mrs. Shorter?" Hank asked. "Didn't you once say that colored jurors tend to resent, even though slightly, a defendant who is rich or successful?"

"Yes, but by the same token the Negro is more likely to be sympathetic toward someone who is facing a hostile world. Women are generally almost impossible to evaluate as jurors. I wanted some women on the jury in view of what we can show about Janet Porter's life of oppression. Women will sympathize with that, and especially a Negro woman will."

The big man looked doubtful. "I'm not so sure, Sam."

"Another thing about Mrs. Shorter, Hank. Did you notice how calm and well-balanced she is? You didn't see her fidget, or pick at her nail polish, or fuss with her handbag, or anything like that. Beware of nervous or fidgety jurors; they have flighty minds and have difficulty in following the evidence. Mrs. Shorter seemed quite intelligent, mature, and self-possessed. She'll make a good juror."

"I guess you're right," Hank conceded.

"And finally, one more principle in picking a jury. Look out for the somber, serious, sour-faced person. He or she often will be harsh in judgment, unless of course the somberness is the result of sadness for the person on trial for his life. That's not easy to find out. In general, though, it's safer to pick the amiable, smiling juror. Mrs. Shorter is a pleasant, humorous woman; not dour or sour. I think she'll be fine."

"Okay," Hank said. "You've convinced me."

"The tactics are going to be simple," Sam instructed his assistant. "We are going to do little or no cross-examining."

"What!" Hank was aghast.

"You heard me. Little or none."

"Why?"

"The evidence that Janet killed Kevin Porter is ironclad. She did it, and that's all there is to that. Cross-examination will just emphasize it."

"And the State's psychiatrists?"

"Cautious cross-examination, and not much of it, about the possibilities of premenstrual tension as causation, and about psychotic aspects. They'll be there to argue that she is perfectly sane, and I don't intend to play into their hands. If their testimony is perfunctory, as it may be, I may not cross-examine them at all."

"Then how will you defend?"

"With just two witnesses. Rubenfeld, as spokesman for our team of psychiatrists, and Janet Porter herself."

"That's all?" Hank asked quizzically.

"That's all," Sam answered with finality.

Trial work calls for a kind of generalship, Sam thought—a kind of tactical maneuvering that has much in common with military strategy. Many times Sam had been struck by the parallels between military planning and trial planning. It was not surprising when you thought of the basic similarity of the situations. In both cases there were two opposite and contending forces. Both were adversary situations—two armed camps, facing and opposing each other. Each side meant to overwhelm and defeat the other.

In the Porter case the lines of battle were clearly drawn. Tomorrow morning the guns would open up. It was a set-piece battle in classic military style. The operational plans were drawn, the available forces marshalled, and now they would fight out the issue. Of course, Sam realized, as in any kind of combat there were imponderables and unexpected developments. But the competent commander—or lawyer—tried to anticipate and be prepared to meet every contingency that he could foresee. Sam knew, from experience that the main factors that a commander, or lawyer, could and should control were two: one, the plan and order of battle, and, two, the timing of the use of his available forces.

The guiding principle of combat, he thought, is to apply your major force against your opponent's weakest point. The ideal tactic is to use a concentration of your force against one after another of your opponent's weaker forces; that is, to defeat his units piecemeal, one after another. Put another way, this means that you apply your heavy force on his flank, for instance, where all your guns can be brought to bear, while only some of his are able to hit back. So, too, in a trial, your opponent's forces should be defeated piecemeal if possible. The ideal tactic is to take him unexpectedly (on his flank) and to overwhelm him with your full force where he cannot resist effectively.

An interesting analogy, Sam thought, smiling to himself.

There was time for a snooze before going out to dinner. He put his feet up on his desk, leaned back in his chair, closed his eyes, and drowsed.

He dreamed.

His company had the lead in the advance, that day. They moved in spread-out V formation—fourteen medium tanks echeloned right and left, with his command tank and two assault guns back inside the V where Sam could see and control them. His front was almost a mile wide, with a hundred yards between tanks. Behind him, a mile back, a company of armored infantry rode in half-tracks. The Germans were running for the Siegfried Line. There had been no contact all day, nor yesterday.

His command radio crackled a message as the afternoon sun sank toward the western horizon behind them. It was Lt. Harper, up at the point of the V. He could see Harper's tank stopped near the crest of a long, straight ridge-line dead ahead. The Champagne fields were almost ideal tank country, Sam thought.

"Blue Fox. This is Harper. Do you read me?"

"I read you, loud and clear," Sam answered.

"There is a line of woods ahead, to my direct front, about a mile ahead of me. I see enemy vehicles moving there. About ten of them. They're tanks. Enemy tanks, to my front. About two thousand yards. What shall I do?"

"Halt!" Sam's voice was urgent. "Stop where you are. All tank commanders, all platoon leaders, this is Blue Fox. All stop!

/ 215

Wait, where you are. I am moving up to join Harper and take a look."

He switched his radio to intercom. "Sandy, move up near Harper—about fifty yards to his right—and stop in hull defilade." Annabelle, his command tank, lurched forward as his driver gunned the engine and they ground forward to the ridgeline. Sam signaled Pearson, his platoon commander on the right, on his radio. "Pearson, this is Benedict. Turn your turrets right and cover our flank." Then, to Roth, his left platoon leader, "Roth, cover us to our left. Acknowledge. Over." Both lieutenants answered quickly. He could see their turrets turning their long 76-millimeter cannon towards the flanks.

Just below the crest Sam ordered his driver to stop while he studied the terrain ahead through his field glasses. Sure enough, ten or twelve German tanks were visible near the line of trees on the other side of a long dip in the plain. There was a swale to his right, half-a-mile away. More woods to his left, also about half-a-mile away. Far behind, the infantry half-tracks were waiting expectantly. The sun was behind him. That was good. The swale to the right was big enough to hide a whole company of tanks. That was good. The woods to the left were too thick for tanks to get through quickly. That was a question mark.

Figure about six Tiger tanks and six Panthers, Sam said to himself as he computed rapidly. Eight-inch bow armor against our four-inch. High-velocity, 88-millimeter tank cannon against our 76s. Not good at all. They'd murder us in a frontal assault. Can we get them to come after us and then hit them from the flank by moving around into that swale on the right?

Yes, we can, he answered himself. He switched on his radio, to his platoon leaders.

"Pearson. Pearson. Back down and move around the ridge to the right. There is a big dip there. Go into it in line and move forward a thousand yards. I'll draw them to us. You get them on their flank when I give the word. Do you understand? Acknowledge. Over."

Pearson answered quickly. "Blue Fox, I understand. Flank

them on the right when they come at you. Wilco. Over and out."
Pearson's tanks moved away towards the right.

Sam spoke next to Harper, telling him to back away, and then to follow Pearson to the right flank. Then he told the two assault-gun commanders to move closer to him and prepare to fire. Finally, he gave orders to Roth, his left platoon leader. "Roth. Move up to the crest of the ridge-line when I tell you to move. Run along it at high speed, firing at the Krauts as you go. Then drop behind the ridge top, into hull defilade. We will be the base of fire. We'll draw them into attacking us. Do you understand? Over."

"I understand, Blue Fox," Roth responded. "Waiting for your order." Roth's tanks moved gingerly up to near the top of the ridge as the other two platoons rolled to the right and disappeared into the big swale in the ground there.

Sam waited a few minutes. Then he snapped his orders out. "Roth, Roth. Move out! Commence firing! Assault guns, move up and commence firing." Guns boomed, out to Sam's left, and the roar of engines echoed as the tanks ran along the ridge-top.

At the woods up ahead, the German tanks were moving into line as explosions shattered the trees behind them. Sam could almost read the enemy commander's mind: "Five American mediums. Meat on the table for heavy Panzers." They were coming on, in line, stopping to fire every minute or so. Armor-piercing shells screamed over Sam's head.

Roth's outgunned Shermans raced and bellowed desperately along the ridge-top. Then they turned as they neared Sam's tank and dodged back below the ridge-line. Their guns kept firing as though in frantic fear.

One tank was still and silent on the ridge, hit and dead.

The Germans were out, moving down into the long dip in the terrain, coming straight at him—twelve huge Nazi tanks. Then they were close, less than a thousand yards away.

"Now, Pearson," Sam shouted. "Now, Harper. Move out. Commence firing. Commence firing!" Sam shouted above the din, into his throat microphone.

And then all Hell burst out from his right. Ten American Shermans came roaring up from the swale, their long cannon spouting flame and steel. Right on the flank of the astonished Nazi line. Hurtling projectiles smashed into the thinner hull sides of the trapped Panzers. Thick black smoke billowed from one after another of the Tigers and Panthers. Desperate men leaped from burning tanks and ran for their lives. The sunken plain shook with the roaring of cannon and the thundering charge of the huge, metal monsters. Sam's own turret gun was blasting insanely, deafening him with its roar. The recoil slid and hissed past his shoulder as the gunner fired shot after shot.

In minutes it was over. Burning tanks lay drunkenly on the plain below, a pall of greasy smoke drifting above them. Far to his left, two German tanks were running for the woods. One was moving slowly, obviously hurt. Sam called Pearson. "Two Krauts running for cover off to the left. Go after them. Finish them off." Sam watched as Pearson's tanks drove forward over the ridge-top. Just to make sure, Sam called back to his accompanying infantry to send a platoon into the patch of woods in case his tanks could not get through it safely. As Pearson's platoon moved off, Sam called to his other platoon leaders to cease fire and to assemble, ready to move on.

A good afternoon's work, Sam thought. A nice job, well done. He felt pleased and tingling with the thrill of combat. Only one tank lost, he thought. Just about perfect. A classic tank action.

It was beginning to get dark. They would bivouac and refuel in the woods. He was pleasantly tired. The acrid-smelling air tasted good.

He woke. The memory of the smoking field in the Champagne was sharply etched in his mind. But this was here and now. Tomorrow would be another kind of battle. Tomorrow, he would fight again—for the life of Janet Porter. He closed the office and went downstairs to Paoli's for dinner.

CHAPTER

10

"The Prosecution rests." Barney Rosvalley ended his presentation. The case for the People was complete. And *how* complete, Sam thought. Barney had a nearly perfect case. He had proved with witness after witness that Janet Porter was guilty of the murder of her husband. There were no "ifs" or "buts." There was nobody else who could possibly have done it. He even had shown motive, through evidence given by the Porter's friends, of her icy-cold relationship to Kevin, and his to her. The most damning evidence of all was that which showed that she had struck Kevin not once but probably four or five times. And the State's psychiatrists had sworn she was sane. "A murderous rage," Rosvalley had called it.

He was right, Sam thought, righter than he knew.

Sam straightened the points of the snowy-white handkerchief in his breast pocket. He stood up and looked back at the people seated in the spectators' section of the courtroom. "I call Dr. Irwin Rubenfeld to the stand."

When Rubenfeld had taken the stand and had been sworn in, Sam began. "Doctor, will you please state your full name to the Court and jury?"

"Irwin S. Rubenfeld."

"Where do you reside?"

"719 Bigelow Place, San Francisco."

"What is your profession?"

"I am a physician."

"Duly licensed to practice in California?"

"Yes."

"Of what colleges or universities are you a graduate, Doctor?"

"I have a Bachelor of Science degree from the University of Michigan and a Doctor of Medicine degree from the University of Indiana."

"And how long have you been a physician?"

"Thirty-one years."

"Have you taken any postgraduate work of any kind?"

"Yes. I had seven years of postgraduate work in Chicago, in Dallas, and at the Menninger Clinic in Kansas."

"In any particular line, or specialty, Doctor?"

"Yes. For the first four years I was in general medicine; what people call a general practitioner. Then, for three years I studied and worked with nervous and mental diseases, as I mentioned."

Barney Rosvalley broke into the questioning. "The State will admit the witness' qualifications as a psychiatrist if Mr. Benedict wishes to save time."

"Thank you," Sam answered Rosvalley acidly. "It may save time, but it also will prevent the jury from being fully apprised of the fact that Dr. Rubenfeld is one of the leading physicians in the world."

"I'm just trying to save time," Barney explained, innocently.

"Your kindness is overwhelming," Sam snapped, his annoyance rising. "Do you mind if I conduct my own examination of the defense witness?"

"Gentlemen, gentlemen," Judge Alberts broke in, tapping his gavel lightly.

Sam turned to the judge. "If the Court please, no doubt some of the jurors are not familiar with Dr. Rubenfeld's standing. I would like to have him tell us, briefly, about his background and experience.

"Go ahead, Mr. Benedict." The judge settled back.

"All right, Dr. Rubenfeld," Sam resumed. "The Menninger Clinic is a celebrated psychiatric institution, is it not?"

"Yes," Rubenfeld agreed, "world famous."

"And how long have you specialized in the study and treatment of nervous and mental diseases?"

"Twenty-four years. That is, after leaving the Menninger Clinic."

"Did you come to San Francisco then?"

"Yes."

"Did you hold any official positions in these twenty-four years?"

"Yes. I was Director of the State Psychiatric Hospital."

"For how long?"

"Fifteen years."

"And then?"

"And then, about nine years ago, I went into private practice in San Francisco."

"Did you retain your connection with the hospital?" Sam asked.

"Oh, yes," Rubenfeld answered. "I am still a member of its staff."

"Have you written any articles on the subject of mental illness, Doctor?"

"Yes, many, for such journals as the *Bulletin of the Menninger Clinic*, the *Pennsylvania, Cleveland-Marshall*, and *Tulane Law Reviews*, and others."

"Have you written any books on the subject?"

"Yes. One book, in collaboration with Dr. Carruthers, of this city."

"On what precise subject?" Sam looked at the psychiatrist expectantly.

Rubenfeld replied slowly and distinctly. "On 'Law and Insanity.' "

Sam looked at the jury significantly and waited for the answer to sink in before asking, "Anything else?"

"I now am working on a text on the subject of the M'Naghten and Durham Rules of forensic insanity. It is not yet ready for the printers."

Sam's voice sounded respectful as he went on with his next question. "Will you tell us about your practice, please, Doctor?"

Rubenfeld made an arch of his fingers with both hands pressed together, and answered, "My practice is entirely in the field of nervous and mental diseases. I see patients regularly at my office, of course. In addition to my staff connection with the State Psychiatric Hospital here, I am also an attending psychiatrist at San Quentin Prison and at a sanitarium located at San Jose. Besides this, I am often called in as a consultant in other hospitals, in patients' homes, and as an alienist for legal matters such as this case."

"Have you ever instructed or taught medicine or psychiatry?"

"Yes. I am Associate Professor of Mental Diseases at the University of California Medical School, and Adjunct Professor of Legal Medicine at the University of San Francisco."

"How long has this been, Doctor?"

"Eight years at the Medical School and five years at the Law School."

Sam turned to the jury. "That should be enough to explain to the jury your qualifications as an expert medical witness and psychiatrist, I should think."

Leaving Rubenfeld still on the witness stand, Sam turned to Rosvalley. "Mr. Prosecutor, I have a suggestion which will save the time of the Court and jury."

Rosvalley was gallant. "We are glad to cooperate to save time."

"Dr. Rubenfeld made his study of Mrs. Porter as a joint study with Dr. Carruthers, his associate. The report on her is their joint report, in which both physicians are fully agreed. We should like to have Dr. Rubenfeld alone speak for both as to their joint report, and thus avoid having Dr. Carruthers simply repeat the same testimony. Is there any objection to that?"

"But I will not have the opportunity to cross-examine Dr. Carruthers," Rosvalley protested.

"You will have the opportunity to cross-examine Dr. Rubenfeld. That cross-examination, like Dr. Rubenfeld's report and expert opinion, will bind both. It will save much repetition and time."

"Well, all right." Rosvalley sounded uncertain.

"Good. Thank you."

Sam turned back to the witness stand and the waiting psychiatrist. "Now, Dr. Rubenfeld, you and Dr. Carruthers have examined and studied Mrs. Porter quite thoroughly during the past month or so, have you not?"

"Yes," Rubenfeld acknowledged, "but you understand that that is not much time for a full study of a patient in cases of this kind."

"I understand that," Sam agreed, "but you have had a month of study of this patient, have you not?" Then, without waiting for answer, he continued, "Will you tell us, please, Doctor, what your findings are? You may use your notes and memoranda, if you wish, to refresh your memory as to details. I shall offer appropriate records into evidence as you mention and discuss them. Please try, Doctor, to tell the jury and the Court your findings in simple, nontechnical terms."

"I will deal first," Rubenfeld began, "with her physical-report findings and their effects on her mental health. Mrs. Porter has a long history of severe premenstrual tension. That means that regularly every month she suffers biochemical, endocrine, and other changes in her body. Her blood-sugar level drops—what we call spontaneous hypoglycemia. Her electroencephalogram record of nerve and brain reactions changes. But I have only two such tests available, unfortunately. There is an estrogen-progesterone imbalance, too."

"What does this mean in symptoms, in layman's words, Doctor?"

"She becomes extremely nervous and tense. The symptoms are great irritability, depression, hair-trigger temper, and personality changes."

"What kind of personality changes?"

"Catatonic-like depression. A dazed, trance-like state."

"Does this mean a temporarily manic condition?"

"It can."

"And this happens regularly, every month?"

"Yes, I think so."

"Have you observed this yourself, in her?"

"Yes, this past month."

"Does she have any control over this condition?"

"No. It is a function of the menstrual cycle."

"And it is severe in her case?"

"Yes."

"Does this sort of thing occur in other women, or is she a special, rare case."

"It occurs in many women. Some cases are mild, some severe."

"Her case is severe?"

"Yes."

"Severe enough to affect her mind."

"Yes. I think so."

"And Dr. Carruthers concurs with you in this finding?"

"Yes, he does."

Sam paused and looked at the psychiatrist thoughtfully before going on with his next question. "You say that this condition is of long standing?"

"Yes, it is," Rubenfeld answered in a definite tone of voice. "Besides Mrs. Porter's own account of her medical record, we have other records. The one from N.Y.U., for instance."

"I show you this piece of paper, Doctor. What is it?" Sam showed him the photocopy of Janet's employment record at New York University.

Rubenfeld glanced at it briefly and said, "It is a record of Mrs. Porter's employment at N.Y.U., and it shows her regular monthly absences."

"Do these absences support your diagnosis of regular premenstrual tension?"

"They are not conclusive, but they support it."

Sam handed the paper to the bailiff. "I offer it in evidence. Defense Exhibit A." The bailiff showed the paper to the judge, who nodded and sent it over to the jury foreman.

Sam waited until the paper was marked and then circulated among the jurors. "Go on, Doctor."

"There is also a record of medical tests taken some years ago at the Cleveland Clinic. It also reports severe premenstrual tension."

Sam showed him another photocopy. "Is this the record from Cleveland Clinic?"

"Yes, it is."

"Does it show severe premenstrual tension?"

"Yes, it does."

Sam handed this paper to the bailiff. "Offered in evidence. Defense Exhibit B. Go on, Doctor."

"I have here the tapes of our electroencephalogram record, blood-sugar levels, and so on." Rubenfeld held them out.

"Do these show premenstrual tension?"

"They indicate it."

Sam took the paper rolls and sheets and handed them to the

bailiff. "Offered in evidence. Defense Exhibits C, D, and E."

Barney Rosvalley was suddenly on his feet. "Objection. I object to all these papers being offered in evidence. They have not been properly authenticated."

Sam bristled. "Does the Prosecutor insist that I bring officers from New York University and Cleveland Clinic here, in order to lay a foundation for introducing this evidence?"

Judge Alberts called the bailiff to his Bench. "Let me see the two first exhibits again." He looked at them. "They are clear photocopies of official records, readily identifiable and showing no tampering or alterations. Dr. Rubenfeld's records have been made by himself. I will admit these exhibits. Their weight is for the jury to decide."

Sam resumed his direct examination. "So, Doctor, there is recorded evidence of Mrs. Porter's severe premenstrual tension, as well as your own and Dr. Carruthers' findings by examination?"

"Yes."

"And can you project the dates of her suffering from this condition?"

"Yes. It follows a regular, predictable pattern."

"In other words," Sam said, slowly, "you could tell us when she will be ill again next month?"

"Yes, I can."

"At the same, regular period of time?"

"Yes."

"And could you tell us when she was last ill?"

"Yes. I have the record of it."

"And could you tell us when she was ill the month before— in early August?"

"Yes, I can."

"When was that?"

"From August first to August fifth, give or take a day, according to my extrapolation of her graphs."

"And Kevin Porter was killed on August third, was he not?" Sam queried.

"So I have been informed."

"Which means that Janet Porter was ill, severely ill, perhaps in a catatonic trance, at that time?"

"She was ill at that time," Rubenfeld agreed.

"And, for all we know, quite possibly, was in a state of mental confusion, or even mania, at that time?"

Rubenfeld nodded slightly. "Quite possibly."

"She was ill with premenstrual tension then?"

"Yes."

"You are sure of that?"

"Yes. I am sure of that."

Sam stole a glance at Barney Rosvalley, who was busily scribbling notes at the Prosecutor's Table. Rosvalley's assistant was leafing through a sheaf of papers that looked like medical reports. Sam guessed that they were preparing for cross-examination on the surprise question of premenstrual tension as a basis for a possible finding of insanity. Good, he thought, let them worry. He went on with his direct examination of Rubenfeld.

"Now, Doctor. Besides the finding of severe premenstrual tension about which you have told us, did your examination reveal any other significant findings?"

"Yes, there were other findings."

"Please tell the Court and the jury about them."

"Mrs. Porter shows signs of a possible schizophrenic condition. This means a mental disorder characterized by indifference and withdrawal which is sometimes accompanied by delusions of persecution. It is common in such cases for the intelligence to be unimpaired. In addition, there are indications, during her premenstrual stress cycle, at its peak, of catatonic symptoms."

"What does that mean?"

"Catonic, or catatonic, refers to various schizophrenic syndromes which are characterized by trancelike phases of stupor, often alternating with phases of excitement and muscular rigidity or spasm."

"And Mrs. Porter exhibits these symptoms."

"She exhibits *indications* of them," Rubenfeld said cautiously. "We have not yet actually seen her in a complete catatonic state."

"You mentioned delusions of persecution. Can you be more specific?"

"Yes. Mrs. Porter revealed indications, old and deep-seated, of fear and antipathy directed towards her father. More recently, she showed similar reactions toward the name or figure of her husband. These indications cannot be described as conclusive, of course, but they are significant to a psychiatrist."

"Do you mean that she has, or had, delusions of persecution by her father and then by her husband?"

"Yes, but it is an unresolved question whether these are delusions or are based on actual events. I cannot reach a conclusion on that. However, I will add that this fear of hers seems to be related to the work she does, which is legal research. Somehow, in ways which we cannot pinpoint accurately, her fear revolves around her father, her husband, and her work."

"This is an emotional symptom, I take it, Doctor, rather than a biochemical reaction such as is involved in premenstrual tension?"

"That is correct."

Sam stepped back, put his hands on his hips, and said slowly, "Then your findings from your actual examination of Mrs. Porter are twofold, are they not? One, a biochemical type of illness; and two, an emotional or psychosomatic kind of illness?"

Rubenfeld nodded. "That is right."

"And do these two types of illness affect each other?"

"Indeed they do." The doctor was emphatic. "The physical or biochemical symptoms can trigger emotional reactions, and the emotional symptoms can trigger biochemical reactions. It is a kind of vicious cycle each feeding on the other."

"And do these have cumulative effects?"

"Yes, they do. Each one tends to heighten and accentuate the other."

"To a dangerous degree?"

"Yes. The cumulative effect can be to produce reactions that may be explosive."

"Dangerous to other people?"

"Oh, yes. The results can be quite unpredictable."

"And is there any particular time when these reactions are at their maximum?"

"Yes," the doctor said. "At the peak of her premenstrual-tension cycle."

"Which, last August, was the time during which her husband was killed, is that correct?"

"That is correct."

"All right. Now, Doctor, assuming the facts that you have discovered in your examinations of Mrs. Porter—that is, her condition of premenstrual tension and her emotional reactions as you described them—can you tell the Court and the jury whether Mrs. Porter at the time of the killing had the mental capacity to form the intent to kill her husband?"

Rubenfeld leaned forward in his chair. "Yes, I can. In my opinion Mrs. Porter is suffering from a schizophrenic condition that can become acute at any time, and most likely so at the time of her peak premenstrual tension. As to the time of the death of her husband, it is my opinion that she was in a state of acute schizophrenia—probably catatonic in nature—when that occurred."

"Do you mean that she was mentally incapable of having the intent to kill her husband?"

"In the psychiatrists' meaning of that term, yes."

"And that her mental capacity for forming such intent, in respect to her husband, or someone else, is still the same?"

"Yes."

"Do you mean by that that she did not know right from wrong at that time?"

"I cannot say that," Rubenfeld demurred. "It is quite possible that she did not know the difference. I cannot be more specific."

"Do you mean that she did not know the nature and quality of her act?"

"Quite possibly. But I cannot be certain."

Sam persisted, "If I ask you to answer the question with only a 'Yes' or a 'No,' what would you answer? Was she unaware of the nature and quality of her act?"

Rubenfeld shrugged his shoulder and answered, "Probably."

Sam nodded thoughtfully. "I understand, Doctor, that that is as concrete an answer as a psychiatrist can give to that question, put in that way. Is that so?"

"Yes."

"Putting the question in a different way, was she, in your opinion, temporarily insane—at least, at the time of the death of her husband?"

"I cannot be certain, but my answer is 'Probably yes.' . . ."

Sam smiled. "That is good enough. Thank you, Doctor." Then he turned to Rosvalley. "Your witness."

Barney Rosvalley approached the witness stand like a panther stalking his prey. Sam watched him with interest. He had a lot of respect for Rosvalley as a cross-examiner.

"Tell me, Dr. Rubenfeld," Rosvalley began, "do you view the State's alienists as competent psychiatrists?"

"Yes, I do."

"And you have seen their reports on Mrs. Porter, have you not?"

"I have," Rubenfeld acknowledged.

"They report that, in their opinion, Mrs. Porter is perfectly sane, do they not?"

"They do."

"But you say they are wrong?"

"Yes."

"You believe that you are right and they are wrong?"

Rubenfeld nodded stiffly. "Yes."

"I see. You base your opinion largely on your finding of premenstrual tension in Mrs. Porter, do you not?"

"Yes."

Rosvalley's voice was suddenly scornful. "That is a rather novel basis for a finding of insanity, Doctor, is it not? It isn't a well-established basis recognized by court decisions, is it?"

"I suppose not."

Rosvalley looked surprised. "You *suppose not?* Have you ever seen or heard of an actual court decision that rested a finding of legal insanity on a basis of premenstrual tension?"

"No," Rubenfeld replied stubbornly, "but that does not mean the courts should not do so."

Now Rosvalley was suddenly affable. "Oh, you believe that this Court should make new law in this case? Is that what you mean?"

Sam sprang to his feet. "Objection. If the Court please, the Prosecutor is putting words in the mouth of the witness."

Judge Alberts nodded. "Sustained. Mr. Rosvalley, I suggest that you rephrase your question."

Rosvalley bowed slightly towards the Bench, and returned

to the psychiatrist. "You will admit, will you not, that there are no court decisions of which you know that rest a finding of insanity on a basis of premenstrual tension?"

"Yes. But I think . . ."

Rosvalley interrupted him. "Please, Doctor, just answer my questions with a 'Yes' or 'No' unless I ask for a detailed explanation."

Sam was on his feet again. "I object to that. We are dealing with an expert witness who is entitled to explain his reasons for his opinion."

Judge Alberts disagreed. "This is cross-examination, Mr. Benedict. We must allow the cross-examiner to confine his questions to narrow points if he wishes to do so."

Rosvalley drove on. "Your finding of schizophrenia is based largely on the premenstrual tension, too, is it not, Doctor?"

The doctor shook his head. "Not entirely. There also are the emotional and situational factors which I reported."

"You mean that she didn't like her father and her husband?"

"A great deal more than 'didn't like.' . . ."

"Hated them, perhaps?"

"Yes, hated them."

"And is hatred of someone proof of insanity?" Rosvalley prompted.

"Not necessarily, but it often is strong evidence of it."

"Not necessarily," Rosvalley echoed. "And you recall that she continued to live with her father and then with her husband, did she not?"

"Yes."

"And do you remember that the reports of the State's alienists made no mention of Mrs. Porter's premenstrual tension other than to say that it is a common trouble of many women?"

"I remember that."

"So you will agree that premenstrual tension is not an accepted basis of court finding of insanity, will you not?"

"I have said that," the doctor acknowledged.

"And the matter of emotional causation of schizophrenia, which you say you found, is contradicted by the State's alienists, it is not?"

"Yes."

"But you stated that you found that Mrs. Porter probably was temporarily insane when she murdered her husband, so that she could not have had the mental capacity to form the intent to kill her husband?"

"Yes, I did."

"You said 'probably,' did you not?"

"Yes."

"You cannot be sure even of that, can you?"

"No."

Rosvalley was looking very pleased with himself. He went back to the Prosecutor's Counsel Table and picked up a paper covered with notes. Then he strode forward again and resumed. "Tell me, is it your view that the rules in M'Naghten's Case are the proper rules, or that they should be relaxed?"

"I think they ought to be relaxed."

"You have written articles and are writing a book on that matter?"

"Yes."

"You have advocated a revision of the Rule?"

Rubenfeld hesitated. "Not exactly. My difficulty has always been to offer an alternative," he said.

"Have you not advocated the Durham Rule?"

"Yes, I have."

"Is the Durham Rule the law in this State?"

"No, it is not."

"So the M'Naghten Rule, which has been followed since 1843 is still the law in this State today?"

"Yes."

"Do you believe that the knowledge that an act is punishable is one of the restraints upon people doing such an act?"

"Certainly."

"Do you say that the accused did or did not know, or did not possess the power of knowing, that her act was punishable?"

Rubenfeld corrected him. "I think it is quite possible that she did not know that what she was doing was punishable."

Rosvalley pressed him. "The question we are upon is whether she knew at the time she did this act that this was an act punishable by law?"

"Yes."

"She remained in the room with the body of her husband and made no attempt to leave, did she?"

"Yes, but that suggests that she didn't realize what she had done."

"Or didn't care?"

"Or didn't care."

"She had the murder weapon in her hand when discovered, did she not?"

"Yes."

"And that suggests that she didn't care, doesn't it?"

"It does," Rubenfeld conceded.

"All her acts were consistent with the idea of disregard of the consequences, were they not?"

"Or unawareness of them," the doctor countered.

"They could have been disregard, though?"

"They could have been."

"They could indicate that she knew the act she had done was punishable by law, and that she didn't care?"

The psychiatrist was hesitant as he answered, "I suppose so."

"Is it your view that if she did this act under the influence of insanity, it was a sudden frenzy?"

"Yes."

"Are you suggesting here, as an expert, that the present case is one of irresistible impulse?"

"No I am not. I do not know. It might have been a catatonic state."

"Catatonic means rigid and immobile, does it not?" Rosvalley said sharply.

"Yes."

"She hardly was immobile when she struck her husband, was she?"

"No."

"And you are aware, are you not," said the Prosecutor, "that the theory of irresistible impulse as a defense in a criminal charge is not accepted by this State?"

"I am aware of that." The psychiatrist sounded defensive.

"Aside from premenstrual tension and the emotionally triggered schizophrenia you have mentioned, is there any form of insanity that you can suggest to the jury which would cause her to take her husband's life?"

"She may have had homicidal tendencies at that time," Rubenfeld suggested, a little uncertainly.

"Is that the same as irresistible impulse?"

"No, it is not."

"What is the distinction between homicidal tendencies and irresistible impulse?"

Rubenfeld shifted in his chair as he answered. "I think a homicidal tendency is usually a condition that arises in conjunction with another form of insanity. You may get a homicidal tendency in many different forms of insanity by itself."

"What form of insanity would there be in homicidal tendency?"

"You might meet it in delusional insanity or states of melancholia."

"Do you suggest any of those in this case as being the cause of homicidal tendency?" Rosvalley's voice was challenging.

"I think she had delusions," answered Rubenfeld, stubbornly.

" 'Delusions' is the only suggestion you can make?" Rosvalley said, with a look of surprise on his face.

"Of course I consider she was unsound aside from delusions," the doctor added quickly.

"I am afraid that you are wandering away from the question; the question is the actual act of murder. What form of insanity in your view caused her to do the act of murder?"

"I think it was an episode in the form of insanity which arose in chronic premenstrual tension plus emotional stress."

"Premenstrual tension again?" Rosvalley's tone was almost mocking. "Now this was not only a brutal murder, but a deliberate one. There were four or five separate blows, were there not?"

"Yes."

"Imagine for yourself, without your experience even, that a person in a frenzy might strike a violent blow?"

"Oh, yes."

"But then she proceeded to strike four more blows?"

"Yes."

"That took time and effort, did it not? She is not a very big or strong woman?"

"Yes."

"That seems deliberate and continued over more than a split second?"

"I suppose."

"She wanted to make sure?"

"Possibly." Rubenfeld's voice was almost inaudible.

"Does that not strike you as deliberate?"

"Not necessarily," the doctor protested weakly.

"Now, you seem to attribute some importance to the fact that she appeared to be calm after the awful event?"

"No, I did not."

"Calmness is certainly not an uncommon incident in sane persons who have committed murders?"

"Oh, certainly not," Rubenfeld admitted.

"So that there is nothing in favor of insanity in the fact that she is calm?" The D.A.'s voice was triumphant.

"Nothing that I attribute any importance to."

Sam was feeling unhappy. Damn that Barney Rosvalley, he was thinking, with grudging admiration. He's a crackerjack cross-examiner, unfortunately. Barney was slowly and steadily breaking down Rubenfeld's testimony to a lot of "ifs" and "maybes."

Rosvalley was hammering at the psychiatrist again. "Do you suggest, Doctor, that the accused was unaware of what she was doing?"

"I suggest that."

"But you do not know that, do you?"

"No," dryly. "I was not there."

"So you can only conjecture?"

"I suppose so."

"You suggest that her mind was deprived of any sense of the meaning of what she was doing?"

"Yes, I do."

"Do you agree, or do you not, that she must have been conscious—not in a catatonic trance—in order to be able to see her husband, pick up the statuette, and strike him with it?"

"Yes, she must have been."

"But you say that she was insane then?"

"Yes, probably."

"Not certainly?" Rosvalley raised his eyebrows in mock astonishment.

"Not certainly." The doctor's tone was becoming harried and very uncertain sounding.

"Do you agree, or do you not, that a person can be both insane and criminally responsible for a crime?"

"You mean," Rubenfeld parried, "that she may know the nature and quality of her act, know that it is wrong and punishable?"

"That's exactly what I mean."

Rosvalley pressed the question. "And might she not be certifiably insane at that very time?"

"I can give you an illustration."

"I want an answer to that question," Rosvalley snapped. "Do you agree with that?"

"Yes."

"So that the mere act of certifying a person as insane—if it were done, and it has not been done here—would not show that she is not criminally responsible?"

Rubenfeld shrugged. "No. I do not think that that fact of itself is sufficient."

"Do you think that it is possible the prisoner may have been aware that what she was doing was an act punishable by law?"

"It is possible."

"Do you at least agree that she was doing an act which was morally wrong according to the recognized social code?" The Prosecutor's voice was heavy with sarcasm.

"I think it is so."

"When you say that she did not know, in your view, what she was doing, do you mean that she was catatonic or unconscious?"

"No."

"What *do* you mean?"

"That she was not aware that what she was doing was wrong, according to the standard in her confused mind at the time."

"She did not know she was doing wrong, according to her own standard?"

"Yes," Rubenfeld agreed.

"Do you say this diminution of the sense of right and wrong is a form of mental disease?"

"I think that this can happen," he answered earnestly. "Some people actually are born with a deficient moral sense. This has been recognized for about a century by medical men. It has been recognized by an Act of Parliament in England, the Lunacy Act."

"Would that refer principally to habitual criminals?"

"Yes."

"One witness has said of the accused that she had periods of high spirits occasionally, and periods of great depression. Is that symptomatic of schizophrenia?"

Rubenfeld nodded. "Yes, it is."

"But it is also seen in many people not classified as schizophrenic—normal people—is it not?"

"Yes."

"So, all in all, aside from your theory as to premenstrual tension, you must base your opinion that the accused is insane on her hatred for her father and husband?"

"Yes, principally," the doctor conceded.

"And you do not suggest that hatred of a person is in itself proof of insanity?"

"No."

"Thank you." Rosvalley ended his cross-examination. "That is all."

Sam moved close to the Judge's Bench and beckoned to Barney Rosvalley. When Rosvalley joined him he spoke in a low voice, audible only to Rosvalley and Judge Alberts. "Your Honor—Mr. Rosvalley—as you undoubtedly have guessed, I am going to call Mrs. Porter to the stand. Her defense in large part rests on her own testimony. In order to adduce this testimony I am going to have to question her rigorously. I think that you will agree that that is necessary in a defense based on the lack of mental capacity to form an intent to murder."

Rosvalley tilted his head noncommittally.

Judge Alberts looked concerned. "Within limits, of course, Mr. Benedict."

"That is exactly the point, Your Honor," Sam emphasized.

"That is why I am conferring with you now. I believe that I may have to lead her testimony more than is usual on direct examination. And I believe that I may have to be repetitious at times, and may have to press her hard at times."

"I understand," Rosvalley conceded. "I will not object if it is not unreasonably done in these circumstances."

"It is important that my questioning be interrupted as seldom as possible by objections that break the train of thought."

"Oh, I can't give you any blanket waiver of objection," Rosvalley protested.

"I'm not asking for a blanket waiver," Sam said blandly, "just consideration and professional courtesy. I may sometimes have to press the questions so hard that I may seem to be cross-examining and badgering my own witness."

"You're bound by your own witness' answers. I can't go along with that," Rosvalley objected.

Judge Alberts settled the point, for the moment at least. "If you go too far, you can expect me to intervene."

"Of course. Thank you, Your Honor." That was as much as Sam had hoped for.

Sam walked back to the Counsel Table and picked a Manila folder out of his dispatch case. It was the same blue folder, full of annotated notes on Justice Holmes' decisions, which he had found on Janet's desk in the library of the Porter home. He noticed that Janet, sitting behind the table, stared at the folder with a look of surprise. He placed the folder on top of the leather case.

"I call Mrs. Janet Porter to the witness stand." Sam gestured to her to get up and go to the stand. She rose slowly and walked woodenly to the stand.

Sam lingered a moment at the Counsel Table. "How do I look?" he whispered to Hank.

Hank looked him over critically. "With that black suit and broad necktie you look pretty old-fashioned. I think that your pocket handkerchief is still much more Sam Benedict than Oliver Wendell Holmes."

Sam pushed the handkerchief down in his breast pocket. "How's it now?"

"Better. You look like a 1910 fashion plate."

"Good." Sam turned towards the witness stand. The bailiff already had sworn in Janet.

"Now, Janet, take your time and don't be nervous," he began. He noticed that her face was pale and set. Her hands were clasped in her lap so tightly that the knuckles were pearl white. "You spent your childhood in New York living with your father after your mother died when you were a baby, is that correct?"

"Yes." Her voice was faint.

"Please speak up, Janet, so that the jurors can hear you. And you were cared for by a succession of housekeepers?"

"Yes."

"You had no close relatives other than your father?"

"No."

"And he was away teaching at Harvard Law School very often, was he not?"

"Yes."

"How were you educated? You did not go to high school or college, did you?"

"My father had tutors come to the house," she answered, her voice flat and dull. "He taught me, too. He gave me study assignments, and quizzed me himself."

"Was he a stern, demanding teacher?"

"Yes."

"Did you enjoy being taught by him?"

"No."

"Would you describe your father as a warm, fatherly kind of man?"

"No."

"He was austere and distant with you, was he not?"

"Yes."

"Did you love him," Sam asked gently.

"Well . . ." Her voice trailed off.

"Did you often accompany him on his trips and when he was doing research work?"

"Yes."

"Did you enjoy those trips and work periods?"

"Mostly I just waited for him."

"Did your father put you to work, assisting him?"

"Yes."

"How did you assist him?"

"Copying, making notes, looking up points, typing his notes."

"Did he praise you for your help?"

She shook her head. "No."

"Did he scold you when the work displeased him?"

"Yes." Her voice was bitter.

"You were, in effect, his secretary?"

"Yes."

She paused and took a deep breath. Now he would have to take a dangerous new tack. "Did you enjoy the work?" he asked.

"Sometimes. Sometimes I would get so engrossed that I would forget . . ."

"Forget what?"

"Nothing. Really, nothing." She shrank back in the chair.

"And what was the subject of most of his research work?"

"Legal history. The Supreme Court."

"And the justices of the Supreme Court?"

"Yes."

"Such as Marshall and Taney and Cardozo?"

"Yes."

"And Holmes?"

Her eyes, which had been fixed straight ahead, suddenly turned towards him. Her eyelids flickered for a moment. She was silent.

He repeated the question. "And Holmes?"

Her head moved up and down, in a slow nod. She was staring straight ahead again. Her lips were pressed tightly closed, so that little ridges of muscles under the skin made tiny bumps at the corners of her mouth.

"Your father had great esteem for some of the justices of the Supreme Court, did he not?"

"Yes," she managed in a half whisper.

"He even liked to dress in the style of the early nineteen-hundreds, did he not?"

"Yes." Her voice was sibilant with the s-s-s sound.

Barney Rosvalley stood up lazily and addressed the Bench. "If Your Honor please, this is all very interesting, but I fail to see what point. . . ."

Sam turned on him in a blaze of wrath. "There is such a thing as common courtesy, Mr. Rosvalley. I asked you not to interfere. This is perfectly proper questioning." Then he turned to the judge: "I ask the Court to instruct the Prosecutor not to attempt again to destroy the development of the defendant's testimony by such gratuitous and harassing interruptions for no cause and for no reason."

Judge Alberts agreed. "Mr. Benedict's questions are perfectly proper. His resentment of your interruption is not without cause, Mr. Rosvalley. Please confine your objections to proper ones for proper reasons."

"I only meant . . ." Rosvalley began.

"Whatever you meant," Sam shot back at him, "just remember that we are not playing some kind of legal game here. This woman is on trial for her life." His hand smacked at the edge of the jury box. "For her *life*." He paused in order to cool down. "She is entitled to tell her story without being cut off and harassed."

Rosvalley sat down without another word.

"Now, Janet," Sam began again. "You married Kevin Porter in New York, did you not, and your first home with him was in Cleveland?"

"Yes." She had regained her composure.

"And he was a law professor and legal scholar and researcher, like your father, wasn't he?"

"Yes."

"He, too, was interested mainly in one field of law, wasn't he? What was that field?"

"Legal history."

"Of the Supreme Court, again?"

"Yes."

"And largely of the justices of the Supreme Court?"

"Yes," she said almost in a whisper.

"Like Marshall and Taney and Cardozo?"

"Yes."

"And like . . . ?" He stopped, his question unfinished. Janet

Porter had become visibly tense again. She was looking at him with almost pleading eyes. He changed the question. "Did you assist Kevin, as you had assisted your father, with his legal research and writing?"

She relaxed a bit. Her voice almost sighed, "Yes."

"You were happy when you were first married, weren't you?"

"Yes."

"Did that first happiness last long?"

"No."

"It was gone within a few weeks after your wedding?"

"Yes," she admitted softly.

"Was it because your husband didn't love you?"

She shrugged her shoulders. "I don't know."

"Was he an affectionate, warm, friendly man?"

"No."

"Would you say that he was cold and austere?" Sam suggested.

"Yes."

"Like your father?"

"Yes."

"He was a tall, prematurely gray-haired man, was he not?"

"Yes."

"Your father was tall and gray-haired, wasn't he?"

"Yes."

"In fact, John Duffield, your father, and Kevin Porter, your husband, both looked superficially alike, did they not?"

"Yes."

"And their manner and treatment of you were alike, too, weren't they?"

"Yes."

"Kevin was a harsh, demanding taskmaster, like your father, wasn't he?"

"Yes."

Barney Rosvalley stirred restlessly in his seat at the Prosecutor's Table. He seemed to be about to rise and object, but then apparently thought better of it and let it go.

Sam drove ahead. "Now, let us talk about something else, Janet. I regret that I must bring up this subject in a courtroom full of strange people. Even so, please answer these questions.

First, the physicians who examined you report that you suffer regularly from severe premenstrual tension. Is that correct?"

"Yes."

"When did this illness begin to trouble you?"

"When I was about seventeen."

"Has it persisted since then?"

"Yes."

"Every month, regularly?"

"Yes."

"Is it distressing?"

"Very."

"Tell the Court and the jury how you feel when it happens."

"Sick," she said. "There is pain many times, but not always."

"What other symptoms?"

"Nerves. I get very tense and depressed. Sometimes I feel that I could jump out of my skin."

"Does it ever cause you to collapse?"

"Sometimes. Sometimes I have a fainting spell. Everything goes black. Then it passes."

"Do you ever have memory blackouts during that time?"

"I don't know. I don't think so."

"Now, on the night when Kevin was killed, were you suffering from your regular premenstrual tension?"

"Yes."

"Was it very bad?"

"Yes."

"Did you faint during that day?"

"I don't think so. I felt nauseated several times."

"There is a period of almost an hour during which Kevin was killed and during which you say you remember nothing?"

She nodded. "So they tell me."

"Do you remember that hour?"

"No."

"Is it possible that you blacked out during that hour?"

"I suppose it is possible."

"You don't remember?"

"No."

"What is the last thing you remember before that hour?"

"I was working at my desk in the library."

242 /

"Alone?"

"Yes," she said, her eyes widening.

"And what is the next thing you remember?"

"Kevin was lying on the floor. Then I was out in the hall with a strange man talking to me. Rogers was there, too."

"The strange man was a police detective?"

"Yes."

"Nothing in between those times?"

"No."

"You don't remember?"

"No. God help me! I don't remember."

Sam walked slowly to the Counsel's Table. He picked up the blue Manila folder. Then, holding the folder at his side, he returned to the witness stand, stopped, and stood close to Janet. Janet's eyes followed him all the way, and when he stopped she seemed to keep on looking at the blue folder.

Sam's voice, which had been pitched in its usual slow, soft tone until now, was higher when he resumed his questioning. It was almost a growl, now. "So, you had been unhappy with both your father and your husband, had you not?"

Her voice faltered. "Yes."

"You never really liked the work you did for either of them, did you?"

"Not really."

"And both did the same kind of work, didn't they?"

"Yes."

"And drove you to assist them in it?"

"Yes."

"In fact, didn't Kevin have you working on his notes for his study of the Supreme Court, this past summer?"

"Yes." Her voice was faint.

"And didn't he have you working on the history of the justices of the Supreme Court?"

"Yes."

"At the same time, you still were working on the autobiography of your father, built around the decisions and lives of those same justices. Isn't that so?"

"Yes."

"You were constantly pushed into working on the opinions

and decisions of the Justices—like Marshall and Taney and Cardozo?"

"Yes." Her lips were tightening again.

"Your father had done that too, hadn't he?"

"Yes." The hissing sound in her voice was becoming marked again.

"Your father and Kevin were tall and white-haired, weren't they?"

"Yes."

"They reminded you of the judges of the turn of the century, didn't they?"

"Yes." Her voice was barely audible.

He placed the blue folder on the edge of the witness box, and her eyes followed it, as though she were hypnotized. "Of one of the justices in particular?"

She was silent.

"There was one justice whom both your father and Kevin idolized, wasn't there?" His voice challenged her.

She remained silent, staring dully at the blue folder.

"Do you remember this quotation, Janet? 'We must conform our standards to experience.' Do you know whose quotation that is?"

"No!" she spat out the word.

"You don't know a famous quotation of one of the famous justices of the Supreme Court? Come now, Janet, and you a scholar of the Court?"

"No!" Her voice was suddenly shrill.

"Your father and Kevin looked like him. They dressed like him and they looked like him. Except for his moustache, they looked like him."

"No! *No!*" Her voice was piteous.

"I show you this blue folder, Janet. It has pages of notes in it. They are pages of notes about this justice. They are notes about . . ." He paused. Her eyes were glaring at him. "They are notes about Justice Oliver Wendell Holmes. *Oliver Wendell Holmes!*" He shouted.

Rosvalley stoood up and raised one hand as though about to break in. Sam ignored him. Janet Porter was starting to rise from her seat, her face a death mask.

"Didn't Kevin bring these notes to you that night?" Sam's voice was loud, harsh, accusing. "Aren't these more notes about Holmes? Justice Oliver Wendell Holmes? The man who was the image behind your father and Kevin? Oliver Wendell Holmes?"

Judge Alberts was banging his gavel. "Mr. Benedict, this is going too far."

Barney Rosvalley, too, had found his voice. "I object to this cruel, brutal kind of questioning."

Sam drove on, heedless of Rosvalley or the judge. "Answer me, Janet. Answer me," he shouted. *"Oliver Wendell Holmes?"*

Janet stood stiff and unhearing in the witness box, eyes blank, and her mouth working in sudden spasms. One hand moved towards the blue folder. She grasped it. Held it tightly. Then she tore it in half, and tore it again, and again, and again. She leaned forward towards Sam, glaring. Then she spat, like an animal at bay; saliva running out of her mouth and down her chin. "God damn you. God *damn* you! *Go back to Hell, where you belong!*"

Sam raised his arms defensively. She was clawing at him, her eyes unseeing as she looked through him, her hands stiff, curved into talons, mouthing words. "Damn you! *Damn you! Damn you!*"

He seized her wrists and held them firmly. "Bailiff," he shouted, "Get Dr. Rubenfeld up here fast."

Hank gathered up their papers. The courtroom was still now. Only Sam and Hank and Justice Radcliffe remained in it.

"Don't feel badly, Sam." The austere old judge touched him on his shoulder. "You did what had to be done."

"She'll be all right, boss." Hank murmured, trying to comfort him. "They'll take good care of her. She may be able to be cured, you know. These mental hospitals today can do wonders."

"What choice was there, Sam?" Radcliffe asked. "It was this or the gas chamber, wasn't it?"

"That's what I told myself." Sam's voice was heavy and sad. "But what an end for a fine mind like that!"

"It was a broken mind long before you met her. There's no

doubt of that." The judge put out his hand. "Now you'd better get working on the alienation proceedings—appointment of a committee to manage her property and all that. I'll help any way I can, of course."

"I know." Sam shook his hand, and the old judge left.

"Got everything, Hank?" Sam asked as he started to walk toward the rail gate.

"Okay. For Pete's sake, boss, don't feel that way," Hank pleaded. "You did what you had to do."

"I suppose so. You know, Hank, a quotation keeps running through my mind. It goes like this: 'Insanity is often the logic of an accurate mind overtaxed.' Do you know who said that?"

"No."

"It was the poet—the father of the justice—Oliver Wendell Holmes."

They looked at each other silently for a moment. Then they walked out of the courtroom and started back to the office.